C.S. KENDALL

Descendants of the Curse

Jessie's Awakening

First edition

ISBN: 978-1-7342562-3-9

This book was professionally typeset on Reedsy.
Find out more at reedsy.com

Contents

Prologue

February 4th, 2012

Dear Diary,

Cora got me this journal for my birthday—how'd she know I'd need to vent?

I'm sitting here, trying to lose myself in my character, but my brain won't shut up. I wish I could just get lost in my role and forget my life. That's why acting means so much to me—I get to be someone else. And this time, I am the baker's wife in *Into the woods*. I worked so hard to get this part, and I'd love to lose myself in her agony rather than face my own.

I wish I *could* be someone else. Anyone else.

But my brain won't let me.

This is not how I saw my seventeenth birthday going. My parents just...blew my world up beyond recognition. If I told you the story they told me, Diary, you would never believe it. I still don't know if I can.

What a beautiful world it was...and it just came to a screeching halt. I had the lead in the school musical, great friends, and a cute boyfriend who finally freaking kissed me (we've been practicing a lot of that lately...more on that later). Everything was going so well. *So* well.

That should have been my first clue.

Then my parents sat me down and told me about my heritage—and I don't want any of it! Ugh, I can't even write the words they said...it takes too much energy and forces me to face something I can't even wrap my head around. How do I go on now? How do I learn my lines and go on dates and have slumber parties with Addy and teach my dog new tricks and eat ice cream and choose a college, now that I know what I am...what I'm becoming? I guess none of that matters anymore, does it?

I don't want any of this!!!

Don't I get a choice? Don't I get a say in who I am? I thought that was the point. I thought we got to determine our own paths. I was on the way to doing this for myself. But here I am, a mess of tears and snot and mascara, sitting on my bed, my musical soundtrack playing in the background, my script laid out highlighted on the floor, but my brain won't stop racing.

My head hurts. What I thought was my reality is only an illusion. And I'm freaking out. *Seriously* freaking out. My parents told me the sooner I embrace this thing inside of me, the better it will be. But how the hell do I do that?

Oh, and just to make things interesting, apparently someone wants to kill me now...wants to kill everyone who is like me. Ugh, like *me*. I'm not sure I even know what that means.

And on and on and on and on it goes. The thoughts. The crippling fear. The paralyzing prospect of losing my mind and doing the unthinkable...

Make it stop, Diary. Please, just make it all just...stop.

1

Jessie

"I've never lied to royalty before. I've never anything to royalty before! What a beautiful gown you're wearing. Were you at the King's Festival?"

My own dark gaze peered at me from my reflection in the mirror as I watched myself recite my lines. I exhaled and twisted my face into the pained expression I had practiced so many times before now—the one that had secured me the role of the baker's wife in our high school's rendition of *Into the Woods*. I ran the lines and then I ran them again, practicing with different inflections and intonations to ensure I got it just right. It was a personal goal to have the first two scenes memorized before tonight's rehearsal.

And I was almost there, despite the ungodly early hour of the day.

"Aren't you the lucky one. If a Prince were pursuing me, I certainly wouldn't hide."

My bedroom door flung open and my mom and dad stood there smiling, a plate full of birthday donuts and balloons in hand. They burst into a chorus of 'Happy birthday', my mother harmonizing at the end as she did with every annual performance on this day. Millie, my border collie, wagged her tail at this out-of-the-ordinary set of morning events, happy to have all her pack in one place.

I didn't want them to know how cute I thought this was, how much I looked forward to this tradition, even if it had grown a little embarrassing the older I got. Thank God there were no witnesses.

Wrong again.

My two sisters sprung out from behind my parents, throwing confetti and jumping up and down. Well, my youngest sister, Cora, jumped up and down. My middle sister, Talia, who was in the "too cool for school" stage, threw her confetti with a bored look on her face. And by "threw" I mean she raised her arm two inches from her side and let the chopped up colorful paper fall from her fingertips.

The whole lot of them filled my room now, trespassing on my sacred territory. But, I supposed, I would allow the intrusion for today.

Mom hugged me first. A cockroach set in resin dangled from her neck, and her little pet snake Arnie was wrapped around her arm as he often was. Mom almost always had one of her many pets on her person, but lately Arnie, the baby snake seemed to have taken up near permanent residence around her arm or neck.

"Oh, happy birthday, sweetie. Seventeen! I can hardly believe it." Every time I had a birthday, she could hardly believe it. Like each year this date came as a surprise.

"Eww, Mom. No offense, but I don't like it when that thing touches me." I squirmed out of her grip and gestured toward the bug-turned-jewelry. Then I reached forward and stroked the little snake coiled around her forearm. "Good morning, Arnie. You're such a cute little guy, aren't you?" I cooed, stroking his soft back.

"Oh, come on, Jessie-girl. You know I love to help them live forever. And here! I made you a bracelet this year!" She reached into her robe pocket and dangled a leather bracelet in front of my face, a colorful beetle trapped inside it.

"Thanks, Mom." I pinched the bracelet between my finger and thumb, as if the thing was going to come alive and eat me. This newest piece of jewelry from my mother would join several others in my secret drawer, out of sight, but unfortunately, not out of mind. I shuddered, thinking of all the dead but forever preserved bugs that lived in that drawer.

Dad's embrace was stiffer and more akin to a rough squeeze than a hug. "Almost an adult now. How's it feel?"

Displays of affection were not his thing. I always chalked it up to what he must see in his line of work as a detective. Even though he kept a safe distance—emotionally speaking—from his daughters, there was no doubt he loved us. He just showed it differently from Mom. And it worked for us—she was the buffer, the confidant, the problem solver. We left it up to her what she would convey to our dad and what she would keep between us and her.

"Thanks guys!" I said, sweeping the room with my gaze to indicate all of them. "Now, where's my jelly donut?" I picked through the options on the plate and found my donut of choice. Wasting no time (there were donuts to be consumed!) I stuffed that sucker into my mouth, the strawberry jelly spilling out and staining the corners of my mouth. In all my now seventeen years, I had never learned how to eat one of these things gracefully.

Mom looked from the script lying on my bed to my face. "Were you rehearsing your lines before school? How's it going, baker's wife?" There was a warmth, a pride in her tone.

"I was. And good. Did you know I was the only junior to get a lead? So far, the script is a bit different from the movie, though. I'm just glad I didn't land Cinderella or Rapunzel. I would not a great princess make. You know when rehearsals start, we hit the ground running. Gotta be ready for that."

"Jessie girl, it's your birthday. I love how you commit yourself to the roles you play, but you could take a day off." She winked her approval.

"Besides, no one will be more prepared than you."

That was kind of the point. I had to be perfect, had to show everyone. "I *could* relax a bit, yes, but then I wouldn't be a lead in the school musical, would I?"

Talia rolled her eyes, her irritation palpable. I'd been getting more and more of that from her lately. She wore her usual choice of attire: a superhero t-shirt with jeans. Today it was Captain America who demonstrated her extreme love of all things Marvel.

"Maybe you could take a break from hating me today, Talia. After all it's my birthday." I narrowed my eyes at her.

"I don't *hate* you." But her tone and the glare in her expression said otherwise.

"Girls," my mother scolded. "Let's not start the day arguing, okay?"

I put my hands up to indicate my surrender. I, too, was not keen on beginning my day fighting with my sister.

"We'll leave you to get ready for school. You're driving yourself and your sisters this morning, okay?"

"Planning on it," I said turning away, my mind already back to my lines. My room emptied after that, but my dad lingered behind the rest. When he reached the door, he paused, waiting for the rest of the family to scatter before he turned toward me.

"Jessie, tonight we'll do the usual gifts and cake bit but after all that, we have to talk. Now that you're seventeen, there are a few things I need to make you aware of."

I paused my mental rehearsal and cocked my head at him. "Like—?"

"Just things about this family and your role in it." Though he was obviously trying to keep his tone light, the scowl etched on his face worried me.

I didn't like the sound of this. My heart sped, drumming in my ears, and my skin burned hot. "Am I in trouble? Just tell me what I did now."

Dad softened a little, his posture relaxing, and a smile threatened to lift the corner of his mouth. "No, Jessie girl, you're not in trouble. But you do have some responsibilities you aren't yet aware of and there are some things about this family that you need to know. You're old enough now. It's a privilege, okay? So don't worry all day that I'm going to bring some sort of hammer down on you. You can tell your overactive guilty conscience to give it a rest."

Fat chance of that.

His smile was slight, the hardness on his face making it a tad difficult to detect. Still, beneath that hardness was his usual handsome exterior. I know it's borderline weird to say your day is handsome, but mine really was. I knew this objectively and my friends had confirmed this over the years (eww). He looked younger than all the other dads, with zero gray hair and skin still smooth and supple. Mom looked really good, too. They'd aged beautifully, gracefully. Good genes, they always said. Guess that boded well for me down the road.

I gulped, feeling somewhat reassured by his vague explanation. But a niggling uneasiness shadowed the reassurance. "Roger that, Dad. I shall put it out of my head until the designated time," I lied.

He raised one of his dark, full eyebrows at me. "Sure?" he verified.

"Yeah, I'll be okay."

"Have a good day, Jessie girl. Happy birthday." He kissed me on the head and disappeared through my door, leaving me to mull over what that could have possibly meant. I could think of nothing I'd done lately that would merit a reprimand from my parents. And what was this talk of privilege and family history and responsibility? The more I thought about it, the greater my anxiety grew, rumbling my belly with nausea. I forced myself to finish getting ready for school, doing my best to push aside my growing anxiety about what I might be in for tonight.

An hour later, I was at school, standing at my locker waiting for my best friend to make her appearance. Still preoccupied, my thoughts bouncing between possible scenarios about what my parents wanted to discuss with me and the lines I needed to remember for the school musical. I was so lost in my own head, I didn't see her approaching and jumped when she covered my eyes from behind.

Addy laughed, jerking her hands away as I spun to face her.

"Birthday girl!" she screamed, pulling me into a hug. "How does it feel to be seventeen?"

"Hmm...about the same as sixteen so far."

"So no, like, epic transformations or anything? You didn't go up a cup size or suddenly get really wise?"

"I mean, the day is young so there's plenty of opportunity still but so far..." I crinkled up my face, like I was going to drop some unfortunate news. "It's pretty much the same."

"Boo! At least you pave the way for me. You can take seventeen out for a test drive for a couple of months before I catch up." She pulled her hair through her fingers, a mindless tick I'd grown to find endearing. Her asymmetrical rainbow bob fell around her heart-shaped face with perfection, and her blue eyes popped against all the color.

"You've been saying that since we met in kindergarten! Glad to pioneer each new year ahead of you." I turned toward my locker and sorted through my books.

"Oh, I forgot!" Addy dug into her backpack and pulled out a Caramello and a Dr. Pepper, each wrapped in ribbon. "Can't let my girl go without her favorites on her birthday." She thrust the gifts forward, a smug grin on her face.

"Thanks, ma darling. I can always count on you to fatten me up, today and every day." I took the gifts from her and dropped them into my locker, exchanging them for my script, then slamming the locker shut.

Addy snatched my script from my grip. "Are you already obsessing over this?"

6

"Of course, I am. Do you know me at all?" I plucked it from her fingers and hugged it against my body.

"You're going to kill it. You know you always kill in these things."

"Thanks. But I can't do that without preparing."

"God forbid you forget a line. Or get a 'B'."

My smile slipped. "I don't want to talk about that. It was a disaster."

"Oh, Jess, it was one test. There's no need to freak out. It's okay not to be perfect. Perfection is an illusion anyway. Along with control. You just can't control everything. Sorry to break it to you."

I rolled my eyes at her when a comeback failed to come to mind. She was wrong anyway; I knew it and I had to believe she did too, way down deep. Still, Addy was always just…okay with doing okay. This both baffled me—like literally did not compute in my brain—and caused me to admire her. I daydreamed for two seconds what it might be like not to feel utterly stressed about getting a 'B'. Nope, that was a reality I could not imagine.

We began making the trek down the hall toward our classes, my brain now spinning with trying to remember my lines, the impending conversation with my dad, and wondering how anyone could be okay with anything less than the best, my bff included.

Addy expelled a long sigh. "What's on your mind?" The question came out in a tone of recognition. She knew my tendency to get lost in my head.

"Too many things…as usual. My dad wants to talk to me tonight about something big. And, I still can't figure out how you're always okay with not getting good grades. Like, what would that even be like?"

Addy threw her head back and laughed. "Oh, my darling Jessie, I'm sure this thing with your dad is nothing. You haven't done anything wrong, right? And as for my grades…well, you should try to chill a bit. Heck, I bet your lines are spinning in your head too, yes?" She raised her eyebrows at me.

I shook my head. "You know me too well." I elbowed her in the ribs. "I wish you'd tried out with me."

"And stand securely in your shadow for the next few months? Nah, I'd rather make a bunch of noise at every performance and embarrass you."

She would, too. I could count on it. "Do you think you'll come over tonight?"

"I still have to ask Ralph and Janis, but I'm sure they'll allow me to grace you with my presence on your birthday."

"Why don't you call your parents 'Mom' and 'Dad'? It's been eight years since they adopted you."

"I know, and they're good to me, but you know, they're not *my* parents." A shadow crossed her face. We generally avoided talk of her dead parents.

She looked down the hall and her expression lightened, the sadness either chased away…or sent away. "Ooo, there's Jakey," Addy squealed.

My boyfriend of a solid three months made his way toward us, his tall, lanky frame sauntering down the hall. He caught my eye and gave me a head bob and a smile. It was dumb—it'd been three months—but I still felt the little stir of butterflies in my stomach whenever I saw him.

When he reached us, he put his arm around me. "Happy birthday, beautiful," he said, his too-deep-for-high-school voice sending chills down my body.

"Thanks," I uttered awkwardly, my cheeks burning hot.

"That's my cue," said Addy. Then she turned the corner and disappeared down an adjacent hall. I watched her go, concerned that the mention of her parents may have put a damper on her day. But then, Addy was good at tucking her emotions away.

Silence settled between me and my boyfriend as we made our way, hand in hand, down the hall. It was the comfortable type of silence, the kind that happens when you feel totally at ease with someone.

"So," said Jake. "Big plans for your birthday today?"

"The usual, I suppose. Dinner and cake when I get home. Unless you have something in mind?" I squeezed my eyes shut and turned my head away from him. Was I too obvious?

But Jake smiled, kindness crinkling his eyes. "Nothing much for me tonight. Probably just dinner with the rents and then homework."

"Oh," The word—and the extreme disappointment in my tone slipped from my lips before my internal filter had a chance to catch it. "Cool." I worked to recover, but even I wasn't convinced.

"Why? Was there something else—?"

"No!" I shouted over him, each utterance sinking me deeper into embarrassment as my cheeks burned red. "Sorry." I pressed my lips together, as if it was the only way to prevent any more idiocy from escaping them. I swallowed my disappointment. I'd so hoped Jake would see me tonight. But then, he wasn't exactly comfortable around my family. My dad had all but threatened him when we first started dating, and Cora ogled him like she was into him while Talia pointedly ignored him. I couldn't blame the guy.

"Jess, I like you. And I'm happy it's your birthday. That reminds me." He reached into his pocket and extracted a small, red velvet box. "I got you something." He thrust the box forward, a smile on his face.

I examined him. His short auburn hair—slightly longer in front—fell just above his green eyes and a few freckles dotted his slender nose. He towered over me and I had to crane my neck to look into those eyes, now crinkling with his smile. He wasn't "hot" in the conventional way, but he was cute, and my attraction to him had grown with my affection.

I took the box from him and opened it. Inside I found a heart pendent strung on a golden chain. As the first piece of jewelry I had ever received from a guy, it wasn't exactly my style, but I loved it. "Wow, Jake, thank you!" I exclaimed as I immediately found the clasp and worked to open it.

"Here, let me." He took the necklace from me as I turned my back to him. Chills ran down my spine as his cold fingertips brushed my skin, both from the fact that *he* was touching me and from his icy digits.

I turned toward him and looked down at the heart hanging around my neck. "I love it. Thank you," I said. I stood on my tip toes and gave him a kiss on the cheek.

An immediate blush covered the surface of his skin where my lips had been, and he averted his gaze to the floor with a shy smile. Then, he extended his hand, and I placed mine in his grip as he walked me to my first class.

And that was the last time I saw him.

Well, at least until third hour Chem. That was the only fifty minutes in the entire day we crossed paths—even including lunchtime—and I was forced to go to rehearsal immediately after the school day ended. But considering acting was my passion, and I had prepared for a lead role from the moment the musical selection was announced, I could think of worse ways to spend my birthday.

Rehearsal was a welcome reprieve—it was something I could fully focus on. Despite my promises to my dad, I had been unable to put our impending conversation—whatever it was—to the back of my mind. And the more I thought about it, the bigger it loomed. I couldn't shake the darkness I'd seen on my father's face this morning.

"Hey, nice job today, Jessie. I'm not surprised you've already memorized the first few scenes, but I'm still impressed," Mrs. Ferris, the musical director said as I prepared to leave for home following rehearsal. She pushed her oversized glasses up on her nose and tucked her shoulder-length brownish-gray hair behind her ear. I always thought she looked a little mouse-like. Pointy big nose, protruding teeth. But she was one of the nicest teachers at the school. Her expression held amusement, but I was missing the joke. "Isn't there something special about today?" she asked, looking like she was trying to prevent her lips from cracking a smile.

"Oh, yeah," I answered, surprised she knew. "It's my birthday today."

"That's what I thought. Happy birthday, my leading lady." She dipped into a bow.

"Th—thanks," I said.

"You have a great evening, Jessie." With a wave of her hand, she twirled away from me, leaving me shaking my head. She was most definitely a drama teacher.

Mom had already picked up my sisters, leaving me alone for the car ride home. I welcomed the solitude. It offered ten free minutes to decompress after my long day at school. My stomach rumbled and I glanced at my car clock. It was 6:00 p.m.—definitely time for some birthday cake. I blasted my radio and sang along to show tunes all the way home. When I pulled into the driveway, there were an unusual number of cars there.

One of them was Addy's.

Another was Jake's.

"What the—?"

I parked the car, then walked up to the house, not sure what to expect. When I pulled the front door open, my family, boyfriend and best friend all screamed, "Surprise," scaring the living daylights out of me.

"Geez, guys!" I yelled, but I couldn't help grinning. I was genuinely surprised. "I have to say, I did not see that coming."

Jake crossed the room and gave me a hug. "I meant dinner with *your* family," he said.

"Love you, hon!" squealed Addy. She squeezed me tight, lifting my feet off the ground for a split second.

I smiled at my mom, knowing full well that this surprise had been her idea. But something shadowed her return smile. It didn't quite reach her eyes, and all throughout pizza and cake, she seemed nervous, fiddling with the amber encased bug around her neck, not laughing at anyone's jokes.

Something was off.

My dad's words ran through my memory again, and dread crept over me. I looked from my mother to my father, who sat in the corner, silently observing, a scowl on his face. No, something was not right here.

"Jessie!!" My youngest sister Cora jabbed my shoulder, waking me from my stupor. "I want you to open my present first!" She thrust her gift into my hands.

"Oh, okay." I tore open the wrapping and found an iridescent blank journal inside.

"You said you wanted to get back to keeping a journal, so I got you one."

I smiled, my glance shifting from the book in my hands to my youngest sister's face. "Thank you, Cora. That's really thoughtful. Mom, didn't Cora find the perfect gift?" I tested.

"Hmm? Oh yes, very nice," she dismissed. She jumped to her feet and started clearing away the empty plates, avoiding my eyes.

My dad cleared his throat and checked his wrist. "Well, it's almost nine. Soon time for you kids to head home, I think." It wasn't a suggestion.

Jake held back as my sisters made their way upstairs to their rooms and my parents talked in hushed tones as they cleaned up. Addy made her way out the door first.

"Can you walk me out?" Jake asked. "I have one more gift for you."

"Bye!" hollered Addy as she climbed into her car and fired it up. "Love you! Happy birthday!"

"Thanks Addy! Love you, too!" I waved as she pulled away from the curb, leaving me and Jake alone. A cool breeze kicked up and I silently scolded myself for coming outside without a coat. Between the fun of the birthday surprise and the distraction of my parents' bizarre behavior, I'd forgotten it was February.

"Sorry about my dad. He can be a turd," I said, rubbing my arms to keep warm.

"Oh, no worries. I guess his job as a detective makes him a little suspicious of everyone. Anyway, it is getting late, and I still have homework."

Jake peered down at me and I saw the moon reflected in his emerald eyes. He licked his lips and I could tell what was on his mind—the same thing that was on mine.

I drew closer to him, and he wrapped his arms wrapped around me, reaching down and nuzzling my nose with his, in an Eskimo kiss. Then he went in, laying a soft kiss on my lips. Warmed from the inside, I forgot the nip of the night air as I snuggled into his chest. He squeezed his arms around me, and I gazed up at him, offering my face for more, and he didn't refuse me. We made out on my front lawn with no shame.

When our lips smacked apart, I felt the hammering of Jake's heart in his chest and smiled at the knowledge that I was the one responsible for that reaction. I liked that.

"Thanks for coming," I told him.

He held me tight still, and the scent of his cologne wafted into my nostrils. "I really, really like you, Jess. Like a lot."

"That's good because I really, really like you, too." I smiled and he leaned in for one more good-night kiss.

"Before I go, there's that gift I mentioned."

"Ahh yes." I stood back from him in anticipation.

He reached inside his coat and took out a small canvas, then handed it to me.

Gazing down, I saw he'd painted a picture of a vibrant purple flower. "It's beautiful," I said. "My favorite color."

Excitement lit in his eyes, and he pointed to the image. "Not only that, but it's a violet." He paused, his eyes holding expectation.

"I'm sorry, I—"

"Oh!" he said. "No worries. Violets are February's flower, your birth flower. I looked it up."

Warmth radiated through me at the thoughtfulness of this gift.

"Jake, that's—" But I didn't have the appropriate words to finish whatever I was going to say. My eyes stung with moisture. "That's really thoughtful. I love it. And I love even more that you took the time to make something for me."

"Happy to." He gazed down at me, then leaned in and gave me one last soft, slow kiss. "Happy birthday, Jessie." Tipping his forehead to mine, we froze like this, and the joy of this perfect moment warmed my heart, making me forget for a few minutes about what was waiting for me inside.

"Okay, I don't want to but I have to go. I told my mom I'd be home by 9:30, so I can have time to do my homework."

"That's okay. I'm just glad you came. Text me when you get home?"

"You know it." He withdrew one arm from around me and fingered the heart hanging from my neck. "It looks good on you," he said with a smile and then he turned to go. I waited as he got into his car, then waved as he pulled away, my insides on fire with excitement and affection for this boy.

I was still smiling when I walked through the front door. My sisters were nowhere to be seen but my parents sat, side by side, on our brown leather couch in the living room, waiting for me.

Oh, God . It was time for the *talk*.

"What's—up?" I asked with a tilt of my head.

"Jessie, sit down."

Looked like there was no putting this off. I sank in the patterned chair across from them.

"Do you remember what I mentioned this morning?"

"Yes, Dad." *It had plagued me all day.* I gulped, the anticipation stirring up my belly. My leg started bouncing of its own accord, until my dad gave me a stern look. Palming my knee, I tried to stop the trembling, but I couldn't control the nervous energy racing through my body and was only successful in toning it down a notch.

He nodded. He gave a sidelong glance to my mom, whose endless fiddling of her necklace was now driving me crazy—before returning his gaze to mine. "You're seventeen now."

"I know, and you guys seem to be making a big deal out of it. It's kind of freaking me out."

"We don't mean to alarm you, but we do need to talk. Now that you're of age—"

"Of age? For what?"

My dad squeezed his eyes shut, his irritation apparent. He rubbed his temples before resuming. "Please don't interrupt. Let me get this out."

"Okay, sorry," I mumbled.

"We wanted you to celebrate with your friends tonight and with your...boyfriend..." The word came out as if it caused him physical pain to say. "Because...things are about to change for you. We wanted you to have a fun night with them, share a great kiss good-night...create some memories. Because it's all going to change."

I must have looked dumbfounded, so he clarified. "Honey, you're going to have to break up with Jake. And it would be wise to distance yourself from Addy too. Your life is about to get very complicated and you can't afford any distractions. Do you understand?"

Uhm—no.

2

Jessie

"What do you mean I have to *break up* with Jake? And not see Addy? You're talking about my best friend and my boyfriend," I argued, as if they had no clue what they were asking.

Maybe they didn't. Maybe this was some kind of weird birthday prank. Wishful thinking. But when my parents' only answer was an exchanged look of concern, I continued.

"You can't just forbid me from seeing my best friend and my boyfriend."

My gaze traveled between the grief-stricken eyes of my mother and the stern glare of my father. But still, neither of them offered a word.

"What did I do?" The question came out small, my voice sounding closer to a little girl's than an almost grown woman's.

"*You* didn't do anything, sweetheart," my mother assured me. Tonight, she was pet free, a rare occurrence for her.

"Then—"

"Look, Jessie girl. I have to tell you something, and I know you're going to think I'm joking, but I'm not. This is serious. But you have to

16

understand, so hear me out, okay?" My dad raised his eyebrows, as if asking my permission to proceed.

I didn't have a clue what he meant, but I waved my hand for him to continue.

"We've given you a good life here, no?"

I nodded, my stomach flipping in uncomfortable somersaults, the cake and pizza from earlier climbing up my throat, threatening to make a reappearance.

"We've been able to do that because we've followed certain...*rules*...for our existence."

"Our existence? What does that mean?"

My parents exchanged a glance.

"Jessie girl, I'm going to tell you a story now. It's going to be hard to hear, hard to believe, but it's *our* story." His Adam's apple bobbed up and down in his throat as he gulped, his wary gaze bouncing between my mother and me before settling on my face. "The first thing you need to know is…we're not exactly mortal," my dad said with a rush, pausing for the bomb to drop, watching me closely in case I flew off the handle.

"What?" was all I could think of to say, as the nausea swelled in my belly.

My father cleared his throat and folded his hands together. "Have you ever heard of the Fountain of Youth?"

"Ponce de Leon and all that? Of course."

He nodded, his eyes pinned on me. "Yes, exactly." He paused for effect, obviously hoping his revelation would sink in. But I didn't know what in the world he was talking about.

"What?" I uttered again.

My dad sighed and pinched the bridge of his nose. "I'm doing a poor job of this." He cast a desperate look at my mom.

She bit her lip and rubbed the bug pendant she clutched around her neck. "Sweetie, the Fountain of Youth is a real thing. Its history goes back much further than Ponce de Leon, only it wasn't called by that name back then." She paused, measuring my reaction.

"How long ago are we talking?"

Mom cast Dad a nervous glance, then puffed out a sigh. "As far back as we know. Think origin of humanity, millennia. Back then, life was very different than it is now. Communities lived in absolute harmony. We all had roles to fulfill, and we did them without question. Within our community, your father was a Cataloger. His job was to investigate new discoveries in plant food and animals, learn about them and report back to the community. And I..." She broke up, her eyes welling with tears. "It was my job to work with the animals as a teacher. I knew every kind and breed and I taught the children about them—how to interact with them, how to approach them, what they eat, how to care for them, how they preferred to be talked to."

"Talked to?"

As if on cue, Millie ambled into the room, her collar jingling with her arrival. Sensing the strange atmosphere, she put her ears back and settled at my mom's feet, looking up to her for comfort.

Now that I thought of it, Mom had always been Millie's favorite member of the family. They seemed to share a special connection, something Cora had been jealous of when she was younger—although I was never sure whether my sister wanted to be closer to Mom...or to the dog.

"Life was very different back then. Every creature lived in harmony. We communicated, we coexisted, and we took care of each other. The land produced food to eat and, in turn, we took care of the land. All living things shared a special connection, a reciprocal relationship. No one went hungry, there was no violence, no want. Life was perfect.

"In the center of our community was this beautiful Fountain. No one knew much about it but there was one rule we all knew well—the

Fountain was off limits. We were not to drink its waters or even dip a finger in it. To ensure this never happened, the Fountain was under constant surveillance by the Great Guardian. I mentioned everyone had a job—well, that was his. To guard the water of the Fountain."

"But why? Why couldn't anyone drink from it?" I sat forward in my seat, captured by the story, though I refused to see it as anything but a fairy tale. Still, I'd hear my parents out.

"Our world thrived on balance and the Fountain maintained that balance. To drink would cause a disruption to life as we knew it, and any disruption came with consequences. For most of us, that was okay because life was good, perfect really. Because we wanted for nothing and there were no dangers to us, there was no need to question anything.

But for one person, our peaceful existence wasn't enough. This woman was intrigued by the Fountain, and in the end, her curiosity got the better of her." At the mention of this woman, my mom's tone hardened.

Dad squeezed her hand and took over the story. "She and your mother were friends. Maybe it was because of all the time she'd spent in the garden tending to the plants and being around the Fountain, or maybe it was inevitable...but this woman was the first to take a drink from the waters."

"But what about the Guardian guy? Wasn't it his job to stop her?"

It was Mom who answered. "No, not to stop her. To warn her. To warn us all, to dissuade us from breaking that critical rule. But our will is our own, and she couldn't help herself—she tasted the water."

Millie jumped onto Mom's lap and circled several times before laying down, looking into Mom's face with canine worry as tears trailed down each of her cheeks. "It was chaos after that. It was as if the earth immediately responded. By taking the drink, by committing the one forbidden act, she had brought mortality into our world. She'd shifted the balance."

Mom paused, then cleared her throat and continued, her voice a bit stronger. "A great storm blew up, destroying homes, injuring some of us. It was a terrifying time. Life as we'd known it no longer existed and we suddenly found ourselves in this new, unfamiliar world. No one knew what to do."

She dropped her head and scratched Millie behind the ears.

Dad picked up where she left off. "Because one woman had taken a drink, making us all mortal, the rest of us were given a choice—stay as we were and figure it out, or drink from the waters, too. The Guardian ensured us the water would return us to our immortal state—but there would be consequences.

"We couldn't imagine anything worse than what was already happening around us. People dying, fear and anger, destroyed homes and crops. It was like the land and weather revolted against us, declaring war, and we were desperate to establish peace. We figured that any consequences we'd have to pay would pale in comparison to what we were experiencing."

I rested my chin on my palm, enraptured, my imagination easily engaging with the story. "So, what happened?"

"This is where it gets a little weird," Dad warned.

"Oh, it's already weird, but I need to know what happened."

"Yes, you do," he agreed. "Because this impacts you, too."

His statement sobered me a bit, reminding me that something dire lurked within this fairy tale—something I was now old enough to grasp, apparently. I shifted in my seat, drawing my knees into my chest and resting my feet on the cushion beneath me, figuratively protecting myself from whatever was coming.

"The woman who took the first drink was convinced that if we all drank the water, it would fix everything. Her family was the first to follow her example and then they went door to door, trying to convince the rest of the community to follow suit. Many did, but some did not.

"Those who did drink, your mother and I included, regained our immortality. Broken bones were set back into place, health was restored. Things looked like they were returning to the way they had been. But we couldn't have been more wrong."

Mom's gaze drifted off somewhere in the distance as she continued the story. "The Fountain served as the balance in our perfect world. And once the balance was broken, it had to figure out a way to survive. So it evolved, and we had to deal with the consequences of this evolution. Our Fountain is the true Fountain of Youth, and it exists to heal, to make those who drink from it immortal—just like in folklore. But the stories neglect one critical aspect. They don't mention how the Fountain gets its infinite stores of life-giving power."

She gulped, her gaze still lost in distant memory. Then she shook her head slightly, sat a bit straighter, and continued the story.

"Drinking the water came at a great cost. While The Fountain gives immortality to those who drink, it also awakens a bloodlust within them. To get what it needs, it uses those who drink like puppets. They become killers."

She took another deep breath, obviously having trouble finishing the story. By this point, I couldn't believe what I was hearing…but I had to learn the rest, even though every word brought me closer to throwing up.

After a short pause, she continued. "It's a compulsion deep within that awakens—the voice of the water starts to speak to you until you can no longer ignore it. And then, you take a life. This happened Community-wide, and we revolted against each other. No one wanted to kill another person, but we had no control, and it was inevitable. The only way to break free of the water's compulsions is to kill another immortal person, one who had had a drink. That gives the water the stores of an immortal life and your debt is paid. For many of us…" She gulped, her gaze returning to the present, reaching for my Dad and then meeting my own eyes. "Your father and I included, that debt was quickly paid since so many within the Community had had a drink, so many were immortal."

I raised my hand. "Wait, just wait. I need a second." My heart skittered inside my chest, every feverish beat intensifying the growing nausea in my belly. "No," I said, shaking my head, hot tears stinging my eyes. "I can't...I don't accept what you're telling me." I sprung to my feet, pacing the space in front of my chair. Millie lifted her head, her ears standing up in concern.

"You're telling me you guys are...are...mur— murderers." I stopped in front of them, tears trailing down my face, my breaths coming out short.

Mom stood and approached me, trying to hug me, but I shrugged her off. "Don't touch me. Please!" I screamed. This wasn't real. It couldn't be!

Lifting her hands in surrender, she retreated to the sofa.

"Jessie, I know this is hard to grasp. Please know that this happened a very long time ago—millennia have passed since then—and that we were sick over what we'd done. At the time, we had no idea...we didn't know what the water would make us. But we're free from that now, understand? We need you to know that your parents don't moonlight as serial killers, okay?" Mom's tone carried a plea.

I bounced where I stood, trying to absorb what she was saying, but I was too distracted by the growing nausea in my belly. "I'm going to be sick!" I announced, and ran out of the living room, making it to the bathroom just in time to puke all the pizza and cake and ice cream I'd gorged myself on earlier. I spit into the toilet and wiped my mouth. When I flushed and looked into the mirror, a white face stared back at me. My hands shook as I turned the faucet and splashed cold water on my face and then rinsed my mouth.

This wasn't happening.

It was a dream.

My parents had lost it.

I shook my head, which now pounded, and made my way back to the living room. My mom came to me, wrapped her arms around me and held me. This time, I didn't resist.

"I'm sorry, Jessie, I am. I know this is a lot to take in."

"Why are you telling me this? I don't want to know this about you." I tore from her grip and returned to my seat, pulling my knees into my chest again.

"Because, sweetie, you are the daughter of immortals. The same demands will be made of you."

"What?!" I shot up to my feet. "But I didn't drink any water. I didn't throw off any balance."

"I know." My mom dropped her head as her voice lowered to a whisper. "But you are of pure immortal blood and that is one of the consequences, too—that our offspring would be faced with the same compulsions we had, way back then. I was never going to have children for this reason…"

"Why did you then?" I snapped. "Seems a bit irresponsible."

I saw the impact of my words in her expression and felt an immediate rush of guilt. "I'm sorry, Mom, I didn't mean—"

"You're not wrong," she said. "I ignored the impulse to have children for a very long time. But when I finally decided to settle with your father, the desire for a baby overcame me. He warned me—but I wanted you so badly. I knew we'd have time to figure it out, to prepare. It was selfish of me, I know, and I'm sorry for that." She rushed to me now and took my hands in hers. "But I can't imagine my life without you and your sisters in it. I wouldn't trade you for the world. We're going to get through this. Our people have a way through and that's what we need to discuss."

"Our people? There are more?"

She nodded. "After the dust settled and we gained our bearings—and after we discovered that our murderous impulses had been inherited by our immortal children—we organized. We figured out a way for our offspring to learn to control the water's urges, to work with it rather than against it, and to channel it to more productive uses. We'll get to that later. But you need to know that as you approach adulthood, Jessie, the water's voice will begin to stir within you, too. It's going to be scary, but you're going to be okay. We have an ironclad method for dealing with all of this, okay? We call ourselves 'the Community' and there are pockets of us all over the world, infiltrated into societies everywhere. In our own neck of the woods, there are numerous families spread within a certain radius. We take care of each other, support one another when a child comes of age. And that support is available to you."

"No," I said.

"No?" She narrowed her eyes.

"I don't accept this. I'll fight it. I refuse to kill someone."

There it was again—the look my parents exchanged.

My dad leaned forward and expelled a heavy sigh. "Your reaction is understandable, but I'm afraid you don't get a choice in this. You have to work with us, let us teach you. We don't know exactly when things will change for you, but the water usually starts making itself heard to young people sometime between the ages of seventeen and eighteen. Soon, the water will begin to speak to you. You'll have strange impulses that don't feel like your own until, eventually, you won't be able to fight them. Those urges will take over and you will start paying your debt to the water by giving what it demands—the lives of others."

"No," I objected again. "I can fight it. I have a strong mind."

"You absolutely do. You are brilliant, my girl, but this has nothing to do with strength. This is bigger than all of us."

I huffed and turned from them, trying to process this bizarre tale. I couldn't imagine having bloodthirsty impulses. Hell, I was captain of our volunteer squad at school, the girl who released spiders outside instead of killing them. I was not a murderer, and I couldn't imagine becoming one, any more than I could conceptualize the things my parents admitted to doing.

I shook my head, emotion threatening to get the better of me. "No," I whimpered. "That doesn't work for me. I don't want to be…this." Doing my best to stay composed, I swallowed past the lump in my throat and the heat of my tears stung my face.

My mom squeezed my knee. "I'm so sorry, sweetie."

I thought of my sisters. "What about Talia and Cora?"

My parents exchanged a glance, but it was Dad who answered. "Their time will come. But right now, they aren't ready to learn of their heritage, so it's imperative we keep this between us. Okay?"

I shook my head in disbelief. This wasn't real. "Is that all?" I managed to say as I choked my sobs down.

Dad cleared his throat and leaned back against the sofa. "Not quite. We mentioned that many of us took a drink from the Fountain when it was offered. Many—but not all. Those who did not lost many of their loved ones to the compulsions stirred within those of us who did drink, and they wanted revenge. Ever since that time, they've hunted us. They call themselves The Order of Mortal Defenders. You need to be aware of this because they could be anywhere."

"But…if we're immortal, how are they are danger to us? And isn't everyone who didn't take a drink back then dead by now?"

"They are, but their ancestors are not. The Order is almost cult-like—it's a very secretive organization. Hunting and killing us is their religion." Dad sat up and looked me in the eye. "Remember when we said the Fountain evolved? Well, a plant started to grow from its waters—and that plant is an antidote."

A bloom of hope sprung up in my heart. "I can just take that! I don't need to be immortal."

Sadness filled my mom's expression as she met my hopeful gaze. "The antidote is available to those who *drank* from the fountain out of their own will. But for those of you who inherited it, one taste of that plant and you'll turn to dust."

I gulped. "Oh."

"So, just be on your guard. Be watchful, okay?"

As if finding out I was a murderer-in-waiting wasn't enough, now I was in mortal danger from some invisible force I couldn't see coming.

Sudden exhaustion crushed me. "Can I go to bed now?" I felt a meltdown coming on.

"Just one more thing," Mom said, turning her pleading gaze to Dad.

He cleared his throat and stood. "You can do this when you're ready, but...as we told you: you're going to have to break up with Jake. And you might consider distancing yourself from Addy, as well. It's not safe for them to be around you while you're training. And..." He paused, scratching the back of his head. "As an immortal, you are already promised."

"*What?*" That word had come out of my mouth so many times, it was starting to sound weird. I grappled to wrap my mind around this newest piece of information.

"When two immortals have a family, everyone knows what to expect. They both know what the other one is, they both understand the need to kill and they can work as a team in fulfilling the water's demands. And as long as the bloodline is kept pure, their children will be awakened and commissioned by the water in a predictable way. And we have a system to manage it all. However, if you were to end up with a mortal, there's no way they'd understand what you are. It would pose a risk to our entire Community. And worse, your children would become wild cards—maybe the water will come calling, maybe not. The situation would become impossible to contain, very quickly."

"I can't...I can't handle anymore." I pushed my mother's hands off me. "I need to get out of here." Panic rose inside me, and an immediate impulse to run took over.

Springing to my feet, I escaped to my room and shut the door. I leaned against it and slid to the floor, no longer able to contain my tears as heavy sobs racked my body. My eyes fell on the balloons next to my bed, this morning feeling a lifetime away. If this was seventeen, I didn't want any of it.

But according to my parents, I had no choice in the matter.

3

Jessie

When my alarm went off, I woke with a start and realized I was on the floor. Sometime between the snot and tears, I'd drifted off to sleep for a few short hours, still uncomfortably leaning against my bedroom door. I sat up, rubbing the crick in my neck and blinked, trying to wake up.

Maybe it'd all been a dream.

Groggy from my limited sleep, I considered my options. School, which was my sweet spot, suddenly seemed senseless. What did American history or calculus matter if I was about to become a monster? I shuddered at the thought of that, and the store of tears I thought I'd exhausted welled in my eyes again.

My parents were killers, and I would be too.

Maybe they were wrong. They had been before...although this would a pretty big error on their part. And what about me being *promised* to another immortal?

I couldn't deal with it—any of it! Last night's sob fest had bankrupted my energy reserves, leaving me almost too weak to even think about what last night's revelation would mean—losing Jake, losing Addy...and eventually myself.

I could refuse, could tell my parents I wouldn't meet the guy I'm supposed to end up with, won't train, won't become *this thing* I already despised.

Why did I even have to think about marriage yet, anyway? *I was seventeen.* In my plan, I had at least a good eight to ten years before settling down was on the radar. I was going to finish high school, get my college degree in biology and then do my best to get accepted into the only veterinary school in our state. Once all that was done, maybe I'd have time to think about having a family one day.

Now ALL that had changed.

I thought about my fate—that I was destined to kill, that something inside of me would awaken and *change* me, that I was immortal. Nausea rumbled in my belly and my panic rose. I had to get a grip if I was going to make it through the day at all.

Immortal.

So consumed by the murdering aspect of all of this, I'd almost forgotten that piece. I'd never seen any indication I was immortal before. If I got cut, I bled. End of story.

If I was brave, I'd test it out in a big way—jump out my window or something. The thought sent a nervous shudder through me. Thinking back to my childhood, I'd never broken a bone and couldn't remember having any injuries of note. I'd had a handful of scraped knees and cuts as a kid, but nothing out of the ordinary. Hell, just a couple of weeks ago, I'd cut myself shaving in the shower and it had bled like a mother. A tiny speck of hope teetered on the edge of my heart. Maybe my parents were wrong! If I was immortal, shouldn't I immediately heal? Maybe I could just forget about this whole thing and leave it behind me.

I had to test this new hopeful theory, prove my mortality to myself.

I jumped to my feet, clicked on my desk lamp and rifled through my backpack until I found the pencil bag inside . I carefully slipped the safety pin holding the small tear in the bag open and removed it, the sharp end gleaming in the soft glow of my lamp.

I sucked in a sharp breath, then pierced my finger with the pointed tip of the pin. Glancing down, a small spot of blood appeared. I swiped it away, revealing the tiniest pinprick in my finger. Phew, mortal!

But then I watched it close up, healing entirely...and zapping my short-lived hope.

A soft knock sounded on my door. Staring at my finger, I opened the door, only looking up to meet my mother's gaze when she greeted me. I gawked at her blankly, still trying to comprehend what I'd just witnessed.

She stood there, still dressed in her nightgown. This morning, her parrot Liza rested on her shoulder.

"Hello friend," the bird said.

"I came to check on you. I know we upset you last night, and I—"

"Why can I suddenly heal?" I demanded.

My mom's gaze flicked down to my miraculously healed finger, and the safety pin I held in my other hand. Understanding crossed her expression. "This is why we told you on your birthday. The changes start gradually, and this is the first one. I didn't expect it so soon, but here we are."

"I don't understand. If I'm immortal, why didn't this kind of thing happen in the beginning? Why suddenly now?"

"Two reasons. One, when you're growing, your cells are too and they need to learn how to repair themselves over time. Now that you're of age—"

"I hate when you say that."

"Even so, now that you are done growing, that ability kicks in." She reached for my hand, but I jerked my finger away.

"And the second reason?"

"You'll need your invincibility. Once the water's voice awakens within you, you'll become a hunter and you must have an advantage over your prey. They can hurt you but one of the water's benefits is that you will mend. You cannot die, and any injuries you get will heal."

"Well, I can die, if I encounter one of those Mortal Defender people."

Mom sobered. "Yes, and you must take them seriously, Jessie. Watch those around you, okay? Don't accept any—"

I interrupted again with a dismissive wave of my hand, "—yeah, yeah, I know. No leaves."

She watched me for a moment, compassion in her gaze. "How are you this morning?"

I threw myself onto my bed. "Terrible, Mom. I can't do this. In fact, I've decided I *won't* do it. You want me to break up with my boyfriend, completely alter all the plans I had for my life, and accept that I'm destined to kill people. How do you think I am?"

She sighed and crossed into my room, pulling out my desk chair and positioning it across from me. She covered my hand with hers. "I know it's a lot. I wish there were another way."

"Hello friend," said Liza again, and Mom gave her a treat from the pocket of her robe.

Heat covered my cheeks and a defiant sob rose in my throat. "Me, too," I said, and I could hear the desperation in my own tone. I'd wanted to prove them wrong, but the pinprick told the truth. A sense of defeat overcame me, and behind it, despair. I choked that down and resolved to take control of this. Even if I was immortal, that didn't mean I had to let this water take over my life. It was *my* life and I had control of it. I could do this. And I would do it perfectly, just like everything else I did in my life.

"No!" I yelled, jumping to my feet.

Mom's face twisted in confusion at my outburst. "No what?"

"Just…no. I'm not doing this. I don't care if I can suddenly heal or that I'm going to live forever. I won't become what you're trying to make me be! That's not who I am." My face grew hot as my heart thrashed and tears fell down my cheeks.

Mom closed her eyes and when she opened them again, grief swirled in her gaze. "I'm not trying to make you *be* anything. This is what you are and we can't change it. I don't want to blow your life up or steal your dreams. But it is what it is. Try to view it as a gift."

"A gift?!" My stomach flopped, and I shook with indignation. "How can you call this a *gift*?! You said I was going to *kill* people, Mom!"

My mother stood and took a seat next to me on the bed, but I smacked her comforting touch away. "You can still have the life you dreamed of. You can still go to veterinary school and have a family and—"

"How, Mother?! How am I supposed to go to school while fighting off blood lust? And I can't even imagine having—" I shuddered and gulped, "—sex with some stranger I don't know, so I'll never have children. Why would I want them? Why would I knowingly bring children into this world when I know what they'll become? Why did you?!"

My question hung in the air between us. Tears welled in my mom's eyes, threatening to melt some of my ire, but I narrowed my gaze and focused on my anger. I felt entitled to it and she would hear how I felt.

"I know," she said at last in a calm tone. "I know and I'm sorry. But Jessie, you and your sisters are *my* gift. I know it's hard to accept because this is all new to you, but your father and I have lived with this for a very long time. It's our norm and it will become yours too."

"No." This refusal came out weak, quiet, and I wasn't even sure she'd heard me. Just then, Cora poked her head through the door.

"Hi Mom! Hi Jessie! Can I have those muffins you made for breakfast?" she asked, completely obliviously to the tension in the room.

Mom spared a smile at her. "Good morning, sweetie. Of course, you can."

"Thanks!" She ran down the stairs, going about her *normal* routine of eating breakfast and getting ready for school.

That was normal.

Not this.

My mom turned her attention back to me, and that same crushing sense of defeat threatened to undo me.

"What does it feel like?" I asked, a hollow sigh echoing through me.

"What does what feel like?" She shrugged a shoulder, making Liza move from her left to her right.

"The voice of the water. What should I be expecting?"

Mom was silent for a moment, then said, "It's like a voice from within. At first, you'll notice your emotions getting the better of you. It likes to feed on anger—that's how it often takes control—and then it starts to speak to you. You'll hear its commands and you'll want to resist. You'll be able to hold out for a while but eventually the voice will grow louder, the commands impossible to ignore."

"How—how do I know when that's what it is? How do I prepare?" My pulse sped as a new wave of nausea settled in my gut. I considered the day before me and shook my head. "Mom, I can't go to school. I feel too…raw. This is all too much. What if I get angry? What if I wake it up on accident?"

She reached for me, and this time, I didn't fight her warm touch. "Oh honey, that's not how it works. You don't have control over this, and you can't hold yourself responsible for what's going to happen. You will learn to work *with* the voice of the water. But as for school…" She shifted Liza onto her arm. "I came in to check on you, but also to let you know that you won't be going today. Dad and I think it's important for you start your training right away."

My head snapped up. "Training?"

"Yes, we told you we have a system, a tried and true way of dealing with this. So, why don't you take your time getting ready for the day. We'll get your sisters to school and then tend to all of this. Okay?"

I gave a subtle nod as my mom rose from the bed. Speaking threatened to unleash the flood of emotions overwhelming me. She shut the door behind her, and the second the latch clicked, I burst into tears. Burying my face in my palms, I tried to stifle the sobs that rose from deep within me. I sat there, dissolved into a puddle of my own grief.

Fifteen minutes later, someone knocked on the door.

"Not now," I said, emotion I was still struggling to choke down heavy in my tone. I dabbed my eyes with a tissue and blew my nose. My face felt puffy and worn.

"Jess, it's me, Talia." My sister's muffled answer came through the closed door.

"What do *you* want?" I cringed at how cold that question came out. It wasn't her fault all this was happening, or that it was happening to me first. My acknowledgment of these truths softened me a bit.

The door swung open and Talia leaned against the door jamb, appraising me. Her shoulder length dark hair cascaded around her face, her features betraying our family connection while being uniquely hers. Her slim nose came to a point and her hazel eyes—our mother's eyes—looked me up and down. An assemblage of female Marvel characters—Black Widow, Scarlet Witch, Okoye, Captain Marvel—covered her t-shirt, displaying their superhero girl power.

"Aren't you going to school?" Talia crossed her arms over her chest.

Millie lifted her head and gave her tail a subtle wag at Talia's appearance.

My eyes narrowed into a glare. "Not today, Tal."

"Why not? What about your perfect attendance aspirations?" she challenged.

I'd forgotten all about that during this nightmare I'd aged into. "I guess that's something I'll have to let go of."

Talia cocked her head. "What's up with you?"

She had no idea what her question invited but her time would come, and this wasn't my bomb to drop. A hybrid of aggravation and pity came over me as I stared back at her. My mind reeled, trying to come up with an answer that wasn't a total lie.

"I just had a fight with Mom and Dad, that's all. They're trying to dictate my future."

Her face twisted into a scowl. "Really, Jess?"

"What?" I snapped, thoroughly annoyed by her response. I was too exhausted for this.

"*You're* irritated that Mom and Dad care about your future? At least they care enough to talk to you about it." Her tone was bitter, and she ripped off a piece of nail with her teeth and spat it to the floor.

I had my own angst to wallow in—I didn't need hers as well. "What do you mean, Talia? Of course, Mom and Dad care about your future, too."

"Think so? Seems to me like they don't have time. They're too busy fawning over their straight A, musically and theatrically gifted eldest child, and their athletically inclined youngest one."

"You're an athlete."

"I guess." She crossed her arms and leaned more heavily into the doorway.

I sighed, devoid of energy. "I don't want to fight with you, Tal. Why'd you come to my room?"

She gave a curt nod and thankfully dropped the topic, opting to instead start chewing on her nails again. "There's someone here to see you."

My chest gave a quick lurch. "Who?" I demanded.

"Some guy." Her answer sounded bored, but I knew that was an act.

She was happy to deliver the news to me, obviously hopeful I'd spill on who he was. If only I knew.

"Okay. I'll be down in a sec. But I need a minute."

Talia nodded and disappeared, closing my bedroom door behind her. Despite myself, I checked my reflection. Puffy eyes and a red nose stared back at me, and my hair looked like a rat's nest.

Taking a deep breath, I tried to get a hold of myself. I ran a brush through my long, dark locks and wiped my face with a cool cloth, trying to ease the swelling around my eyes. It was so incredibly obvious I'd been crying. Annoyed that some stranger was at my house at this hour of the day—especially on the morning after I'd just found out about my imminent murderous instincts—I threw on my sweats and an oversized hoodie.

A little warning would have been nice.

My stomach swirled with uneasy anticipation as I descended the stairs. When I rounded the corner into our living room, I found my parents with some boy. His dark blond hair was longer than I generally liked, hanging somewhere between his chin and his shoulders. I did notice that he had a nice, square jawline and blue eyes framed by full brows.

As I walked into the room, his blue eyes met mine and there was a certain kindness in them, but also something else I couldn't quite discern. He didn't smile at me, but just stared as if he was studying me, unnerving my already fragile sense of self. So, I stared back, refusing to be the first one to shift my gaze away. I don't know what his eyes were searching for, but I vowed to keep mine just as fixed as his were.

"Jessie, this is Tyler." My dad's voice distracted us from our staring contest, and Tyler looked away first. His gaze shifted to my dad and he gave him a smile. I decided I liked his smile until he looked back to me and it fell off his face. Jerk. He cleared his throat and stepped toward me, extending his hand. "Nice to meet you."

"Jess," I said, and I took his hand, paying particular attention to ensuring I shook it with firmness, conveying to him that meeting him did not affect me, whoever he was. "I'm sorry, but who are you?" I asked as our hands separated.

Tyler cleared his throat and shifted his stance, casting an uneasy look at my parents.

"Jess, you remember we told you that you're...you are promised to another immortal?" my mom asked.

I looked from her, to my dad...to Tyler. "No," I said.

Mom's answer was an uncomfortable smile and a shifty gaze.

"Look, if it's any consolation, I'm not thrilled about the idea either," Tyler said. "But I'm here to help you train."

"Train?"

My dad stepped forward. "You're going to come with me and Tyler today. We're going to start getting you ready for what's coming. Okay?"

No, it was not okay. None of this was. My head spun. Things were moving too quickly.

"I need to sit down," I said, as specks started to dot my vision. My mom rushed over and eased me into a chair. I put my head between my knees and closed my eyes, fighting to stay conscious, to make the spinning stop.

Somewhere between consciousness and going under, I heard Talia's voice echo through the room. "'Scuse me...rents? Jessie? Strange male I don't know... We have this thing called school. It starts in, like, ten minutes."

Mom's hand squeezed my knee and then she released me. I ventured a look around the room. The spinning had started to ease.

"Of course. Get your coat on, Talia, and have Cora do the same." Mom stood and gave me a reassuring smile. "You okay?"

I nodded, a lie to myself and to her. I wasn't sure I'd ever be okay again.

Before anyone else could speak, Cora skipped into the living room. "Hey guys—oh…" She stopped short at the sight of Tyler. "Hello there," she said, smiling and tucking the strand that had broken free from her ponytail behind her ear.

She walked towards Tyler and extended her hand. "I'm Cora, number three of this wonderful unit." Ever the charmer, ever the boy-crazed pre-pubescent.

Tyler gave her a warm smile—much warmer than any he'd given me thus far. "I'm Tyler. It's nice to meet you, Cora. I'm a friend of your…" He looked from my dad to me and back at Cora again. "Well, I guess I'm a friend of your sister's."

"I'll be your friend!" Cora's hand shot up in the air as she volunteered.

Tyler laughed. "I'm sure we'll be getting to know each other. too." And he gave her a wink which elicited visible delight from her.

"Cora, sweetie, we need to get going." Mom, now in her warm winter coat, poked her head back in.

"Oh sure, Mama. Catch you later, Ty."

Already at nicknames.

She skipped from the room, and a little wave of jealousy rolled through me at how simple life still was for my two sisters. They were blissfully unaware of what would be coming for them one day.

Dad cleared his throat. "Well now, I guess you've met the whole family, Tyler. Sorry—we probably should have done our first meeting elsewhere. Still, it's done now. At least you two have been properly introduced and as soon as you're ready, Jess, we'll head to our training facility."

"Dad," I managed to say, still feeling entirely drained. "Do I have to go today? I just…I can't…"

Tyler's face tightened and his jawline flexed, as if I'd offended him. But I didn't care.

Dad approached me where I still sat in the chair. "Jess, I'm sorry, but

I need you to push through. We have to get on this."

My head dropped, and I gulped past the knot in my throat. This was my life now. Try as I might to fight against it, to deny the reality, I was going to have to train, with a strange boy I was supposed to one day marry, for a task I couldn't even comprehend.

Seventeen really sucked so far.

4

Jessie

Happy Birthday again, beautiful. I hope you liked my painting. Maybe we can grab a Dr. Pepper after practice or something. I'd like that. <3

Jake's text was a welcome distraction on the car ride to wherever this training would happen. But as I sat in the car, thinking about the stranger I was supposed to one day marry, I couldn't help feeling guilty and I tapped and deleted about fifty responses before settling on one I could send.

I love your painting. It's by my bed. Not feeling well today so won't be at school but would love to see you tomorrow.

I rounded out my response with a kissy face emoji.

I didn't care if my parents wanted me to break up with him, that they already had someone chosen for me. Somehow that knowledge only intensified my desire to get closer to Jake, not end things with him. I wouldn't let the reality of who I was—of what I was supposed to become—take Jake away from me.

"Who you texting there?" My dad's gaze didn't shift from the road as he peeked at the rearview mirror, at Tyler's silver Honda Accord trailing behind our vehicle.

"Just Jake," I said, hugging my phone close to my body.

My dad didn't respond, but I didn't miss the way his eyes narrowed in disapproval.

I fixed my earbuds in my ears and searched on my phone for the mp3's of the songs I would solo for the musical. Eyes closed, I rested my head against the back of the seat and listened. At least when those songs were playing, everything felt like it might be okay in the end. I could lose myself in my character. Oh, to be the baker's wife. To have my only worries be to have a child and survive a giant's descent down a beanstalk. That I could handle. But my own reality? Not so much.

We were in the car longer than I anticipated, which was fine by me. The longer the ride, the more time I had before I had to face all of this. After about thirty minutes, the car finally rolled to a stop and I opened one eye to survey my surroundings.

Our car and Tyler's were the only ones in the lot. Before us stood an old building that looked like it may have housed a school at one point in time. The pavement of the parking lot was cracked and there were deadened weeds growing through the broken asphalt. Since it was the dead of winter, the withered plants were brown and dusted with snow. The building itself stood several stories tall but appeared abandoned. A sign out front was stripped of any labeling, confirming that this building had fallen into disuse.

Open fields flanked either side of the abandoned school building and the only other sign of humanity was a gas station across the way.

"Are you sure this is the right place?" I asked my dad.

"Of course, I am, Jessie."

"Where are we?"

"Headquarters." He didn't look at me, but kept his eyes focused ahead.

"Of???"

He gave me a swift glance. "The Community."

"It has headquarters?" The enormity of this fact dawned on me.

His jaw tensed, but his expression softened when our eyes met.

I couldn't help the fresh round of tears pooling in my eyes. I hadn't cried this much in…well, I couldn't remember. And I was getting tired of how weak this all made me feel.

Dad reached over and patted my shoulder—his attempt to convey warmth, comfort. My mother was better at this. "I'm sure this is a huge shock to you, Jess. Take whatever time you need to process it. To grieve the life you had."

"The life you and Mom blew up," I spat.

Dad tipped his head and expelled a sigh. "I'm sorry," he said, almost inaudibly. "But Jessie, it's coming for you. I have to be honest—" His voice wavered, something I'd never heard before in my life. He punched the steering wheel lightly. "I'm sorry this is happening to you. I'm sorry you feel like we 'blew up' your life. That wasn't our intention, but you have to be ready. When the water starts speaking to you…" He broke off, eyeing me to ensure he had my attention. "It is inescapable. Don't you think we've tried everything, as a Community, to find a way that our children don't have to suffer through this? But there is no way around it. And when you start to experience the water's call, you will know what it is. I'd much rather you be prepared than think you're losing your mind all together. Because it can feel like that. We're doing our best to help you with this. If it's going to happen anyway, I want you know how to handle it."

My heart shifted a minuscule amount. What he said made sense but didn't bring me any closer to accepting it as my truth. Still, I saw the anguish in my dad's expression, heard it in his voice. This was hard for him too, and that fact softened me some. But only a little. I doubt it was harder for him than it was—would be—for me.

"So why does this place look abandoned? I can't be the only kid aging into this."

"You're not, but we use as much discretion as we can. So, families with children around the same age, though perhaps within proximity of each other, do not mix. We keep the training separate too. You'll come here at scheduled times to avoid overlap."

A third car rolled into the lot, a sleek black Charger, with a stranger behind the wheel.

"Who's that?" I asked, weary of all these surprises, dreading meeting another person today.

"His name is Rodney Dougherty. He's the main guru in our area for the kind of training you'll be doing today. Time to get out," Dad said, and he opened his door.

I eyed Tyler as he followed us out of his vehicle, the hardness in his expression remaining. He didn't acknowledge me when he saw me, but he gave my dad a subtle head nod.

Rodney Dougherty approached and extended his hand to my dad. "Greetings John." His palms met together in a prayer position and he gave a slight bow. "And this must be Jessie." Turning to me, there was a warmth in his expression. He looked to be around my dad's age and had short brown hair. When he smiled at me, his amber eyes lit up. I decided he was handsome and felt an instant comfort by his demeanor.

I extended my hand and he took it with a firm grip.

"Pleasure, Jessie." He did the same weird bow thing toward me. "I'll be working with you and Tyler today on one particular aspect of training. Many would agree it's the most important when it comes to what we are, what we can do."

Appraising him, I got a Zen vibe from him—not what I'd expect from someone who was going to train me to kill other people. He wore jogger sweats and a hooded blue fleece.

Together, the four of us approached the abandoned building in total silence, which gave the place an even more ominous feel. I would never want to admit this to my dad, but I huddled a little closer to his protective form as we made our way to the door. The crisp, dark morning and creepy building had me a bit on edge and my dad's presence gave me a sense of security. We reached the back door, which we found chained shut with a padlock. Dad reached for the lock, moving it right then left then right and finally snapped it open. He unwound the chain from around the handles and last, inserted a key. The lock turned with ease and the door swung open.

I could see my breath as we walked inside and was dismayed to find the interior wasn't any warmer than it was outside. Shivering, I rubbed my arms but neither of the three men seemed fazed by the arctic temps. I was relieved when Dad approached the thermostat on the wall and kicked up the heat.

Looking around the area, I didn't find abandoned, rusted lockers or the series of old classrooms I'd expected. The place had been gutted, wide open and pristine. I was reminded to never judge a book. Several doorways jetted off from the walls and I wondered what each of them held. White tile covered the floors and the walls were painted a light gray. Modern lights hung overhead. The area we walked into from the back door didn't have much by way of furniture, save for a couple of couches in one corner.

"Okay, Jessie, this is where I leave you," my dad declared.

"What? You're leaving?" Panic gripped me.

Dad stationed himself between me and the other two men, then gripped my shoulders, and looked me in the eyes. "I trust your life to these two men, okay? Tyler is your partner now and he's going to help you. And Rod—he's going to train your mind to work with the demands that will soon enter it. Okay? I will be back this evening to get you."

I nodded, choking down yet another rising sob. If these men were good enough for my dad, they'd have to be good enough for me. Dad kissed my forehead and gave a nod to the other two before walking out the door.

Rodney smiled warmly at me and gestured in front of him. "Okay, Jessie, come this way with us." I gulped and followed, taking it all in. He led me and Tyler through one of the doors, into a room that looked like a gym. Internally I grimaced, my energy still low due to all the crying I'd been doing over the last twelve hours. I didn't think I had a workout in me.

Mirrors stretched between floor and ceiling on one side of the gym and equipment lined the opposite wall. Everything from exercise bikes to ellipticals to treadmills and every weightlifting device imaginable was available for our use. Along one of the other walls, a row of punching bags hung from the ceiling.

Fitness was really my sisters' arenas. They both seemed to have inherited the athletic genes of the family. I was into academics and the arts, myself. My poor parents encouraged me to try out for teams, and individual sports, but I fought them at every turn. We finally saw eye to eye when it came to dance. It was the one physical activity that made sense to me. Just my body, moving with music. I didn't consider myself extraordinary at dance either, but at least I enjoyed it. Still, I hadn't taken a dance class now in three or four years. If I was going to have to be at the mercy of the water's strange and murderous demands, I could only hope it came with some supernatural strength and agility as a side effect. Otherwise, I was screwed.

Rodney walked to the center of the room, Tyler and I at his heels. The floor beneath my shoes was comprised of foam and was squishy. I liked the feeling of my feet sinking into the surface.

"Alright, Jessie, we're going to take a seat here," he said, squatting down to the floor and crossing his legs. Tyler sunk beside him, arranging his feet in kind.

I followed suit and gazed at them with expectation. "Aren't we going to train?" I asked, confused by our kindergarten rug circle.

"Yes, that's why we're here." Rodney smiled again and closed his eyes.

I looked from him to Tyler, who mirrored Rodney. "I'm confused. We're in a gym. Doesn't 'training' require us to be on our feet? Moving? Aren't you going to teach me to kick ass?"

Rodney opened one eye, his expression suggesting amusement on his part, but I didn't get the joke. "Tyler will teach you how to kick some ass, but today, we're going to work on your mind."

He closed his eyes again and rested his palms on each of his thighs. Tyler mimicked Rodney, and the two men sat still as stone, their eyes closed. Utter confusion swirled within me. I was too tired for these kinds of games.

I let a few beats of silence pass before I couldn't take it anymore. "Are you guys pranking me or something? My god, all I've gotten from my parents is how serious this is and you two are sitting here napping."

One side of Tyler's mouth twitched, a smile threatening to break out, which only served to irritate me further. But neither of them answered me. So, I decided to copy what they were doing and closed my eyes, breathing deeply and trying to quell the burgeoning anger inside me.

In the darkness, a million thoughts crashed through my brain. I wondered if I was supposed to be trying to hear the 'voice' of the water. I strained, listening, but I was met only with my own random thoughts. I thought about how the room smelled like cleaners and that reminded me of my school—they must use the same stuff to clean there. The thought of school took me to my musical and a twinge of guilt resounded in my brain as I reminded myself that I was skipping school for this, which meant I couldn't go to practice either. Then I was reminded of how trivial going to school felt on the heels of the news I'd just received. And then the news struck me again, saddening me. My stomach let out a terrible rumble, reminding me that I'd neglected to eat breakfast. Immediately embarrassed by the growl of my stomach breaking the silence, I peeked and clutched my midsection. Neither man was fazed by my body's complaints and they remained locked in their silent postures.

I checked my watch, steadily growing impatient, uncomfortable with this sitting in inexplicable silence with two strange men. I was told we'd be training. I could be doing *this* back in the comfort of my own bed, where I'd rather have been, with my covers drawn over my head. Alone.

"I don't mean to be rude," I said finally. "But what gives? I don't understand what we're doing here. I don't understand any of this."

"Do you want to be all done?" Rodney opened his eyes, as did Tyler, and they both stared at me.

"Yes. I don't know what I'm supposed to be doing. I certainly don't know how to defend myself by sitting here in a circle with you two."

Rodney nodded. "We can be done, but it's important you understand that it's not you who needs defending."

I scrunched up my face. "What do you mean?"

"We'll get to the physical stuff later. Tyler can help you out with that. For now, we need to train your mind, help you get in touch with it so you can learn to discern your own voice from that of the water. You need to be able to work in harmony with the demands that will be made of you."

"Harmony?" I uttered stupidly. The idea seemed asinine to me. I had every intention of fighting the voice, of controlling it. Not working with it.

Rodney' face contoured with aggravating patience. "When the water comes calling, it will be strength of mind you need, not of body."

"Well now I just feel like you're talking in riddles." I sighed and ran my hands through my hair as my face scrunched. This was a waste of time, as far as I was concerned. This was apparently so critical that it had to begin right away, taking me from school, from the things and people I loved to just…sit.

Rodney watched me, the calm patience never breaking from his expression, but it was Tyler who spoke up.

"Think of it like wild Africa. The lion is the king, right? He doesn't sit in fear of anything because he knows nothing hunts him. No one is stronger than him. He sleeps all day because he doesn't need to train to catch his prey. When the time comes, he will overpower whatever he hunts. In this scenario, you're the lion. But you have to learn to recognize the voice of the water—and understand how to work with it."

"So, to do that, I have to sit here in silence with you two. I'm still not following."

Tyler's hard exterior didn't crack. "You're the lion. I'm the lion. When the water comes calling and the compulsions grow, your strength is not your own. For a few seconds, you'll almost feel like a superhero. You don't need to train to overpower people because you will be able to. Even people much bigger than you. It's like the water…takes over."

"Then why are we here?"

"Because," Rodney said. "When you start to hear the early whispers, it will only be strength of mind that allows you to contain what it asks of you. That keeps you from acting impulsively. Untrained, you will fight its compulsions until it overcomes you. You must learn to manage the commands as they enter your mind because they will take over, they will force your hand. It's important you understand that this is not a fight for control, but a lesson in cooperation with what's inside of you."

I grimaced, the thought of cooperating with murderous compulsions incomprehensible to me.

"So we're going to spend the morning in silence, Jessie, and we'll take turns choosing a focal point for our thoughts. We'll start with sound. I want you to choose one sound in the room and focus on it. When your thoughts try to distract you (and they will), refocus your attention on the sound you've chosen. We're going to do this for one minute."

"But it's completely silent in here," I protested.

"Just listen," Rodney encouraged, and he and Tyler closed their eyes.

I shut mine too and the only sound I could hear was the deafening protests of my own thoughts. I listened around me, and my efforts were met with more silence…

Then…I heard it! A steady tick tock of someone's watch. It was faint, hardly discernible otherwise but here, as I focused, as I put forth some effort, I detected the sound. I did my best to keep my attention there, but my thoughts kept pulling me away. The minute stretched on as I struggled to keep focused on the watch's sound.

"Time's up," Rodney's voice announced after what felt like a year and I opened my eyes to find both him and Tyler peering back at me.

"How'd you do?" asked Tyler, a serious expression on his face. Did the guy ever loosen up?

"Terrible! I kept having thoughts that pulled me away from the sound and I'd have to find it again."

"What did you hear?"

"Someone's watch."

Rodney gestured toward his wrist, pride swelling in his smile, like I'd accomplished something great. "You did well."

"How can you say that? The minutes were long and grueling, and I was distracted."

"You are training your brain. The fact you were able to notice when your mind drifted and bring it back to the ticking you heard, is key. You are paying attention. This is the skill you need to develop. The goal isn't to empty your mind—the goal is to notice it, become very familiar with it, exercise your dominion over your thoughts so you can decipher which voice is yours and which is the water's. By giving your mind something to focus on, you can work through the compulsions. Then, when the time comes to act, you'll be ready."

I gulped at that last statement. I couldn't imagine a scenario where I'd want to kill someone so badly that I'd have to focus on a ticking watch to keep myself from committing murder. This was all so strange, and I didn't get any of it.

We continued with the exercises, focusing on other senses, bringing attention to a visual focal point in the room, to a sensation in my own body, to a texture I held in my hand. For me, it was sandpaper and I'd run my fingers over the rough surface whenever my mind wandered, bringing my attention back to the feeling of the sandpaper. At one point, Rodney passed out a potent peppermint candy for us to suck on, the flavor our focus. Another exercise involved keeping my nose buried in a candle, to come back to the scent. Fortunately for me, it was an ocean breeze scented candle and not something gross like frosted sugar cookie or something.

The morning melted into lunchtime and by then, my stomach was really protesting. And I was growing weary of these practices, no closer to understanding how any of this was going to help me when the time came.

"Can we have a break, please?" I issued my plea before Rodney launched us into another exercise.

"Absolutely." Rodney gave an easy smile. "I'm famished myself. It's important to fuel our bodies, too! There's a sandwich place down the road. Tyler, you mind taking her for something to eat?"

Tyler spared a quick glance at me before giving Rodney a curt nod. But I didn't miss the protest in his eyes, even if it didn't reach his lips.

"Let's go," he said, getting to his feet and not bothering to wait for me.

I waved at Rodney and jogged to keep up with Tyler.

I did not want to be alone with him. I'd rather sit and think some more about a ticking watch. Another uncomfortable rumble of my stomach pressed me onward and into Tyler's silver Honda. Buckling my seat belt, I prayed this would be over fast.

My phone buzzed in my pocket as I buckled, and I found I had several concerned texts from Addy.

Where are you today?

Jess?

Jess!

Jessie!!

Lunch is boring without you. Also, I brought you a Dr Pepper.

Where. Are. You?

Thinking for a moment, I tapped a quick response:

Sorry, was tired today. Had a fight with my parents—they want me to break up with Jake. Will tell you more later.

At least there were some half-truths in there. I hated lying to my best friend.

5

Tyler

I looked at her out of the corner of my eye, trying my best to stay focused. The sweet mercy of our lunch outing was that it was only two minutes away—two minutes steeped in uncomfortable silence. She seemed nice enough, if a bit overwhelmed by all of this. But I got that...I remember how I felt when it was me for the first time.

I knew I had the ability to help ease her in, to make things a bit easier for her, to tell her she's not alone...

But my own walls held me back. I'd had a couple years lead time to adjust to the idea of being *partnered* with another immortal for life, but meeting her finally made it real, made it weird.

"So, what do you like to do for fun?" Jessie said.

I cleared my throat. "I don't get a lot of time for fun."

I felt bad shutting her down, but I also was not interested in getting to know her a whole lot. It was nothing personal against her. We just needed to stay focused.

Catching a glimpse of her out of the corner of my eye, I watched her slump against the back of the seat and glower at the road ahead, presumably angry at me for being such a dick. Sorry, kid.

"You know, I didn't ask for any of this. I still don't even quite understand what all *this* is. The least you could do is be nice to me. Don't you remember what it was like? How scary and confusing?"

I glanced her direction and she threw me a look of disgust when I adjusted my eyes back to the road, refusing to answer.

"Whatever," she snapped.

Then her phone buzzed, and she reached into her pocket for it. Whatever it was, whomever it was from, it made her smile. She did have a beautiful smile—I'd give her that.

She tapped a response, which thoroughly annoyed me. This was what I was talking about—she wasn't taking this seriously enough and it grated on me.

"What's that?" My tone was sharper than I intended, and I pressed my lips together with regret.

She cradled her cell against her chest, and I immediately averted my eyes to the road. "My phone." Her tone told me she thought I was an idiot.

"Give it to me," I demanded, my hand outstretched.

But my command was met only with the tightening of her grip around her phone. "You aren't my dad," she answered.

"*Your dad* should have told to leave that thing at home. It's a distraction. Today is about focus."

She leaned close to me, close enough that I could smell the coconut fragrance of her shampoo mixing with the vanilla of her deodorant. "The only thing getting in the way of my focus is this bad boy." She jabbed a finger toward her stomach, which grumbled in agreement.

We'd just arrived, and I put the car into park. Huffing loudly enough to convey my irritation, I opened my door with a forceful push and got out. I heard her following behind me.

The sandwich shop was like Subway, with a counter running along the front where you could give your order and specify which fixings

DESCENDANTS OF THE CURSE

you want, and they would build your sandwich.

"We're getting these to go, I assume?" she asked.

"For here."

"Ooo, caveman almost make whole sentence," she snarled, and I couldn't help but be amused by her attempt at an insult. It was almost...cute.

I snapped my attention toward the sandwich counter, shaking that last thought free.

"Did Rodney give you an order?"

"He did. I've got it." Keeping my eyes trained ahead, I avoided her dark gaze.

She placed her order (a club on wheat) and I watched out of my periphery as she filled her cup with a fountain drink and plopped down in a booth. Once my sandwich was made, I got my own beverage and joined her in the booth.

"So, you're a Dr. Pepper man, eh?" she said as I sat down across from her. She'd been paying attention. I made a mental note of this. The fact that she was attentive to detail would bode well for what was ahead. I narrowed my eyes and took a long draw from my straw.

Jessie sighed and rolled her eyes. "Look, you clearly have a problem with me, even though we've just met. All this was dumped on my lap *yesterday* and I'm trying here. The least you could do is be polite." She tore a hearty bite off her sandwich, her cheeks swelling with the quantity of food in her mouth. She narrowed her eyes, chomping hard, tying to look as if she'd taken too much on purpose. Trying and failing.

I huffed an amused laugh. "Bite off more than you can chew?"

She tried to speak, but the half a sandwich she'd shoved in her mouth prevented her. She put her finger up and I waited a good thirty seconds before she could finally swallow. "In so many more ways than one," she finally answered, looking proud of her response.

I shook my head and fought a smile. Maybe I should throw her a bone here. She wasn't wrong. She had done everything Rod had asked of her this morning and I remembered how stupid I'd thought this part of the training was. I was far less gracious with Rodney than she'd been. And she hadn't asked for this any more than I had. I looked up to find her staring at me.

"So do you like ever smile, or…?"

"Do you?" I countered, locking eyes with her dark gaze as I bit into my sub.

She flashed me an exaggerated, cheesy grin. "See? I smile all the time. But I do have to admit that since last night, I have less to feel happy about," she said, her tone going flat.

A solid two minutes of silence settled between us as we ate our sandwiches and I decided I was good with that, even though we had things we needed to talk about. I should just open the conversation. I didn't want to, didn't want to have to be in this position. It all felt so unnatural to be betrothed to someone in this day and age. I bucked up and cleared my throat.

"I don't have a problem with you," I said as we hit our third minute of dead air.

She raised her eyebrows in response.

I expelled a heavy sigh. "This thing…this thing we are? I hated it too when I found out about it. I still hate certain aspects of it." My gaze flickered up to meet hers and then moved back down to my sandwich. "I'm sure this training seems dumb to you. It did to me. But stick with it—you'll need it when everything starts."

"Yeah, but I'm not even sure what to expect. I've never experienced anything like this and it just seems so…so far-fetched." Her dark brown eyes met mine.

"Like a fairytale?"

"Yeah. Or a horror story. I can't imagine dealing with what they say is coming. Hearing voices. Isn't that usually reserved for, like, psychotic people?"

I laughed at this. "I felt the same way. Before I heard the voice for myself, I thought my parents had lost it. That my true legacy was one of insanity."

"Yes!" Her face lit with a smile, a genuine smile, and I saw, for the first time, just how beautiful she was. This would be a whole lot easier if they'd paired me up with someone I didn't find attractive.

Focus, Tyler.

I sobered, my tone matching the intensity of the topic. "The best advice I can offer you is to practice what we've worked on today. Every day."

She straightened her posture in her seat and furrowed her brows. I wondered what had occurred to her, but she merely took another bite of her sandwich, and I chose not to pry.

"Anyway, I wanted to have lunch with you because I wanted to talk to you about this...arrangement."

Her eyes bulged in her head and I could tell the topic made her as uncomfortable as it made me.

I soldiered on. "I just want to make sure our expectations match." Appraising her with my gaze, I waited for a response.

She didn't offer one, but shrugged instead, waving her hand for me to continue.

"I'm sure you're a wonderful person, so I don't want you to take this the wrong way. If we're to be teamed up to help each other with this...plight...we share, that's fine. I will be your guy. Our training is going to involve more than just focusing our minds. I'll teach you some self-defense and you'll also learn how to focus the bloodlust inside of you so that it's productive. I've gotten quite good at it, and you will too. And I'm perfectly fine with being a team for that."

I was rambling, hoping this wasn't coming off like rejection. I wasn't interested in hurting the girl's feelings, but it was important I let her know where I stood.

"Look," she interjected. "I'm not going to feel rejected by you. I don't know you and you don't know me and we've just been thrown together in this thing."

It was like she'd read my mind, and that came as a relief. I leaned against the booth, tension easing from my shoulders. "That's good to hear. I was going to say that, while I'm good with being partnered up with you to manage our immortal impulses, I'm not looking for anything romantic. I know the idea is that we'll settle down one day, have each other's backs, if we want children, we'll do that together too..." I drifted and cleared my throat, having ventured into uncomfortable territory. "But right now, I'm not interested in any of that."

Jessie's shoulders eased and a look of utter relief crossed her face. "I can't tell you how happy I am to hear you say that." She gave me another (beautiful) genuine smile.

"Really?" I said, not quite believing we were in agreement on this. It couldn't be this easy. "I'm happy to hear you're happy. I was worried you'd feel slighted, and that wouldn't be such a great start. I think it's best we focus our energies on learning together. Okay?"

"Deal," she said and extended her hand for a shake.

I frowned first and then broke into a smile, taking her hand. We shook, and I did my best to ignore the soft texture of her skin, and the way her hand curved perfectly into my larger one.

"Ahh, you do know how to smile!" she exclaimed as she withdrew her hand from mine.

I bit down, stifling my grin. "Sometimes," I muttered. "Alright, you done with your sandwich?"

"Let's get to it."

We collected our trash and made our way back to the training center to round out the afternoon of training, a weight seeming to have been lifted from both our sets of shoulders.

6

Jessie

The first day of training melded into the weekend and soon I'd missed three days of school. Now it was Sunday, making it four days since my world had been turned on its head. The lessons so far with Rodney and Tyler had been more of the same and I was determined to practice them in my free time too, since everyone seemed to think these skills critical ones for me to acquire. I would not only be good at them; I would be the best.

So, I worked at it when at the training facility and when at home at night and in the morning. I committed to it like it was my job, but in doing so, I was neglecting almost everything else. My parents decided to give me Sunday off from going to the training facility, so long as I promised to keep working on my exercises.

I rolled over in bed that morning, happy to have slept past five a.m., and found a text waiting from Jake. And several from Addy, who I'd given up on responding to. I couldn't deal with her litany of questions that I had no answer for. I'd settled on telling her I'd been sick and had left it at that. But I was eager to answer Jake's.

Jake: *I assume you're busy again today. Would love to see you sometime. I miss you.*

My heart lurched inside my chest. As if to punctuate how much and how quickly all of this had changed my life, his assumption clearly told me that I needed a day to be normal, to see my boyfriend. He hadn't been getting the time he deserved, and my guilt deepened at the recognition that I had instead been spending my time with Tyler.

But I pushed my guilt aside, eager to see my boyfriend and take a break from the rest of it. I hoped being with him would allow me to feel normal again, if even just for one day.

Me: *I'm dying to see you! Meet at Great Lake Roasting at 10:30?*
Jake: *See you there.*

The reply was almost instantaneous and was accompanied by a kissy face emoji. A tremble of excitement fluttered in my belly and I swung my feet over the side of the bed and gave Millie, who was content to continue snoozing away, a pat on the head.

"Today I'm just a normal teenage girl, Mils." I kissed the top of her head and rose to my feet to get dressed. Donning jeans and a crop top, I skipped down the stairs in a much-improved mood from the last couple of days, the gold heart pendant Jake had given me swinging from my neck.

"You look chipper this morning," my mom greeted me. She leaned against the kitchen counter sipping her coffee, her little baby snake Arnold coiled around her hand.

"That's because I'm going to spend the afternoon with Jake. Cool?"

Her expression sobered. "Jessie, you're just making this harder on yourself."

My insides instantly restricted in defense. "Let me have this, Mom. Besides, Tyler and I have an agreement."

She frowned and ticked her head to the side. "What kind of agreement?"

"Neither of us is interested in exploring the romantic component of our arrangement at this time." My words came out so official sounding.

"Hmm," was all she responded, and she turned her back to me to top off her mug of coffee, her disapproval apparent.

Frankly, I was happy she didn't give me more of a fight. I skipped over to her, kissed her cheek, and sang goodbye as I grabbed my parka and headed out the door.

The crisp February Michigan air burned my lungs as I made my way to my frozen car, but the morning could not have been more serene. Large, silent flakes fell from the sky and landed gently on my surroundings. The simple quiet of winter held a special kind of beauty, and the cool touch of her air brought me alive. Today I felt better, lighter. All this immortal fountain of youth killing stuff had consumed all my time and I was happy to have a day to see Jake and just be myself.

When I arrived, Jake was already there, leaning against his car waiting, and he gave me an easy smile. I got out of my car and he approached, wrapping his long arms around me and encasing me in a hug. I loved how small I felt when we were wrapped up like this. It made me feel like everything would be okay. We separated our bodies, all but our hands, and went inside, placing our orders. Jake hugged me from behind as we waited for our drinks at the counter.

"Are you feeling any better?" He nuzzled his face in my hair, the question spoken softly in my ear.

I felt my body stiffen. I had no interest in discussing the last few days. "Um, I am, yes."

He released me and took my shoulders in his arms, turning me to face him. "Why haven't I heard from you much? I was worried."

Crap, did he know? Did he somehow know I was a vicious serial killer in the making and that I'd spent the last few days with a cute boy

I was supposed to someday marry? I felt panic climbing up my throat, and it was keeping guilt for a companion. I didn't want to lie to my boyfriend any more than I wanted to lie to Addy.

I smiled at him. "I—I'm sorry I worried you."

He ticked his head to the side, and I could tell more questions were coming, so I changed the subject. "What'd you do yesterday?" I asked.

My abrupt change of topic seemed to irritate him. "I painted for a while, played video games and then my family went out to dinner."

"Sounds like a pretty good Saturday." *Better than mine.* A little quiver of jealousy occurred to me—gone were the days of casual game play and family dinners.

Our drinks were up just then, and we grabbed them, taking the side by side leather chairs in front of the fireplace. We sipped our drinks in silence, which grew thicker as it settled between us. An unusual tension filled the atmosphere. Already my mood was dampening which disappointed me since I'd been so looking forward to this time with Jake.

"So…" I said.

"So…" he answered.

I gazed into the fire and then back at him. He was staring off into the distance with a concentrated scowl on his face. "What's on your mind?" I asked him.

"Hmm?" He dragged his gaze to meet mine. "Oh…nothing."

I reached over and squeezed his arm. "Are you sure? You seem a little distracted, or annoyed or something."

The corner of his mouth twitched, as if he was trying for a reassuring smile but the attempt fell flat. "I don't know… It's just…are you going to break up with me?"

My stomach dropped and I sat up a little straighter in my seat. Heat covered the surface of my face as my heart sped its tempo. "Um, I don't have plans to. Why would you ask that?"

"Addy."

"*Addy?*" I parroted.

"We were playing Apex together yesterday and she was acting really weird. Like, super sensitive to everything, asking me if I was okay and kind of fishing around for something. I didn't let it bother me at first because, you know, that's Addy. But she finally asked me about you and if you were acting weird or if you had talked to me since your birthday. You hadn't but I couldn't just let her off the hook after the way she was acting and what she said."

I gulped, the nervousness in my belly morphing into irritation.

"So, she came out with it and said she thought you were going to break up with me and was worried how I was doing. And then I thought about how you've been blowing me off since your birthday, and it makes sense. So, are you, Jess?"

"Oh…" I slumped back into my seat and pinched the bridge of my nose. "Jake, I can see how you'd worry about that, but I promise that the only reason I haven't seen you is because I—I haven't been well. And Addy should have never said that to you." My jaw tensed and I hammered my leg with my fist.

"Uh oh, did I just start a bff battle?"

"*You* didn't start anything, Jake. It wasn't her place to say that to you."

"Well?"

"Well what?" My tone was sharper than intended.

"Are you going to break up with me?"

Forgetting my sudden blast of anger with Addy for a moment, I softened when I saw the worry on his face. "Oh, Jake. I don't want to break up with you. My parents have been on me lately about my future. *They* think it would best if I was…singularly focused."

"That's ridiculous. You're the most focused person I know. You want something, you go for it, you get it. They think I'm a distraction?"

"Yeah, they would like it if I concentrated on preparing for my future a bit more." *Oh, and they've already got a husband lined up for me.*

"Okay, so you don't want to break up, then? It's just your parents being parents?"

I angled my body his direction and reached for his hand. "Exactly. I'm into you, Jake. I really like you and that hasn't changed."

His face broke into a smile and he ran his hand through his hair. "I'm relieved to hear that because I really like you too, Jess...Do you want to...um...get out of here? Maybe go somewhere else and then see a movie this afternoon?"

I gave a vigorous nod of approval.

Today would be all about me and Jake and it would be awesome.

After that? I would need some answers from Addy.

I pulled into my driveway later that night, my thoughts fixed on the make-out session I'd just surfaced from with Jake. Lost in the memory of it, I touched my lips and thought about his gentle kiss. When I got out of the car and locked the door, I couldn't help the smile forming on my lips. Today was exactly what I'd needed—an escape from all the madness I'd aged into on my birthday. And Jake had given me the gift of forgetting what I was during the time I was with him.

Maybe I could find a way to handle it all. I refused to lose Jake—today fortified my resolve. I would figure out a way to keep it all under control—to continue my training without having to sacrifice the things I loved.

Still smiling, I grabbed the mail from our box and shuffled through it absentmindedly as I approached the front door. Filed among the junk mail was one envelope, addressed to me.

I turned it over—no return address. Just my name and address on the front. Tucking the junk mail under my arm, I opened the envelope, eager to see who'd sent me a letter.

But when I pulled the paper out, I was so shocked, I almost dropped it. Black letters typed in creepy font stared back at me from the white page.

I know what you are. I'm watching. You try to hurt anyone and you're dead.

My knees went weak as I read the note over and over again, memorizing each threatening word. I stumbled onto the porch, dropping the rest of the mail into the snow as I fell. The world around me faded away, everything went silent and all I could see were the words, now burned on the backs of my eyelids.

I couldn't breathe and the thunderous beating of my heart made it feel like it might explode out of my chest. This had to be the Order of Mortal Defenders. How did they already know about me? I hadn't done anything. Hell, *I'd* only known about me for five days!

I closed my eyes, trying to calm my erratic breathing, my frantic heart. "Mom!" I screamed from outside. "Dad!" All the happiness Jake had brought into my life that day was sucked dry by this brutal reminder that I was no longer myself.

The front door opened, and the worried faces of my parents appeared. My mom came over to me and Millie bounded out the front door, licking at the tears on my face.

"S—someone left me a note," I stammered, and I held the paper into the air. "I don't want to die, Mom. I don't want to hurt anyone. Take it away, make it go away, make it go away!" I rocked back and forth, cradling my head between my palms. Arms surrounded me, pulling me to me feet and ushering me into the warmth of my home.

My safe place.

But not anymore.

Someone knew.

And they were watching.

7

Jessie

The next morning, my alarm rang ridiculously loud, and after hitting snooze for the third time, I finally relented and turned the thing off. Millie was curled up alongside my body and she lifted her head and wagged her tail. I sat up and pulled her head into my lap, giving her a good ear scratch. Last night had been a blur. After finding the note, I'd stayed holed up in my room, too freaked out to leave the safety of my space. Luckily, I was able to practice my lines for *Into the Woods*. Nothing else—not my mother's homemade cookies, not Dad's attempt at joking with me, nor the invitation to join in a family board game snapped me out of the headspace I'd been in. But running my lines, singing my solos—those provided the escape I needed.

But now, it was Monday morning and back to reality. And how different it looked than it had six days ago.

Six days.

That's all the time that had passed since I'd turned seventeen...and I hardly recognized myself anymore.

My parents had given me permission to stay home again, even though my training sessions were moving to the evenings and weekends. But I couldn't bring myself to miss any more school or rehearsal.

I groaned as I snuggled Millie, the warmth and security of my bed keeping me there. "Good girl, Millie," I said in response to her doggie kisses. Swinging my legs over the side of the mattress, I looked at the line of theater posters adorning the blue walls across from me.

"Elphaba, Christine and Alexander." I saluted the characters on my walls, all of whom had faced their own share of obstacles. The characters stared back at me, silently encouraging me. I'd loved these characters for so long, and I admired their strength in overcoming the difficulties they'd encountered. I would overcome too. When the water started to speak to me, I would get control of it and beat it into submission.

Standing to my feet, I stretched and then slowly got dressed, trying to regain some semblance of a routine. I made my way to my Pontiac Vibe on autopilot and got ready to start my commute to school.

I slouched in the driver's seat as the frigid Michigan air bit my skin. I wished I had the forethought to let my car heat up, but I was living in survival mode and barely making it as it was. I checked the clock and sighed in irritation. Despite running late myself, I'd beat my sister yet again.

Laying my whole arm on the horn, I held it down for a solid five seconds. Talia sprinted out the door with an annoyed look on her face. By the time she arrived, the heat level inside the car had just started to turn from ice cold to lukewarm, a modest improvement. She opened the door with no small amount of force, tossed her backpack into the rear seat and dropped down beside me.

I started pulling out of the driveway before she was buckled, which elicited protests from her.

"Hey, you want me to die?" she snarled.

I rolled my eyes and brought the car to a rolling stop. "Of course not.

But we're late," I snapped back.

"Shut up. I overslept."

I bit my response back. I didn't have the energy to get into a fight on so little sleep.

Once her belt was securely fastened, I continued the slow reverse crawl out of our driveway.

A few moments of silence passed between us, which was fine by me. Most drives to school were like this, both of us struggling to wake up before arriving at school. This morning, my mind was a million other places, and I appreciated the quiet.

So when Talia broke the silence, it was out of character. "Where have you and Dad been since your birthday?" Her tone held accusation and I didn't appreciate that.

"Away." I gave a cryptic answer on purpose and rubbed my eyes.

"Obviously." She crossed her arms in front of her body and scowled out the windshield of the car.

"Why do you care?" I asked, observing her defiant posture.

"I don't care," she said in an unconvincing tone. "I just don't appreciate all the weird secrecy lately, the strange people in our house, you and him disappearing without any kind of notice for days at a time."

She couldn't veil the jealousy from her tone. This was about her perception that I was the favorite again. Oh, if only she knew just what was really going on. She would soon enough, and then she'd have to eat her words, her envy.

"You don't even want to know," I sputtered with irritation. And it was true. The truth would horrify her, like it had me, and I felt a sense of duty to protect her from our dark family reality.

"Whatever. You and Dad can have your secrets. I don't care." She turned her gaze out the passenger window, probably to hide the fact that she did care very much indeed.

At this, I decided I was done with the conversation. Exhausted and fragile, I lacked the energy to come up with excuses for my whereabouts to another person. I made a mental note to mention Talia's questions to my parents. They could deal with her.

I turned up the dial on my car and *Moments In the Woods,* the solo I'd be rehearsing at practice today, rang out over the speakers.

Talia reached over and turned my song off.

"Hey!" I shouted at her, then turned it back on, this time cranking up the volume.

"I don't want to listen to your stupid music!" she snapped and turned it off again.

"Ugh!" I screamed, gripping the wheel with angry force, my exhausted rage finally letting loose. I hated this person I was becoming. It was like my emotions were constantly teetering on the edge and anything could cause them to spill over. Mercifully, we'd arrived at the school just then, so I tore into the parking lot and slid into a spot. Choking down a new sob, I killed the engine and jumped out of the car, snatching my bag from the back and refusing to dignify my sister with a farewell as I made my exit.

Arriving at my locker, I still struggled to maintain my composure. But surrounded by the student body, I channeled my frustration and took my anger out on my books, cramming them into my bag with force.

"Hey!" Addy's voice sounded behind me, grabbing my attention. I turned toward her and found that her hair had changed since my birthday. It had gone from rainbow colors to purple and blond. She wore a black t-shirt with a matching black choker and stonewashed jeans. I made a mental note to compliment her on her new hair when I was in a better emotional place.

"Oh, hey…" I sighed and turned back to my forceful rearrangement of textbooks in my locker.

"Whoa there, what's up?" she said, hands lifted in surrender. "You mad at me, or something?'

I zipped my bag and threw it over my shoulder, remembering that I *was* mad at her! My brush with that threatening note made me forget her major friend blunder where Jake was concerned but seeing her now brought it all back to mind. "Actually, I am. Did you tell Jake I was going to break up with him?"

Her cheeks responded with an immediate blush. "I'm so sorry, Jess. I didn't mean to—"

"That's not how Jake tells it, Addy," I challenged, my glare deepening. I knew it was an overreaction, but it was good to have something other than my terrifying future to focus on.

"I—I don't have an excuse," she said, and her gaze dropped to her hands.

"That wasn't cool. Don't you think you'd be the first to know if I decided to do that? When I heard it from Jake...well, I really felt betrayed." Saying those words out loud left me feeling vulnerable again.

"I'm really sorry, Jessie. I am. But can we talk about how you've been MIA since your birthday? You've barely responded to my texts, and you're ditching school? What's going on with you? Yours are not the only hurt feelings." She crossed her arms and planted her feet, a mixture of injury and anger in her expression.

"Good morning, beautiful." At that moment, Jake slid up to me and gave me a peck on the lips.

Thankful for Jake's timing, my face broke into a smile. I turned to Addy. "I have to get to class." And then to Jake, I added, "Walk me?"

"Of course." He took my hand in his and we turned away from Addy.

"Jess, don't you want to talk about this more?" Addy called after me.

"Later," I answered, without sparing her a glance. I couldn't deal with her. Not now.

The school day did little to lift my spirits. The one bright spot was third hour when I got to see Jake, but avoiding Addy was making up a big part of my day. I even took my lunch alone in my car, just in case. I knew she had good reason to be mad at me, and really, I understood why she was poking around about my potential breakup. I hadn't exactly been a great friend lately, ignoring her texts and blowing her off. But with as much as I adored Addy and was thankful for the way she'd *always* been there for me, always took care of me, always showed me her love with gifts of candy and pop, I didn't have the energy for the millions of questions she'd throw at me.

We'd always been there for each other, even through the hard stuff, like when her parents died and she was adopted in third grade, as well as that short period of time in fourth grade when I was bullied.

I didn't want to lie to her. But I couldn't let her in on this—it was too big, too horrifying. Ignoring her was the only thing I could think of. Control was slipping from my fingers in every corner of my life, but Addy had always been my constant. I needed to protect her from knowing these ugly truths about me, even though I missed her. But I didn't know how to reach out to her without blowing my cover.

The day passed in a blur following lunch in my car. Knowing what was coming for me, school felt tedious and pointless. I did look forward to rehearsal, however. I welcomed this break from reality—the chance to get lost and forget my real life. But first, I had to account for my absences last week.

"Mrs. Ferris? Can I talk to you?" I approached the director, fiddling with the zipper on my jacket.

She looked up from her clipboard and gave me a smile. "Ahh, Jessie, I'm so glad to see you. Are you feeling better?"

"Um, yeah, I am," I lied.

She narrowed her eyes in appraisal. "Are you sure? You don't look so well."

There wasn't enough undereye concealer in the world to hide the fact that I'd traded sleep for tears lately. I gulped. "Yeah, yeah, just still recovering. Listen, I wanted to apologize for missing practice last week. I want you to know you can count on me."

"Jessie, you were sick. It's a shame, though, right after your birthday."

"What does that mean?" My stomach clenched with defensiveness, with fear. "How did you know?"

Mrs. Ferris narrowed her gaze and fiddled with her necklace. "How did I know that you were sick? Because your parents called the school. But what I meant was that it wasn't the nicest way start off your seventeenth year." She smiled and glanced down at her clipboard. "Listen, it's forgotten, okay? I know you'll bring your best, Jessie. Why don't you get ready now? We're going to start with *Moments In the Woods.*

I gulped and nodded, embarrassed at my defensive tone. But when I nailed my solo, it was all forgotten. Especially since Mrs. Ferris was not discreet about singing my praises and making an example of me to the rest of the cast.

When it was time to practice my duet, *It Takes Two,* with Colin, I had forgotten all my angst. In fact, I had boundless energy. Here, in this happy place of mine, I was saved from myself, from my family secrets, my fight with Addy and my constant worry of turning into a serial killer. Mrs. Ferris wanted us to try the duet without our music this time. That was no problem for me—I pretty much had everything memorized already. Too bad the same couldn't be said for Colin.

Two phrases into the song, it became clear he didn't know more than the opening lines. We had to start and stop four different times, and each time, a fresh wave of irritation stole some of my joy. The fifth time he messed up, I let out a little scream and stormed over to the side of the stage, snatching my sheet music from my belongings.

I marched back to Colin. "Here!" I said, fuming, and handed him the music.

I nodded at the pianist while everyone else, including Mrs. Ferris, stared at me in disbelief. With a gaping mouth, the pianist looked from us to Mrs. Ferris, who signaled for her to begin the song for the fifth time. She started playing and we tried again. All went well until the third stanza, where even having the music in front of him proved insufficient for Colin to get through the song.

This time he struggled with the melody, slaughtering the would-be beautiful refrain. The actual notes, just inches from his nose, somehow alluded him. The pianist stopped again.

"COLIN!" I screamed. "COME PREPARED OR DON'T COME AT ALL! THIS IS A WASTE OF EVERYONE'S TIME!!"

A foreign rage—different from any I'd ever felt—sprang up inside of me. I ran out of the auditorium, shaking in anger, and busted through the front doors of the school. Once outside, the cold slapped me in the face and awakened me from my angry fog.

Still, something unfamiliar stirred within me...a deep longing I couldn't quite pinpoint. The desire was both a part of me and separate from me.

In my head, a word formed. It was like a thought...but it wasn't. The word sprang forward, sounding almost like an audible voice that echoed through my entire body.

Take, it said.

I jumped and looked around but found myself alone.

Take, I heard again.

I gripped my head, confused. "What?" I asked. "Take what?"

My question hung in the chilly air, unanswered.

Fighting to keep my grip on reality, I remembered my training. I closed my eyes and focused on how the cold air felt when I breathed it in. With each breath, the frigid oxygen filled my lungs, distracting me from my anger and my fear, which fought back with a vengeance.

My irritation, and a host of other indiscernible emotions battled for my attention and I worked to calm my erratic breaths by allowing the freezing cold to saturate my lungs until I calmed.

Once I breathed like a normal person again, I convinced myself that the weird experience I'd just had was no more than a result of my lack of sleep and frustration at Colin's failure to prepare. Still, I was horribly embarrassed. I could not believe I had just screamed at my co-star, especially since I had missed rehearsal three of the five days last week. I buried my face in my palms, unsure of how I was going to go back in there and face everyone.

I was trying so hard to maintain control... I had to do better than this. I *was* better than this. And poor Colin—it wasn't his fault everything in my life sucked. Still, my reaction was completely over the top.

And totally unlike me.

I had an impulse to hop into my car and go home, but all my stuff and my keys were still inside. I had no choice but to face everyone and to take responsibility for what had happened. And the longer I waited, the worse it would be. Unless I quit the musical altogether...

I paused, considering this. Maybe I should quit. Maybe I wouldn't be able to find my way in this new reality of mine if I was still trying to keep a grip on my old life.

But this musical was my one escape, the only thing that helped me cope with it all. And leading a theatrical production had been one of my goals forever.

Then again, what did my goals matter now? A week ago, when I looked ahead, my future was ripe with possibility, and everything I did was to ensure I made the best one for myself. But now...

I pushed all that aside, afraid I'd break into yet another crying spell. No—this was exactly why I had to see the musical through. Sighing with resolution, I swallowed my pride and made my way back inside. They'd gone on without me. Colin now belted out his part with confidence, probably because I wasn't there to shame him. This made me feel even worse. Because the guy was good, really good, and he didn't deserve my rudeness.

When the song finished, everyone turned to stare at me, making me feel even worse. My cheeks burned hot and my stomach clenched. It was now or never.

"I'd like to apologize to everyone, but especially Colin, to you. I don't know what came over me. I've had a lot going on and I... lost my cool. It shouldn't have happened, and it won't again. Mrs. Ferris, I'm sorry for the disruption."

Colin gave me a nod, but I saw legitimate fear in his eyes. I wondered how this would translate on the stage. We were playing husband and wife, after all.

"Thank you for your apology, Jessie. Colin, I'd like you to go through that again. Chorus, practice the forest dance and Jessie, I'd like a word with you."

I gulped, hoping she hadn't decided to boot me off the musical, but I followed her over to the corner of the auditorium. Before she opened her mouth to speak, I was already rambling.

"Mrs. Ferris, please don't kick me out of the musical. I'm so sorry. I'll never, ever talk to anyone like that again. You have to know that's not like me." I took a breath and braced myself.

Mrs. Ferris' mousy face warmed with a smile. "Of course, I'm not going to kick you out, Jessie. I just wanted to check on you. Because, as you say, that behavior was not typical for you. I just want to ensure everything is fine. With the time you were out last week and then this today, I was just wondering if anything is going on at home?"

I cringed on the inside and lied my butt off. "Everything is the same as it's always been. My parents and I aren't getting along right now, though, and I've been having some conflict with my boyfriend and best friend. But other than that, nothing major." I guess some of my utterances were half-truths. Add Mrs. Ferris to the list of people I lied to now.

"Okay, sweetie. But if there's ever anything you need to talk about, just know that I'm here."

I appreciated this woman so much, but she had no idea what she invited with that offer. "Thanks for being such a great friend, Mrs. Ferris."

She clasped her hand to her heart, her warm smile spreading. "You made my day! Why don't you go ahead and go home. As soon as Colin's done with this song, we're going to wrap up anyway."

I nodded, torn. Part of me wanted to stay, to make amends. But the other part of me wasn't quite sure I could handle it. In the end, I decided to take the out she gave me. "Thanks, Mrs. Ferris. I'll see you tomorrow."

I collected my belongings and as I exited the auditorium, I found Addy outside the doors waiting.

I stopped in my tracks. "Hey."

"Hey. I just finished with volleyball practice, so I thought I'd come here to see if we could talk. You've been avoiding me all day."

I'd forgotten all about Addy and what she'd told Jake. At that moment, I wanted nothing more than my best friend. I pulled her into a tight embrace. "I'm sorry I've been a crappy friend, but I really need you right now."

She hugged me back and when she pulled out of my grip, she put her finger up the air and then rifled through her backpack, her hand drawing out two bags of chips. "I have snacks! I'm starved. How about you?"

"Always with the food, Addy."

"You know I come prepared. And I take care of my girl." She winked.

She opened both bags, handing one to me and attacking the other. We approached the door leading to the parking lot as we ate.

"I'm sorry I mentioned a breakup to Jake." She played with the long side of her hair, twirling the purple and blond strands around her finger in between bites. "You weren't answering my texts and I figured your weird behavior had something to do with him."

I waved my hand. "Forget about it, Addy. I know I was a little out of sorts last week."

"A little?"

We'd reached the doors and a shocking burst of cool air welcomed us outside as we made our way toward our vehicles.

"Listen," said Addy when we reached our cars. "You are my best friend in the world. You have always been there for me and we both know it's been rocky at times—" She broke off and took a deep breath.

"I know it's still hard to talk about," I offered.

When her blue eyes met mine, tears had pooled and she nodded. "I'm sorry," she said. "I just miss them so much, you know? I was old enough when it happened, to remember. I have very concrete memories of them."

I put my backpack and Doritos bag on the hood of my car and hugged my friend. She did a good job keeping her grief at bay most of the time, but now and then, it snuck up on her.

"I just—when I didn't hear from you, I got scared that I'd lost you. And Jess, I can't lose you, too. *You* are my constant."

I squeezed her tighter and resolved that I would be a better friend to her. A good girlfriend to Jake, a good costar to Colin. I could do this. I could be all those things and beat this thing inside of me. I had to, for the people I loved.

"And you're mine, Addy."

Addy pulled out of my embrace and dabbed her eyes on her sleeve. Clearing her throat, she said, "So, tell me about your day."

I wanted to tell her about my week, to confide in her, but my new reality was too dark. Silence settled between us for a solid five seconds, as my mind sifted through just what, exactly, I *could* share. "Okay, so something weird happened at practice today."

"Did Colin hit on you? I'm telling you—that kid has liked you since the eighth grade."

"Ha, no. I'm pretty sure I fixed that." I shook my head in disgust as I remembered my outburst.

"Fixed what?"

I cringed. "Him liking me... I yelled at him during practice. Like, I screamed. I totally lost it. It was weird."

Addy's face lost a little bit of color. "What do you mean you lost it? You never lose control. What happened?"

I cocked my head at her. "Nothing. I yelled at him, like I said. And then I stormed off and

cooled down."

Addy laughed. "I'm sure nothing you could say would change the way that boy crushes on you. In fact, it probably turned him on. Maybe he'll start to see you as some kind of dominatrix or something. I wouldn't worry about it."

"Yeah, you're probably right," I said, keeping the rest of my unsettling day to myself. Especially the word I'd heard. Had that been 'the voice' of the water everyone talked about? Was it already starting to stir inside me? I swallowed the bile down that collected in my throat at this thought. If it was, I would control it, just like I had that afternoon. If anything, that experience proved I could.

Yes, I had this. I may not be able to change what I was, but I would hold on to every piece of my old self that I could. For Addy. For Jake.

For me.

8

Jessie

When I got home that day, I found Mom in her studio, crafting more bugs into jewelry. Liza cawed on a branch next to her; Arnie, the snake was coiled in his terrarium and Millie, who had been sleeping in her dog bed in the corner, jumped up and ran to me with an enthusiastic greeting. After scratching her behind the ears, I removed my coat and slumped down on the chair next to where Mom worked, heaving a weary sigh.

"How was your first day back?" She pulled off her gloves and clicked the work light off.

"It was…kind of pointless?" *And maybe I heard the water's voice.* I should probably have told her, but it felt better to deny that that had been what it was, even though in my gut, I knew. So far, I was able to contain it, control it. And keeping it to myself gave me one more thing that was mine in a time when everything felt like it was slipping away.

"I can understand how it would feel that way. There's this big thing looming ahead of you, and you have to still pass calculus."

I shrugged, my gaze unfocused.

"And how are you feeling about the note?" Her voice lowered with the question.

"I don't know, Mom. It terrified me, you know, and now I can't help feeling like I have this invisible threat hanging over me. I don't know what to look for or who to watch out for…" I took a deep breath. "But I know it's there, waiting."

"Just be careful. If you see anything out of the ordinary, make sure you tell us, okay? The Order has been quiet in our area for years, and we've lost touch with who is still involved with them. Just take note of anything weird you see happening around you. Especially when you're out and about. Promise me. Okay?"

I looked up and saw her face contoured with concern.

"I promise, Mom."

She squeezed her lips together and nodded, giving my leg a light smack. "Dinner is almost done and then Dad is going to take you to training tonight."

I rolled my eyes and tipped my head against the sofa. "Do I have to go? I'm so tired."

"I know, baby. I know." She got to her feet and disappeared into the kitchen. Just then, my dad came in with Cora.

"Hey there, little sis. How was practice?" I asked without moving a muscle.

She bounded over and plopped down next to me, excitement bubbling from every pore. "Uhhh-mazing. Coach is going to let me start for A team next game." She bounced out of her seat, then ran into the kitchen to ask Mom what was for dinner before I could even respond.

Dad lingered in the doorway, studying me. "You good, Jessie girl?"

My shoulders lifted in a subtle shrug, not feeling in the mood for a heart to heart. "Fine, Dad." I got to my feet, passing by him in the doorway and walked into the kitchen to see if Mom needed any help with dinner.

"Where's Talia?" I asked once in the kitchen.

"Right behind you," she answered in a groggy voice. "I took a nap after practice." Her shoulder length waves had a distinct bed head look, and her oversized Wakanda t-shirt hung to her knees. I shivered, wondering how she wasn't freezing. Talia rubbed her eyes and yawned.

"Everybody to the table. We're having meatloaf tonight." Mom said, dishing mashed potatoes into a bowl. Millie was at her feet, obviously hoping a scrap would fall to the floor.

I took my seat with reluctance and Talia watched me.

"*I'm* grateful for this family meal together, Mom. Thanks for your hard work." She cast me a look and I rolled my eyes at her.

"You're welcome, Talia," Mom said as she scooped a heaping pile of mashed potatoes on each of our plates and passed the meatloaf around. "Now eat!"

This directive was easy to follow—my mom was an amazing chef, and her meatloaf and garlic mashed potatoes were no exception.

"What's everyone want to do this weekend?" Cora piped up as she poured herself some gravy, drenching the potatoes and meatloaf on her plate. "I thought maybe we could see if the Reddys or Perezes can come over. We could do multifamily pizza and game night. We haven't done that in a while."

My mom and dad exchanged smiles, but it was Dad who answered. "That's a great idea, Cor, but Jess and I are busy Saturday and Sunday."

Talia froze mid-bite, glaring at our father. "*Why?*"

Dad wasn't fazed and he finished chewing before answering. "Jess and I are getting plans in place for her future. She's coming up on the end of junior year and she'll be done with high school before we know it."

"And you can't do that here at home?" Talia's question sounded like a challenge.

"No, Tally, we can't." Dad's answer indicated that his word was final. No more questions.

She turned her glare on me. "Figures," she spat.

"What is your problem lately?" I countered.

"Girls!" My mom held her fork mid-bite, clearly irritated at our ensuing squabble.

"My problem is you, Jessie. Perfect Jessie. Center of attention Jessie. I try to hang out with you, and you exclude me. I want to support you, but you won't let me. I'm tired of all these secrets!" She shot up from the table.

I sprung to my feet, too. "Where is this even coming from? You couldn't handle knowing what's going on!" Something stirred in my stomach, encouraging me to rise to her challenge, somethingn reminiscent of what I had felt earlier that day at rehearsal.

"You won't even give me the chance to find out!" Talia countered.

"Girls, enough!" Mom said, but we both ignored her.

"YOU DON'T HAVE A CLUE ABOUT WHAT I'VE BEEN DEAL-ING WITH!" My voice boomed, startling my youngest sister, Cora. I saw her jump out of the corner of my eye, but it did little to soften my rage. Whatever it was that had initially stirred in my stomach, it now sprang to life. I felt an energy not my own and a whisper form in my mind.

Talia balled her fists at her sides. "That's because you won't tell me. You just keep secrets."

I cracked my neck and narrowed my eyes into a glare. "You're going to have to talk to Mom and Dad about that."

We both turned toward them, and they became the new targets of our fury. As I thought about what they'd kept from us, what they'd dumped on me *on my birthday, no less,* the little seed of rage in my belly put down roots, sprouting and erupting through me.

Take, I heard.

Like the first time, the word formed in my mind, but it wasn't my own thought. Something spoke to me. Something hungry. But it wasn't clear what it wanted me to take. The more I focused on my anger, allowed it to grow and fester, the louder the voice resounded in my mind.

I turned toward my parents and saw the nervous glance they exchanged.

Dad stood and put his hand out, as if he was negotiating with a terrorist. "Okay, Jessie, remember what you've been working on with Rodney and Tyler?"

But I didn't care. I couldn't think about my breath or the ticking clock in the kitchen or the mingling scents of garlic and beef. All I could *feel* was a hunger deep within me. A desire for something, though it remained unclear what. But I yearned to satisfy the unidentifiable craving growing within me.

"It's time for us to go," Dad said suddenly, abandoning his plate and family dinner and rushing to grab our coats and shoes.

If I had been able to think straight, I would have protested, but my earlier exhaustion had been replaced by a raging fire burning hot in my belly, radiating waves of energy through me. What was happening inside my mind, my body…it demanded my focus. I had no choice but to keep my attention fixed on those sensations I was experiencing, which both frightened me and made me want more.

Dad took me by the shoulders, turning me toward him. "Look at me, Jessie!"

There was a small part of me that tried to obey but my eyes only stared through him, his voice a faraway echo in my head.

Then he shook me, forcing my gaze to snap to his, almost waking me from my strange, momentary stupor.

"What's wrong with Jessie?" I heard Cora cry, a hint of panic on the edges of her question.

"Nothing, sweetie. She's okay." My mom drew my youngest sister to her, wrapping her up in a hug, shielding her maybe? From what?

"We're leaving now," Dad repeated, and he thrust my coat and shoes to me. I put them on mechanically, there, but not really. A tiny hint of a headache was starting at the base of my neck—not painful yet but enough to nag and annoy. Still, I felt that yearning, that calling inside of me dying down, present but fading.

I didn't remember saying goodbye to my family or climbing in the car. I heard my dad calling my name, talking to me, but his voice seemed to come from a distance. He did his best to pull me back from this strange state I was in, which felt as if I was trapped inside my own head, standing at the edge of two paths. One took me back to myself, the present, my life. The other was less defined but I had a feeling it ventured deeper into my dark new reality. I somehow knew that if I followed this path, I'd hear more of what the voice had to say to me, learn what other demands it might make.

Demands.

Something about that word snapped me back to the first path and into reality. I came to. The sound of the highway and Dad's 80's music filled my ears. I touched my face, my body. I was here.

"You okay?"

I looked at Dad, his voice clear, no longer an echo, concern in his expression.

"Yeah, I think so."

"You heard it, didn't you?"

I let the question settle because I wasn't ready to answer. I'd heard *something*. "Does the water ever say something else? Does it only ask a person to kill?"

He sighed and rested his head against the seat as he clutched the bottom of the steering wheel so tight, his knuckles turned white.

"I knew it. I knew it was speaking to you."

"But it didn't ask me to kill anyone," I protested, desperate for him to be wrong.

"It doesn't always start off with that. It needs to know you hear it first. Only then will it make *those* demands. It's both a part of you and its own entity."

I shivered, disturbed by the idea. It was like a parasite.

When I turned my gaze to him, his eyes were back on the road, but I could still detect the sympathy on his face. "I'm sorry, Jess. The water only asks for one thing."

But that hadn't been true. Sure, I'd lost my mind for a second, but nothing within me wanted to *kill* anyone else. The only word I'd heard, now twice, was *take*. And it had only stirred a curiosity in me, not a murderous appetite.

But take what? My sister's share of potatoes? I had no clue what that word meant but when I heard it, everything within me was desperate to oblige. But I wasn't ready to admit that that experience was the same thing my parents had been warning me about. Both times, my anger had fueled what was happening inside me. Both times, I'd heard different directives, however unclear they were.

We endured the ride in silence as I mulled this over. If it had been the water's voice I'd heard, it wasn't so bad, not like I'd imagined. Swallowing down the sense of comfort that brought, I reminded myself that I had this. I could do this. Having now heard *the voice* twice, I was more convinced than ever that I could keep control of myself. If it asked for someone's life, I'd simply tell it 'no'.

When we pulled into the abandoned lot, my dad didn't kill the engine. Instead he turned to me. "How's your head?"

"My head?" Then I remembered the tiny headache that followed the whole strange encounter. It still nagged a little, but it wasn't too bothersome. "It's fine."

"Jessie, this is important. Does your head hurt at all? Even a little?"

I couldn't hold his gaze.

"That's what I thought. How bad is it?"

"Barely there," I conceded.

"Be honest, Jess. Before this morning, have you had any episodes when it feels like your anger is out of your control? Any other whisper that sounded like what you heard this evening?"

My mind instantly went back to rehearsal. "Kind of," was my feeble response.

"Why did you not say anything?" My dad's voice now took on a severity I'd rarely heard.

"I—it was just today, earlier. I didn't know what it was for sure. And I barely had a chance to process any of it, let alone tell you." I shrugged, turning to look out the window.

"*Anything* out of the ordinary is a big deal, Jess. You must pay close attention and you have to tell me and your mother about what you experience. There is a progression to these things and if we know what's happening, we can help you navigate it."

"That's great, Dad, but you'll be happy to know that I was able to calm myself. What Rodney is teaching me works. Maybe I don't have to kill anyone."

My dad huffed a breath of air out and pinched the bridge of his nose. "I asked you if you have a headache because when you resist, the water, it...*punishes* you."

"What do you mean?"

"If you don't give it what it asks for, it will inflict pain. The best way I can describe it is the worst migraine of your life. Only you feel it not only in your head but in your entire body. And as things intensify, as it asks and you refuse, the pain will grow so severe that you'll do anything to stop it.

And if you still hold out, the water will take over. You will not be in control of your own body. Today was just a tiny taste—it's nothing compared to what this can become. I'm happy you were able to use what you're learning, but you need to be realistic. There is no controlling this. That's why you have to master your mind, to work *with* it, not against it. To let go of your control."

I recoiled, a hot streak of defiance striking me. He was wrong. I'd managed to find control today. And if I kept working at it, I knew I could beat the water's urges.

As if he heard my thoughts, Dad added, "Our way of handling this works. We've had millennia to perfect it and, though it's been close at times, we've done a pretty good job of keeping the Community safe and out of prison."

"That's great!" I snapped, my tone dripping with sarcasm. "But what about all those murder victims over the years? Where's their justice?"

"That's the second part of your training. We only kill people who deserve it. Bad guys."

I huffed. This wasn't some superhero movie, and yet my dad had just reduced this major life crisis to one. "Bad guys, huh?" I argued. "I thought that was your job as a police detective—to clean the streets of the bad guys."

"It is my job, and I do it well. But there are…limitations as to what I can do as a detective. Limitations that don't apply to an immortal killing machine. But like I do in my job on the police force, I play a central role in keeping our Community safe."

Those words sent a shiver through me. I had yet to come to terms with the idea that my parents were, in a former life, murderers. Given that, I guess it should not have come as a shock that my dad was also a dirty cop.

With a look out the window, I thought that the apple hadn't fallen far from the tree. One of the biggest things bothering me about this whole situation was the dishonesty it required. "What am I supposed to tell people? Talia is all over me and I'm lying not only to her, but to Jake and Addy, to Mrs. Ferris."

"If you'd broken up with Jake like we told you to, it would be one less problem. You're choosing to make this harder than it has to be."

His words lit a fire in me. "Are you kidding me, Dad? I've barely had time to adjust to your big revelation. Excuse me if I've failed to immediately fall in line and uproot everything I've ever known, just so that I can become a freaking killer." I glared at him and angled my body toward the door, indignant.

His hand was on my shoulder and he gave it a gentle squeeze. "Jess…"

I squirmed and shrugged his hand off my shoulder.

"You're right," he said, and I spared a side glance his direction.

"I'm listening…"

"It's not fair to expect you to give everything up all at once. Take your time, do what needs done. But know that we only asked you to break up with Jake and distance yourself from Addy for everyone's protection—theirs and yours. All I can say is that you'll soon understand. We're concerned about you—how this changes things for you, the danger that's out there. That note you received only confirms our fears and it's crucial that you be careful."

I rolled my eyes and shook my head.

"In the meantime, Mom and I will take care of Talia. When it comes to Jake and Addy, I don't see a way to be honest with them without blowing your cover. I'm sorry about that. But you can tell them we're working hard on your future. That, at least, has a shred of truth to it."

Didn't he realize that I was most suspicious of my parents, who'd lied to me my entire life, who had this secret murderous past? He just didn't get it. Kids weren't like they were when he…oh wait! He'd basically lived on a different planet when he was my age. There was zero chance of him understanding any of what I was going through.

Zero.

Tyler's silver Accord pulled in the parking lot, sending a surprising ripple of relief through me at the sight of him. Without thinking too hard about my reaction, I unbuckled my belt and raced out of the car like it was on fire.

9

Tyler

As Jessie walked into the training facility ahead of her dad, I could tell she was pissed about something. Not wanting to find out why, I decided to give her space and let her pout in the center of the training room while we waited for our exercises to commence.

Rodney strolled in and shook everyone's hands.

"There's something I need to tell you guys," Mr. Mason said, pulling me and Rodney over to the side, away from Jessie. "Today she heard the voice. Twice. You know we never know when it's going to start exactly, but this seems quick. She's only been seventeen for a week. I'm telling you this because you both understand how fast this can escalate. Tyler, I'm going to need you to check in on her, okay?"

I nodded, and something weird happened in my belly. I couldn't tell if it was worry about things revving up or...excitement maybe? Casting a look at Jessie, who pulled the long ends of her dark hair through her fingertips, I focused and leaned back into the conversation.

"And Rod, you've been doing great with her, as expected, and she's been practicing quite a bit, but I think we have to kick it up a notch. I don't want to rush this process, but we also can't afford for her not be ready. So, do whatever you need to do to get her where she needs to be. And Tyler, you'd better start on the self-defense section. I'll be back later tonight to brief her on what comes next. Be prepared to pull an all-nighter. Okay?"

"You got it, John." Mr. Mason nodded to Rodney, then with a concerned glance toward his daughter, he left the building without a word.

"Okay, Jessie, are you ready to get started?" Rodney asked, approaching the center of the mat.

Jessie looked up, her eyes meeting mine. When I forced my gaze away, she turned to Rodney. "I guess as ready as I'll ever be."

Rodney chuckled and we each took a seat on either side of her. There was something unsettling about her demeanor, but I couldn't put my finger on it. Rodney opened our practice with a review of the exercises we'd done last weekend, and then he pushed us with more advanced level stuff, practices I'd learned a month or two into my training. And yet, it had been less than a week since this girl had stepped into her birthright.

She was an overachiever; I could tell that much about her. A 'go big or go home' type of person. Since the water's voice was already stirring in her, some advanced practice would serve her well. She'd need to be ready. Still, I didn't like the way she stayed on my mind when I wasn't with her.

After more than two hours of mind training, Rodney got to his feet and checked his watch. "It's about 8:30. I'm going to run out and get some snacks for tonight. Jessie, your father indicated that we might be here much of the night, okay? While I'm gone, I think it's a good time for you to start working with her, Tyler."

"Wait! All night?" she said, hopping to her feet. "I thought this would be like it has been. Home by 10, in bed by 10:15."

"I'm afraid not, Jessie. If the water has already begun speaking to you, we need to redouble our efforts."

She didn't respond but I saw the dismay on her face.

Rodney gave a smile and a slight bow toward the both of us and then left.

"I need to go to the bathroom," Jessie announced and disappeared.

I threw my hoodie aside and decided to warm up at the punching bags. I attacked the bag with jabs, crosses, uppercuts and roundhouse kicks as the cool sweat and my accelerating heart rate woke my body up, making me feel alive.

Jessie was gone almost ten minutes before she returned from the bathroom, her face splotchy and eyes heavier than before. I should have asked her if she was okay, but I already knew the answer. I wasn't okay when this was happening to me. I watched her eyes travel the length of my now bare arms, shoot up to meet my gaze, then shift to the ground. I huffed in amusement at her not so subtle checking me out.

"Did—did Rodney already leave?"

"Yeah—" I puffed, landing a strike to the bag. "He said he'd...be back...in a couple hours." I performed an uppercut/side kick combo and the bag rocked precariously back and forth from the ceiling.

"What are we going to do for a couple hours?"

I cast a glance at her. She looked so small, almost...scared, as her gaze bounced around the gym.

"Ever worked with one of these?" I asked, indicating the bag.

"Nope. I did taekwondo for a few years when I was little and I've done some kickboxing aerobics with my mom, but that's the extent of my exposure."

I stopped the bag with my hands and approached her. I'd worked up a good sweat by now—my arms glistened with moisture, and my tank was damp. Her gaze took in my arms again, then bounced away, eliciting a smile from me.

"While it's just us, you and I are going to work on some basic self-defense."

"I thought you said it was all about the mind."

"It is *mostly* about your mind. And once you learn to work with the water, you'll get stronger. When the time comes to kill, you will be nearly invincible. But when the water is dormant in you, satisfied, the strength it gives you also goes to sleep. So, I think it'd be good to learn some basic moves. We immortals tend to get ourselves into some pickles because of how we choose to give in to the water's demands."

"Oh, you mean because the bad guys might be ready for us," she quipped.

"You got it. That's why your dad wanted me to teach you self-defense. I'm an instructor down at Rico's gym. Heard of it?"

"I haven't but I'm impressed that you teach this stuff." She regarded me with interest.

"Thanks. I also volunteer at a couple of the retirement communities around here, helping the elderly learn techniques that can prevent them from becoming victims of petty crime. Unfortunately, violence against society's most vulnerable is commonplace." Images of my first kill sprang to my mind, and I found myself gritting my teeth.

"Huh!" she exclaimed.

I scrunched up my face, unsure how to take her response. "Huh, what?"

"Nothing. I just didn't peg you as the benevolent type."

"Oh no? Well, I guess you don't really know me, do you, Mason." Her last name emerged from my lips before I thought about it. Maybe I was flirting or maybe it was a way to create camaraderie, so I didn't have to admit that I felt an attraction to her. Whatever the reason, I was going with it.

"Alright…" She paused, her eyebrows lifted in expectation, and I realized she was waiting for me to tell her my last name. It was ironic—I was supposed to one day marry this girl, and she didn't know my last name. A chuckle escaped me.

"Emmanuel." I squared up and walked in a slow circle around her, narrowing my eyes, as if she was my prey.

"Tyler Emmanuel is your name?" She mirrored my stance and we circled each other in the middle of the room.

"Yeah, what about it?"

"Uh, nothing. It's a nice name." She put her fists up, but she looked uncertain. It was...cute in a way.

I cleared my throat and shifted into teacher mode. "So, the key to defending yourself is to focus on the other person's vulnerable areas. I'm talking nose, eyes, throat, or groin. You never want to aim for the chest..." I patted my own, "...or the knee. The chest won't get you very far, especially if your opponent is bigger than you, and catching the knee just right requires more training than we're going to do. You with me so far?"

"Eyes, nose, throat, groin are a go and chest and knees are no fly zones."

I gave a nod of approval. "Okay, so let's start with the nose and throat." I demonstrated, thrusting my left palm forward at face level and simultaneously twisting my body and propelling my right palm. It was a quick move, a simple enough start. "For this to work, you'll want to get in front of your attacker as much as you can. And then..." I demonstrated the move again. "Wind up with your non-dominant hand, then thrust your dominant hand as you twist your body. That'll give you stability and momentum. Try it with me."

We stood side by side and watched ourselves in the mirrored wall as we thrusted, twisted and propelled a few times.

"You want to make sure you're turning your hips like this, and that your knee twists with the movement." I approached her and gripped her hips, unnerved to find something stirring in me. I ignored the sensation and turned her body the direction it was meant to go for the move.

She threw her hands up and shifted out of my grip. "Whoa, what are you doing?"

I backed away, taken off guard. "What do you mean what am I doing? I'm teaching you. Proper form is important." My tone came out business-like, properly shielding the personal offense I felt.

"Okay, sorry. I just didn't realize you were going to *touch* me, that's all." She turned back toward the mirror, a look of determination on her face as she practiced the move I'd just taught her.

"Relax, Mason. I'm your teacher. You may as well be an eighty-year-old lady."

"Thanks a lot," she chuckled, the tension melting from her posture.

"Permission to touch you in order to teach you?" I lifted my hands in the air.

"Permission granted."

I gripped her hips and took her body through the motions with proper form, ignoring the intoxicating vanilla-coconut marriage of scents coming from her. Her hair flicked me in the face as we moved, tickling my cheek and forcing my heart rate up a few notches.

"Okay, so I'm going to come at you now and I want you to use that move on me, okay?" I stepped back from her and opened my arms, crouching in attack mode. I circled her again and she pivoted, trying to get in front of me. But I was too fast for her, landing her on her back before she knew what had happened. We repeated this dance four more times and every time, I landed her on the mat. I could see her frustration mounting and finally, she let out a groan through gritted teeth.

"Ugh, you're too fast. Is everyone I come up against going to land me on my ass as quickly as you do?"

"First, you may never come up against anyone. This is a just in case.

And second, probably not. Remember, I do this for a living. Most people you encounter won't be trained. That doesn't mean they're not dangerous, but they'd likely consider a young woman like you an easy mark. You have to prove to them that you're not."

She hopped to her feet and nodded. "Okay, again." She cracked her neck and started circling me.

I advanced on her and she executed the moves I'd taught her. I danced out of the way in time, but she would have landed her attempted strikes on a slower opponent. *And* she remained upright.

"Good!" I yelled with genuine excitement. Though it was rewarding anytime a student mastered one of the moves I taught, the pride I felt at her accomplishment seemed just a little too much. I told myself that it was because she was like me—immortal—and my success depended on hers if we were going to be partners in this. Still, I didn't want to examine the feeling too closely.

"Well, that's one of six attempts. Not bad for a noob! Again!" She danced on the balls of her feet, ready and waiting.

Impressed but not surprised by her determination, I put my fists up in defensive stance. "Okay, come at me."

She narrowed her eyes and this time, she saw me coming. She struck so quickly, I didn't have time to get out of the way and the heel of her hand met the tip of my nose.

"Ouch!" I howled. I bent at the waist, blood pouring from my freshly broken nose, my eyes filling with water, the pain of the fracture overwhelming.

Jessie gasped, dropping her hands and rushed to my side.

"Oh my god, I'm so sorry!" She looked around frantically. "Do you—is there ice anywhere?"

I stood up straight and tipped my head back. "Don't bother." I could feel the deformed shape of my nose, well aware relief would come. And sure enough, the bones shifted themselves back into place, until the original composition of my face was restored, the pain ceasing in an instant.

I sniffed, wiping the tears that had formed in my eyes and gave her a smile. Snatching my discarded hoodie, I wiped my face clean with it.

"Did you...did that—?" she rambled, as her brain worked to reconcile what she'd just witnessed. "That was unnatural... I'm really sorry I broke your nose, but that was..." Her words trailed off as she grimaced.

I fought a smile as I regarded her, lifting my fists as if preparing for a fight. "Yours should do the same. Want to find out?"

She narrowed her gaze, her attempt at a threatening look coming across as nothing more than adorable. "Are you threatening me, Emmanuel? Because I'll warn you: I'm a recently trained self-defender."

I dropped my fists and burst into laughter. "Are you now? That's funny, Mason."

"Should we clean this up?" she asked, gesturing to the bloody floor.

"Yeah, be right back." I disappeared to the bathroom and grabbed fistfuls of paper towels. When I returned, we worked side by side to clean up the mess. Once that was taken care of, we picked up where we left off.

She circled me, both of us automatically shifting back into fight mode, and so I advanced. Even with the break in rhythm, she thwarted my attack for the second time. Only this time, I was sure to duck her blows.

"Good, good. I think you've got it. Let's move on to the next move."

Her face twisted into an apologetic expression. "I really am sorry about your nose."

I dismissed her apology with a wave of my hand. "Don't worry about it. It happens." My lips cracked into a smile.

"What's that I see? Did you just *smile*?"

"I see Mason has jokes for days."

I shrugged. "I have my moments of hilarity."

From there, I taught her a series of elbow jabs that would serve her well in close combat. I was impressed with the way she mastered those with relative ease. And finally, I showed her a bear hug escape, and an easy way to get away from her captor if her hands were trapped.

I lifted my palms as I approached. "I'm going to wrap my arms around you now, but it's to demonstrate the escape maneuver, okay? I just want you to be prepared, since you freaked out a bit earlier."

A flicker of defensiveness occurred on her face and was confirmed by her tone. "I did not freak out; you just surprised me. Isn't it better that I'm hypervigilant?"

I huffed a small laugh and shook my head. "Yeah, it is. I was just giving you a hard time. Come here and turn around," I said, grabbing her wrist and spinning her around so that she stood in front of me. I checked our forms out in the mirror, mine towering several inches over her. Locking my arms around her waist, our bodies melded together in close contact, sending unwanted vibrations through me. She nestled in, not seeming to mind our proximity, but I refocused my attention on the task at hand, ignoring her scent and the way touching her made me feel.

We took position this way repeatedly as I tried to overcome her and she tried to break free. When we'd again reached a point where she was able to free herself multiple times from my hold, I stepped back from her and smiled.

"You're a pretty quick study, Mason. Well done." I gave her a high five, our fingers lingering for a split second longer than necessary.

"Has to be my strong foundation in taekwondo," she joked, bending at the waist and panting.

We had both broken a sweat and we sat side by side on the floor in front of the mirrors as we took a well-earned break and sipped from our bottles of water.

"Can I ask you something?" she said after a moment's silence.

"Sure. Though technically, you just did."

"Oh my gosh, that's so hilarious," she mocked. Then she took another sip of water and launched in. "Did your parents just spring all of this on you one day, too? Did you have any idea about this world we came from?"

The memory had my jaw clenching and I stared ahead, reminded by her question of everything the water had taken from me just two years ago. I would let her in just a little, just enough so that she'd understand she wasn't alone. "I had no clue. My birthday is in the spring and my basketball team had just made state. They told me, and then pulled me from the championship game. They were afraid I'd lose my cool on the court."

Her eyes bulged. "That...SUCKS."

"Yeah, it did. But that was two years ago, and a lot has changed." I couldn't keep the bitterness out of my tone.

"Like...what?"

I turned my gaze toward her as anger rose inside me, even two years later. "Like, a lot of things. Enjoy whatever is still normal for you now, Mason, because life as you know it is almost over."

She froze, wide eyed and staring. "WOW."

"Sorry." I shook my head, annoyed with myself for how quickly I'd switched back into jerk mode. "Look, I wish someone had told me plainly what to expect. You met me right away but I had to *wait* for you. Sure, the Community helped to train me, but they are always so cryptic about everything, telling us just what we need to know. It's been lonely." I picked at a string in my shorts, unsure if being vulnerable to her was wise if I intended to keep my distance. That was seeming less desirable the more I got to know her.

She reached over and patted my arm in an awkward display of comfort. "Our parents kind of suck, don't they?"

I chuckled and shook my head. "They do. I mean, why couldn't we have been born into a normal family, you know?"

"Right?! Is it too much to ask for my blood to congeal like a normal person's or to eventually get wrinkles? I know most people would die for what we have..." She broke off, sobering as her words landed.

A beat of silence passed where neither of us said anything, the shift in the mood apparent.

"I'm scared," she admitted, her voice low and sounding small.

I turned toward her. "I know, I was too. But you're going to be fine, Mason. This Community really does have your back. Not to mention, you have me."

She smiled at me before shifting her gaze down to her hands. "So...how did you come to volunteer at retirement communities? That's not a common pastime for a nineteen-year-old guy."

"Actually, I came into that because of what we are. Your dad was the one to train me how to channel my impulses toward the 'bad guys' as you called them. And I was with your dad my first time. He put me on the case of a guy who would infiltrate the lives of the elderly, manipulate them, steal from them, and eventually kill them. He was a sick SOB. The things he did..." I broke off and bit my knuckle with a grimace as the images flashed through my mind.

"Anyway, we watched him for a while—a couple of months—and then I couldn't hold it off any longer. Your dad saw the worst of my struggle, helped me through my early compulsions, even almost found himself a victim of them."

"Whoa." Jessie put her hand up between us. "What do you mean?"

"Eventually the water gets what it wants. If you're not ready for it, it will overtake you. That's why everyone keeps saying you have to learn to work *with* it, not against it." Concern flashed in her eyes, and I quickly added, "Don't worry, he's your *dad.* He knew exactly what to do, what to say."

She nodded and cast her gaze to the floor.

I looked over at her. "Jessie," I said, commanding her attention and locking gazes with her. "He taught me what to do, how to take control of my urges, to channel them. You'll get there, too. I'll make sure of it."

"I guess that's why he trusts you," she said. "So what happened?"

"So this dude targeted the elderly and the night I thought I was ready to 'uncage the beast within' so to speak—to make my first kill—he was stalking some poor old woman through a department store. Only he was really bad at it. His intended victim escaped before he could follow her, and he gave up and headed for home. It was really kind of anticlimactic. I was looking forward to saving someone."

Her head snapped up, and her gaze held interest and sincerity. "Well, you did, you know. Save someone. Probably lots of someone's."

"Yeah, but I had this whole picture in my mind of busting in and saving the day, you know?"

"But it didn't happen that way?"

"No. The water was livid with me for not giving in to its demands the day before, when I almost came at your dad. But that lesson was my final one—I gave up control. It feels unnatural at first, like you're resigning yourself to be a killer. But once I figured out that the goal was not control but surrender, it all came together beautifully, effortlessly even."

She gulped, drawing her knees into her chest in a protective posture. "And then what happened?"

"We had a van. You know those paneled windowless ones you always think belong to pedos? Your dad had wrapped the entire interior with plastic to protect everything. We and the van were uniformed as flower delivery guys and we intercepted our guy on the way to his car and lured him into the van." I laughed, remembering how guilty the guy looked.

"How did you do that?"

"We told him we saw him following his grandmother through the store and asked him if he wanted to buy her some flowers. See, we'd followed him long enough to discover that he liked to butter up his victims, gain their trust and then do his worst. We led him around back, to where there were very few cars and no witnesses."

"How did you—?"

"I choked him. Got him in a hold and didn't let go. Turned out the van wasn't terribly necessary because it wasn't messy at all, except to conceal any DNA we may have left behind. Not that we have to be too concerned about that anyway."

"What do you mean?"

"Mason, our Community has a huge network. We are covered at every turn by cops like your dad, to lab analysts, to lawyers to judges, to forensic specialists. If we do slip up, there is a fail-safe at almost every turn of the process."

"WOW." Her mouth fell open. "So not only can we never die, we can never be caught doing what we do."

"They've pretty much thought of everything. But then, they've had since the dawn of time to fine-tune the process." I watched her as she sat there, looking a bit stunned. "Are you okay?"

She nodded slowly. "I mean, I'm okay as I have been since I learned about all of this. But every new piece of information I take in proves to turn my world on its head. Everything I think is true…isn't."

"I know. This whole thing takes some getting used to. Anyway, that's how I got into volunteering," I finished, finally coming around to answer her question.

When she squinted and listed her head in confusion, I quickly added, "Oh, sorry. I mean, I saw a need for the elderly to learn how to defend themselves and that's how I started teaching self-defense."

She smiled. "I think it's nice you do that. Most people only think about themselves…" Pausing, she looked into the distance, deep in thought. "About the killing…how often do you have to…?" Her question hung in the air.

"Take a life?"

"Yeah." She shifted, looking uneasy.

"The demands come up about once a month."

"Wow," she said, as the answer landed. "It's like having a period."

I pulled a face at this comparison.

"Sorry—it was the first thing I thought of. Like a cycle."

"I guess it is kind of like a cycle. But as you get to recognize the water's voice in your head and you continue to practice, you'll learn to cooperate. You are the hands, the water personified, and it has to feed. If you resist, it descends into panic, like a starving rabid dog and it will do whatever it needs to do to get its needs met. Even if it means taking you over."

She was quiet for a moment and I imagined she didn't like the sound of that any more than I had. But it was the truth. And that truth was critical for her to understand.

"Do you know anything about the Order of—the Order of—" She looked upward as she grappled to find the name.

"The Order of the Mortal Defenders?"

"Yes!" Her eyes gleamed. "Have you had any run-ins with them?

"Can't say that I have, but they are out there. They're a small group but they are very determined to end us. They haven't been very active in recent years. Some people in the Community have suggested they've died out."

She stared at me, obviously trying to say something. Finally, she took a deep breath and got a hold of herself. "They haven't died out."

I gave her a strange look. "How would you know?"

She gulped and crossed her arms. "I received a threatening note."

This had me sitting up straight. "What did it say?"

She gulped again. "Something like…I know what you are, and I won't let you hurt anyone. Something along those lines."

My heart raced and a sudden—and surprising—desire to protect Jessie came over me. I leaned toward her and grasped her arm. "Are you okay? Do you have any idea who is behind it?"

She shook her head. "My parents have told me to be cautious and suspicious of everyone. I just don't understand why they hunt us."

"Well, we do kill people."

"I know, but from what you guys have said, we kill *bad* people. And it was their ancestors that had the problem, not them. I don't hold people I go to school with responsible for, say, the Civil War, if their families and mine were on opposing sides. Just like I would never consider someone from Germany or Japan an enemy because of World War II. It's overkill."

"It's probably easy for us to feel that way—we're the ones they want dead. But we have to remember…they descend from the beginning, too."

"So their ancestors were around at the same time as our parents? Still, it's not like they, themselves, were actually around back then. I don't get it."

"It's like they're a secret society, indoctrinating their children from birth. It's creepy, almost cultish."

She shuddered. "My parents said it's their religion."

"Exactly. And that's why we need to watch out for them, especially if you're already on their radar. Promise me that if you get any more notes, or see something that doesn't seem right, you'll let me know right away."

She nodded. "You and my parents, both. Scout's honor."

Her assurances were relieving. I didn't know if it was because of the strange pull I'd felt toward her all evening, or because she was the first person I'd met in two years who seemed to really understand just what I'd been through. But I vowed, then and there, that I wouldn't let anything happen to Jessie Mason.

Scout's honor.

10

Jessie

Throughout the entire self-defense training session with Tyler, I couldn't shake the feeling that something had changed. It was like...he *saw* me. And if nothing else, I appreciated the opportunity to talk to someone my age who had already gone through this nightmare.

I guess, as far as arranged marriages went, my parents could have chosen worse. But, I reminded myself, I was still with Jake. And nothing was going to change there.

When Rodney and my dad returned, I turned my attention back to the work I still needed to do. I couldn't say I was thrilled about the fact we were going to be there most of the night. A quick peek at my phone revealed that it was almost 11:00. But at least they returned with bags of snack food, including a couple of cold Dr. Peppers. Starved, I chowed down on an apple, some Doritos and a granola bar. My unfinished dinner seemed like a long time ago.

Once we'd finished eating, my dad led us into one of the spaces adjoining the gym. The area had the look of a conference room, with a big oval table in the middle and padded black chairs encircling it. A large screen hung at the front of the room, and the walls were covered with corkboards all the way around, with various pictures, handwritten notes, and strings connecting things in all kinds of crazy patterns. It looked like a serial killer's lair.

A wave of nausea rumbled in my belly at the realization that it was. And we were the serial killers.

I grimaced as this cruel reminder of what I would become struck me. A sudden flash of emotion came from out of nowhere, forcing me to face the fact once again that I was going to have to *kill people.*

"Okay, Jessie, take a seat," my dad ordered, interrupting my impending freak-out. It was coming, though—I could feel it.

Tyler and Rodney took seats on either side of me and the screen at the front of the room lit up. My dad controlled the display from his laptop.

"This is the tough part, kid," he said. "I told you before that we, the Community, work to channel your murderous impulses through more…appropriate avenues. Injustices happen every day. The guilty get off or are too smooth to get caught. There are so many parameters around how I can do my job, that justice isn't always served. Sometimes, things fall through the cracks. And not all crimes are discovered. Sometimes, people get away with doing wrong, without any penalty. So, what I want you to understand, Jess, is that there is a place for us in society. We're not monsters—we all serve a purpose." He gestured to Tyler, who gave a slight nod of his head.

"I need to warn you, this part is going to be hard for you to witness. It's not my aim to traumatize you, of course, but I need you to see your place in this and to understand how your particular abilities are useful, even helpful to society."

This was the second time my parents had tried to frame my looming serial killer tendencies as a gift. But I only saw it as a curse. It was as if I'd turned seventeen and had immediately come down with some gruesome affliction.

"You okay so far?"

I snapped to attention and realized all three men in the room were staring at me. I'd drifted off and missed the last bit of whatever my dad said.

"Uh yeah, sorry. Just taking it all in."

Rodney reached for me and patted my arm. "I know that this is a lot, Jessie. But hopefully, you'll be able to see how this all fits together—our work on mindfulness, Tyler's training in self-defense and recognizance, and your dad's intel on the criminal side of things."

"It is a lot. That's becoming my life's motto lately." I crossed my arms and leaned back in the comfy black chair. "But I suppose we need to get this over with."

Dad tapped something on his laptop and a man's face filled the screen. He was big and mean-looking, with a scar above his left brow and green eyes that looked empty.

"This is Teddy Clarkson. Our department had been keeping an eye on him for years, and he was even the prime suspect in multiple murders. But we couldn't ever get any charges to stick. The thing about Teddy was that he was very, very careful. He doesn't look it, but the guy was incredibly smart and calculated. He only killed once or twice every year, but he had a type. Always middle-aged women with dark hair, always a parent. His own mother had been abusive, and we think he believed he was sparing the children of these women the torment he suffered. He, of course, was delusional."

He clicked the keyboard and scrolled through various pictures of tagged, bloody masses of hair.

"I know this is difficult to see, but each pile belonged to one of Mr. Clarkson's victims. This was his M.O., to shave these women's heads. See, his mother had hair down to her waist."

Next on the screen flashed an image of the corpses of these women, bald, with empty eyes and bloodied punctured wounds over their bodies.

"He thought it was fun to kill them slowly. To hear each woman's scream, their pleas for him to stop. Do you see the pattern here?" He used his pointer to draw an invisible line connecting all the stab wounds. He has the same pattern on his body. His mother used to burn him with her cigarettes in those places."

Another picture of Clarkson flashed, and this time his torso was exposed, displaying the patterned scars my dad spoke of.

I shivered in my seat.

"You okay so far?" Dad asked.

"No, this is disturbing. I prefer to think you manage to get all the bad guys off the streets. It's terrifying that someone like this was out there for so long." My face twisted with disgust and my stomach turned over. I looked between Tyler and Rodney, both of whom remained expressionless. Obviously, it was just another day in the office for this group.

"He was arrested twice and both times, was released on a technicality. I knew he was guilty. Hell, our entire force knew he was guilty. But we couldn't ever get what we needed to put him away for good. He had friends in high places, somewhere. And that meant we had no way of stopping him."

Dad clicked the keyboard again, and the face of a girl somewhere around my age filled the screen. She was pretty with dark ringlets and caramel skin. "This is Leah Turk. You may meet her one day, but she is like us. She was around your age when the water started speaking to her. She is responsible for ending Mr. Clarkson's murdering habit."

"Her?" Even though I knew why my dad was showing me this, I still gawked at the picture in disbelief. This girl was young, small, especially compared the monstrous form of Clarkson. It seemed physically impossible for her to take him down.

"I give you this example first because I want you to understand that it is not about your size. You heard your first whisper of the water today, Jess, and it's only going to get louder as time goes on. I know you don't want to be a killer. Everyone in this room feels the same way, but you are one. We all are. It's natural to fight those urges at first, to try and control them, but once you learn to work with the water's demands, you will have the strength to do what needs done. Leah had no problem taking Clarkson down. It happened quietly, and I—as well as others in our Community who are scattered in various positions, offices, and jobs—clean up the mess. You always have our protection."

Nausea stirred in my belly and I suddenly felt queasy. "Can I have a bathroom break, Dad?"

"Of course, Jess, take your time."

I sprung up from my seat, already feeling the cold sweat forming on my upper lip. I made it to the bathroom just in time to puke up all the junk food I'd consumed earlier. Falling onto the bathroom floor, I wiped my face with toilet paper as my hands shook.

He said I *am* a killer. How could any of this be? I couldn't decide if I was more terrified of the monster living within me, or the monsters I'd have to face down the road. And how far down the road? If the voice of the water had been speaking to me for the first time today, how long would it be before the voice grew louder, more demanding?

I stood, steadying myself against the stall wall. At the sink, I splashed cold water on my face and made use of the toiletry offerings of mouthwash and toothpaste to get the disgusting vomit taste out of my mouth.

This thing was happening *to me,* despite my best intentions. Everyone kept saying that trying to control it was the wrong move, but I disagreed. I had to control it. If there was nothing I could do to stop it, I had to, at least, beat it into submission to keep my friends safe. Because I was turning into a killer...

This was worse than any horror story I've ever read.…

Patting my face dry with a paper towel, I made my way back to the conference room.

"You okay?" Dad asked.

"Not really, if I'm being honest. It doesn't feel real—any of it—but after this morning, I realize I have to face what's ahead. And I'm scared." I felt the sob in my throat and blinked my eyes hard to prevent tears from forming.

In typical paternal fashion, my dad gave me a pat on the shoulder. I knew he was doing his best but what I really needed was a hug.

"It's good that you're starting to accept this. The sooner you can do that, the more success we'll have in training you. I want to share a few other stories with you—"

I put my hand up. "Do you mind if we don't? I get it, Dad, but I don't really have the stomach to see much more."

Dad's gaze volleyed between me and the screen, obviously torn.

"If it helps, I can catch her up on some of those when we get together," Tyler volunteered.

I wondered when that would be and what he meant.

"Okay. We can move on then. Are you ready to meet your first victim, Jess?"

* * *

A thick silence hung in the car between my father and me on the way home. I was still floored by the fact that they'd already selected someone to be my first target. From what they told me about the guy, I already didn't like him. But that didn't mean I wanted to kill him.

Yet.

Every detail I took in at that…meeting…further tightened the growing knot in my stomach, and made more real the birthright I was slowly coming to face. It still felt far away from me, intangible. Other than my two episodes that day and the confirmation that I could spontaneously heal, denial had been pretty easy to cling to, since I had yet to experience this killer compulsion they swore was coming for me.

But then I'd heard the voice.

And now, I'd been introduced to an actual living, breathing victim.

"You doing okay over there?" Dad asked, his eyes narrowed on the road.

"I think no matter how many times you ask that question, my answer is going to be 'no'. You guys should really consider hiring an immortal therapist for this process."

"Hmmph," he grunted in amusement. "Not a bad idea. We have just about everything else covered."

"I know you're worried about me, Dad. I'm worried about me, too. I don't know what to expect from any of this and there's only so much you can do to prepare me. If this is going to happen, to change me in some way, then I need to brace myself for it, continuing to practice both the mental exercises and the self-defense moves Tyler taught me." Saying his name brought his story to mind. "And thanks..." When he looked at me strangely, I added, "For not making me quit the musical because of all of this."

At least I had that to be grateful for.

"Mom and I want you to maintain as much normalcy as you can. But it won't be easy."

"Why can't you guys just do what everyone else does? Why can't the police follow these guys and learn their moves, then catch them red-handed? Why do I have to...?" I gulped. "K—kill him."

"Simply put, those things are illegal."

"Oh, well, that makes me feel better."

I spent the remainder of the commute staring out the window in silence, vacillating between trying to accept all of this and clinging to disbelief. When we finally pulled into the driveway at 2 a.m., I was ready to be alone. I should have been ready to sleep, but by then, I'd caught a second wind. My thoughts were too loud for slumber anyway.

Tucked in my bedroom, I blasted the *Into the Woods* soundtrack from my phone, skipping through the songs I had parts in and belting them out. Then I went through my lines, and was pleased to see that all this serial killer business hadn't taken me away from what I'd already worked so hard on.

I was going through one scene, saying my lines to myself in the mirror, when I heard the voice for the third time.

Take

It came through clear as day, as if someone else in the room had spoken the word. Only, I was alone. The voice sounded neither male nor female, and I felt it, more than heard it. I froze mid-line and listened.

Take

I jumped after the second time the word rang through my head.

"What?" I cried out in the empty room. "Take what?"

Life for your life, came the answer

A cold, disturbing sensation crawled down my spine. "No," I said. "Not yet. I'm not ready."

Take

"Not. Yet!!" I yelled. I sat down on the floor, drawing my knees into my chest. Turning up the soundtrack blasting from the Bluetooth speaker, I focused all my energy and attention on the lyrics.

Life

The word hammered in my head over the lyrics, stealing my attention for a second. But I brought my mind back to the music.

I focused on each line of lyric.

Take, the voice answered.

Plugging my ears, I sang over the word, far too loudly for the middle of the night.

Life for your life!

Gritting my teeth, determined, I cranked the volume up another notch.

Take

Soon, the madness in my mind kept time with the song, answering at all the pauses, and interjecting itself above the rest of the sound.

"Ugh!" I screamed. I jumped to my feet and killed the music. Pacing my room, I experienced a mixture of fear and intrigue. The voice of the water called to me, told me what was to come. Images of the dismembered, stabbed women flew through my mind in quick succession. I squeezed my eyes shut to stop them, but that only intensified the pictures in my imagination. I thought of Tyler, of my family, of Addy, of Jake.

Jake.

This was why my parents wanted me to break up with him. Staying with him ensured he would witness me losing my mind, as well as put him in danger. I had resisted doing it since they first told me, but now, as I fought to hold on to my sanity, it became clear what I needed to do.

In order to keep my beloved boyfriend safe, in order to keep myself and this whole Community I'd only recently learned I was a part of secret...I had to end things with Jake.

And I had to do it now.

I snatched my phone off the dresser and dialed his number. It rang three times before his groggy voice answered. "Hello?"

"Jake, I know it's late, but I have to see you," I sobbed into the phone. "Is everything okay?"

His response sent a mixture of pain and guilt through me. I exhaled deeply. "No, it's not. Can you meet me outside your house?"

"Jess, you're scaring me."

"I know, I'm sorry. Just—can you?"

He paused, then sighed, "Yeah, I'll sneak out."

"I'll text you when I get there."

I hung up to save him from hearing the crying jag I wouldn't be able to keep at bay for long. I grabbed my keys from my dresser and crept through my sleeping house and out to my car.

Now that I had decided, I needed to get it done before I changed my mind. Luckily the drive to Jake's was only about five minutes. A minute longer and I might have turned around. My hands shook as I texted him my arrival, and my stomach churned with nausea as I waited for him to come outside.

He emerged from his house in a hoodie and pajama pants, his hands tucked into his front pocket, a cool breeze ruffling his hair. He ran towards me, reaching the car in seconds, and got in. My heart lurched at the sight of his sleepy face and tears burned the inside of my lids. He had no clue what I had come to do.

Jake's face lit with a smile. "Hey beautiful," he greeted me. "I missed you," He reached across and took my hand. "Now, what's going on? Why the middle of the night emergency visit?"

Nervous energy coursed through me and my whole body trembled. Jake looked at our joined hands, mine shaking in his grip and his eyebrows knit together with worry.

I blew out a puff of air and dove in. "Jake, I like you so much..."

He cocked his head, like he was waiting for it.

"But things are crazy right now, and I'm not sure...I'm not sure..." The words, difficult to form, broke off and my attention focused on the Detroit Lions emblem on his sweatshirt.

I squeezed my eyes shut and tried again. "I'm really into you. I may even be falling in...in l—love with you."

He removed his hand from my grasp. "But you're breaking up with me. Aren't you? Even after you said you didn't want to."

"I don't want to!" I yelled, then clasped my mouth with my hands. "Sorry—I didn't mean to raise my voice." I opened my mouth to say more, to offer a better explanation, but choked on the words as they refused to leave my lips. Tears welled and I was tempted to take it all back. But it was too late.

Jake reached for me and pulled me into an embrace across the console. Even as I broke his heart, he was concerned for me.

"Why then?" His question was uttered almost at a whisper and he nuzzled my hair with his nose. "I like you, Jess. I've fallen for you too. I was going to tell you, but I just haven't found the right moment. This is a good thing between us."

"I know," I whispered back. "It is." I paused, the sobs making speech an impossibility as I cried into his chest. My breaths shuddered, and I regained composure, pulling away and looking him in the eye.

"But my life just took a very complicated turn and it's foolish for me to stay with you." I squeezed my burning eyes, hating that answer. It both invited questions and reeked of rejection. I did not want Jake to feel the sting of that.

"I don't know what that means." He searched my face, a million questions in his eyes. "But don't you think that if we're that good together, we can get through any complication?"

"Not this one," I answered, keeping my gaze locked on him. "I'm sorry. You're an amazing guy and I wish I could continue to be the lucky one who is with you."

"I don't…I don't understand," he stammered as tears formed in his eyes.

"I know, and I've done a crappy job explaining it. Just know that you haven't done anything wrong, okay?"

"I—I don't know what to say to any of this. You love me, but you don't want to be with me?" He looked hopelessly confused, which intensified my guilt and made me desperate to get away from him, from this situation.

"I wish I had a better answer for you. This isn't your fault and, if I could change things and stay with you, I would."

"Are your parents making you do this?"

I clenched my eyes again. I wanted to say 'yes'. Oh, I wanted to blame them and give Jake the sweet mercy of not being rejected by me. But I decided, in that moment, that it would only give him hope. And I couldn't leave there without him knowing we could *never* be together. The thought sent a painful pulse through my heart.

"*I'm* doing this, Jake. Me." I leaned away from him. "I'm going to go now. Okay?"

He froze, his eyes still lost, as if he was in shock. I felt nauseous as I peered at him, guilt and regret and sadness all converging in on me, and I knew I couldn't stay there with him any longer.

"I need you to get out of my car now."

The words were cruel, and the expression on his face told me he thought so too. He glared at me, then opened the door and got out. Sparing not a single glance back, he went inside, slamming the front door behind him.

A silent, intense sob hit me the moment he disappeared, and I crashed my forehead into the steering wheel three or four times, letting my silent, mournful wails out. This was hell. I'd just hurt someone I'd only then realized I'd grown to love.

And this was only the beginning.

Through my own pain, I still knew I'd had to do it.

I'd had to end things.

Even if it made me the bad guy.

I guess that was something I was going to have to get used to.

* * *

Tuesday, February 11th, 2012, 4:12 a.m.

Dear Diary,

I can't sleep. Every time I shut my eyes, I see Jake's face.

Jake.

My poor, unsuspecting ~~boyfriend~~—I can't call him that anymore. He's not my boyfriend. I still can't believe I broke up with Jake. What kind of person tells another person they love them for the first time, and then breaks up with him? I'm a monster.

The look in his eyes when I did it nearly killed me. It was so swift and brutal. I didn't offer any answers and, I'm sure to him, made no sense. The last thing I wanted to do was boot him from my car like that, but I knew if he stayed, I'd take it back. The pained look in his eyes broke my heart.

This whole thing is breaking my heart. I never understood that expression before, never knew why people described emotional pain in physical terms. But I get it now. Because it actually feels like someone has split open my chest, torn out my raw and beating heart, ripped it into a million pieces and then threw it back into the gaping cavity, not even bothering to sew me shut.

It hurts.

There's this empty, agonizing sensation that extends from my chest down into my stomach. I feel like I could puke, like I'm hollowed out. I don't understand how I can both feel numb and be in excruciating pain. It makes no sense and yet, here I am.

But I can't stop thinking about how it's only going to get worse. How am I supposed to take a person's life when breaking off a relationship hurts this much? I've experienced the compelling voice of the water and I want nothing to do with it.

What if I'm actually going insane? What if my entire family is a bunch of nutballs and this is how they explain their insanity? What if this is all a delusion and I'm some sort of paranoid schizophrenic descended not from immortals but from other paranoid schizophrenics?

But then I remember the pinprick. Did I imagine that? Did my flesh actually close up? Maybe I hallucinated the whole thing, my brain trying to come to terms with the fact that I will start murdering people out of an inheritance of insanity. Maybe that's how my newly addled mind is going to make sense of all of this. I certainly can't. After all, how is anyone supposed be okay, knowing this is their life?

Sometimes I wonder... Would it be better if I was the one to die?

If only that were possible...

11

Jessie

The last time I glanced at my phone before I fell asleep, it was 4:33 a.m. To say it'd been a long night would have been an understatement. Luckily, my parents didn't seem to care about whether I made it to school these days. Because there was no way I was dragging myself out of bed after what had happened with Jake.

I spent Tuesday trading off sleeping and crying. My mom and her animals would check on me periodically, but I shooed her away. I didn't want to talk about it. When I'd drained my reserve of tears and exhausted myself beyond measure, I'd drift off, only to dream of Jake and the bloody corpses my father had shown me. Waking with fright, I'd remember my heartbreak, which would send me back into another crying jag. The cycle continued until 3:30 in the afternoon, when there was a soft knock on my door.

"Come in," I called, expecting to see my mom poke her head through.

Instead Addy entered my room. "Hey hon," she greeted, crossing to my bedside and plopping down next to me. "You didn't answer any of my texts and I was worried. Especially after I saw Jake today." She held up her phone. "I even used the 'find my friends' app to make sure you weren't in a ditch somewhere. I was relieved to see that you were home."

"You saw him?" I lifted my head off the pillow.

"Yes."

Closing my eyes, a heavy sigh left my lungs and I crashed my head back on the soft surface. "How did he look?"

"Not much better than you. Sad. Your parents finally talked you into it?"

"Something like that. I didn't want to, Addy."

She stroked my hair. "I know you didn't."

"I decided when I was about to do it that I loved him. And I *told* him. What kind of psycho does that?"

She shrugged and swung her legs onto the bed, so she was beside me. "I don't know. I think I'd always want to know if someone loved me. Even I couldn't be with them. It's nice to be thought of that way. I think it's good you told him. Hey, I came prepared."

"What do you mean? And aren't you supposed to be at practice?"

"I skipped it for you, babe." She sat up again and rifled through her backpack, taking two spoons, some Ben and Jerry's ice cream and, of course, a Dr. Pepper out of her bag.

I sat up, suddenly hungry. We opened the carton of ice cream and dug in together.

"How'd you know I'd need you?" I asked.

"Because you're my best friend, Jess. You've always been there for me, too."

She was right and I concurred by crushing another bite into my mouth. "How are Ralph and Janet?"

"Oh, you know. Ralph and Janet. They're going to kill me when they find out I skipped practice today."

I saluted my spoon at her. "Thank you for your sacrifice."

Addy sighed. "I don't know why my parents chose to leave me to them. They weren't even friends. I don't even think they like me sometimes."

I laughed. "Do you remember in fourth grade, after almost a year of living with them, you thought you saw your dad at Meijer? You were convinced he was still alive and for almost two weeks, we came up with every excuse possible to have our parents take us back to that store so we could scope it out."

A soft, reminiscent smile reached her lips, but it couldn't veil the sadness the memory created. "When we figured out it was an employee with an impressive mustache, it was kind of crushing. Almost as if they'd died again." Her gaze was unfocused and distant at the recollection.

We were silent for a moment and then Addy shook her head violently and sat up. "Oh my God! I came here to cheer you up, not bring the mood down further." She heaped her spoon with a massive bite of ice cream, swallowed it whole and then winced as a cold headache took hold. She waved her hands in the air, waiting for it to pass. Shivering, she added, "I want to be here for you, just like you've always been there for me. Thanks for indulging my fourth grade hallucination for two weeks."

"What are friends for?"

We decided to lose ourselves in a ridiculous girl power movie where the girl beats up the guy rather than gets him. Her presence helped me feel normal for the first time in ages, but far too soon, Addy had to get home for "Ralph and Janet's happy family dinner".

Moments after she left, someone knocked on my door, sending a wave of irritation through me. I was just about to lose myself to another nap.

"Who is it?" I called.

Talia didn't answer, just walked in. She narrowed her eyes, her gaze volleying between me and the empty ice cream container on my nightstand. "What are you doing?" Her tone held accusation, which was the last thing I needed right then.

"Nothing Tal. What do you want?"

"I came to see why you skipped school today. Again."

I shrugged. "I haven't been feeling well."

She gestured toward my nightstand. "You feel well enough to hang out with friends and eat ice cream."

I sighed. "I broke up with Jake last night, okay, Tal?"

"Why'd you do that?" She plopped, uninvited, on my bed.

I huffed a sigh, tired of having to explain myself to everyone. "Look, Talia, it was my choice, okay? It's complicated."

"Complicated how? By that boy who was at our house?" She was determined to test me today.

"Why don't you just come out with whatever is on your mind?" I snapped, pulling upright in my bed.

"Did you cheat on Jake? With that other guy?"

"What?! No. I wouldn't do something like that, and I'm insulted that you think I would."

"It's just—he came around and now you've been disappearing all the time and then boom, suddenly Jake is kicked to the curb. It just looks suspicious."

A ball of fury formed somewhere deep within me, and I threw the covers off my legs.

"You know, Talia, I'm getting tired of this. You're determined to pick a fight with me, for some reason. It doesn't matter what I do, it's always the wrong thing."

"It's more about what you don't do," she mumbled under her breath.

"What's that supposed to mean?" The little ball grew and climbed up my insides.

"Never mind."

"Can you get over whatever your problem with me is? Please? I'd love to have ONE PEACEFUL CONVERSATION WITH YOU!" I was on my feet now, but I had no memory of standing, and I did my best to keep my mounting anger at bay. But the feeling was building despite my efforts, burning up my spine and into my head. It ignited an uncontainable energy within me, and I needed a release. I squeezed my fists and dug my fingernails into my palms, trying to focus my mind on the sensation.

Take

The voice came from nowhere, surprising me. This time, though, when the water spoke to me, the burn inside intensified, like it was adding a sensation to the words.

"No," I said out loud.

"No what?" Talia asked.

But her voice faded to the background and I glared in front of me.

Take

Again, the blaze inside of me contracted with the word, and I felt a burning impulse to give in to the demand. But I knew I couldn't. This time I knew what it wanted, and I wasn't ready to give in. I wasn't sure if I'd ever be.

But I did know that I had to get control of this thing. I clamped my teeth down, biting the sides of my mouth to force my attention to the physical sensation. The metallic taste of my own blood greeted my tongue and for a few seconds, I was able to focus on the taste.

A shaky breath left my lungs. "Leave my room. Now."

Talia stood, hands up in surrender, and retreated, throwing an envelope on my bed. "You got mail," she snapped and disappeared.

I paced, the burning sensation now living inside my body and the palpable word being spoken into my head intensifying. I fell to the ground, cradling my head, and fought it.

"Mom!" I screamed. "Mom, I need you!" I rubbed my temples as pain engulfed my skull. "I. Will. Not!" I told the beast within. "I will control you."

My mom busted into my room, Millie at her heels. "Right here, Jess. What do you need?"

But when she saw me huddled on the floor, she ran to my side, skidding on the carpet, and wrapped me in her arms. "It's okay, Jessie. Allow yourself to feel it, to get familiar with it."

But I had no interest in that. It terrified me, both the voice and what it asked. "I can't, Mama," I said, using the name I'd called her when I was a child. I wanted to be a little girl again, cradled in her arms, assured that everything was going to be okay, because I didn't know if it ever would be again.

"I can't take this, and I can't do what it's asking. It's growing in me and I'm scared." Tears burned my cheeks. "And I broke up with Jake and I didn't want to. My heart hurts so bad, Mama. It hurts so bad."

I convulsed with deep sobs, everything hitting me all at once. "I can't do this. I can't, I can't."

Meanwhile, over my pleas, my protests, the voice continued to speak, my resistance only causing me pain. Taking the energy that I could only accredit to the water's power inside of me, it used that strength to inflict pain throughout my skull. I cradled my head now, and my mother rocked me in her arms.

"I know, sweetie. I know. If I could take it all away, I would."

I heard the tremble in her words, the cracking of her voice, and I knew this caused her pain too. My pain was hurting her. This was my life now. Hurting all the people I cared about. Hopelessness crushed me as the burning in my head crawled down my spine. The voice had quieted but it left behind the promised headache, forming behind my eyes and crawling around the perimeter of my head.

Mom rocked me on my bedroom floor, neither of us saying another word as I sobbed in her arms like a baby.

When the influx of emotion had passed, I laid my aching head in my mom's lap. She stroked my hair and I allowed myself to be comforted.

"So, you broke up with Jake, did you?"

"I just couldn't risk it, you know. I'm not safe and there are too many things I couldn't tell him. Even if I could keep myself from hurting him physically, I'd only end up breaking his heart. And the longer I waited, the worse it'd get."

"Losing your first love is tough enough without the curveball we threw you. Look at me, Jessie."

I turned my head so my puffy eyes could meet hers.

"Trust me when I say it's going to be okay. I know it's scary and you feel like you're going crazy, but you'll be okay."

"I wish I could defeat this thing inside of me. I'm determined to. I hate all of this."

"I know, but this is the hand you've been dealt. You're my strong, smart girl and I know you will be okay..."

I turned my head to the side again and she resumed playing with my hair.

"Is it too early to ask what you think of Tyler?"

"Meh," I shrugged. "He's okay. Last night he was nice, helpful. I'm not making any promises about marrying him. I can't even think about that right now." Jake's face flashed through my mind, sending an exhausted trickle of guilt right behind it. At that moment, I didn't know what hurt worse—my head or my heart.

"We don't expect any promises and I won't mention him again, okay?"

"Deal." I sat up, reached for tissue and blew my nose. "Thanks, Mom. I know I've been in bed all day but my head is really starting to hurt. I think I may be done for the night."

She nodded her understanding. "I'll just go grab you the heating pad and some Motrin."

When she left the room, I picked myself up from the floor and crashed onto my bed. My face landed on a crinkle of paper and I opened my eyes to find the mail Talia had tossed at me after our fight.

The envelope was white, my name printed on it by a computer, but I knew. I knew what this envelope contained. With trembling hands, I ripped it open. Typed in the same font as before, I read:

You won't be able to keep resisting. You're losing control. It's my job to keep you from hurting others. And trust me, I'm ready to do what it takes.

I dropped the note to the floor, the fear that suddenly gripped me so intense, it rivaled the vice grip of pain in my head. Who had witnessed my outbursts? I could think of only a handful of people who knew what I'd done, and none of them seemed likely to have left me this note. I crumpled the paper and coiled into a fetal position, wishing for an end to this nightmare.

12

Jessie

Almost a full week passed in a blur, bringing me back to the weekend, back to long days of focused training. The threatening notes had put my parents on edge, making it almost impossible for me to go anywhere alone. That also meant, by default, I'd had to put space between myself and Addy. The threats also motivated me to double down on my training, both the mindfulness and the physical aspect. I had no issue thwarting Tyler's every move now, regardless of which method he used to try and take me down. I was even able to ignore the strange surge of sensation that rippled through me any time our bodies made contact.

Tyler and I had also been studying my intended target, Jimmy Franks. We'd narrowed his place of residence down to two addresses and had figured out where he worked. It hadn't been easy. The guy never stayed at a job more than a month or two, so tracking him down had required some investigative research.

By the time Saturday morning rolled around, I was ready for my long session of mindfulness study with Rodney. As I sat there, legs folded, eyes closed, attention focused on my breath, a feeling of absolute peace engulfed me.

"Okay, I think we can open our eyes now." Rodney's voice reached me through the calm, and when I peeked at the clock, I was surprised to find that a full forty minutes had passed since the last exercise.

I shook out my legs and stretched my arms overhead. Tyler jumped to his feet and disappeared, leaving me and Rodney alone. "Can I ask you a question, Rodney?"

He leaned over, grabbing his toes where he sat. "Of course, Jessie. You can ask me anything."

"I've heard the water four times now. But ever since Tuesday, when I got mad at my sister and it flared up within me, I haven't heard it at all. And after that initial headache when I resisted, I have felt fine. Why would the water back off like that?"

"Ahh, great question. No one immortal's experience with the water is the same as the next. It's a relationship. You've been diligent about practicing your mind exercises and it may be that that is keeping your emotions more regulated. As you've experienced, the voice of the water, grabs on to our most primal emotions, trying to get our attention, causing us to act. But as you've learned to get in touch with your own mind, perhaps the water has quieted, simply because your emotions have."

"My concern is that when it does speak again, will it be stronger than what I've already experienced, so strong that I won't be able to resist it? Is it building up this whole time, getting so powerful that when it calls to me again, I won't be able to fight it off?"

Rodney smiled at me. "You're still thinking of the water as the enemy. It is not, Jessie. Think more of it as a living force within you, fighting for survival. You are learning to work with it, to feed it when its hungry. If its needs are met, there is no reason for it to fight you anymore."

I considered his words and was still trying to figure out how to live in harmony with something that was going to make me do the unthinkable. Was going to make *into* the unthinkable. I thanked

Rodney for his explanations but silently renewed my vow to control this thing. If it wanted to survive, it would do so on *my* terms.

Tyler reappeared, sweatshirt on, car keys in hand. "Ready?" He dangled the keys in the air.

"For...?"

"Today we put into action what we've been studying."

I frowned in confusion, but I got to my feet anyway and put on my coat.

"See you kids later," Rodney said. "And Jessie, remember, you and the water are on the same team." He winked at me, then turned to collect his belongings.

Horse shit. The water and I had very different goals.

I followed Tyler outside and he gestured for me to get into the passenger side of his car. I did, but my anxiety surged. The training facility was nice and safe, keeping everything "out there" at arm's length. The mind work, I could do. Even all the research we'd compiled on Franks had been done 'at a distance'. But going out in the field?

"Where are we going?" I asked, doing a horrible job of hiding the panic.

Tyler threw me a reassuring look and answered as if he'd read my mind. "At some point we have to get out there. Today we're going to go to Franks' last known address and see if we get lucky."

I gulped down the rising nausea that resulted from the fear mounting inside of me. I took a deep breath and observed my surroundings. His car was surprisingly clean and smelled of ocean breeze. I located the tree freshener hanging from the rearview mirror and put my attention on the fresh scent.

"You like it clean, eh?" I asked once my heart rate had slowed some.

He turned the engine over and pulled out of the driveway. "Better that way. I can find things."

My thoughts drifted to Jimmy Franks, and I shuddered, thinking about what we'd uncovered so far about him. Thumbing through the file my dad had put together on him, I said, "This guy is a class A freak."

"There's a lot of those out there," Tyler answered, casting a look at his rearview.

"There's been five victims, so far that they've linked to him, " I continued, reading an update. "Five girls around my age, disappearing, then being discovered, dead, with a note written in their own blood."

"'Now you see me; now you don't.'"

A shiver ran down my spine. "Super creepy."

"Kind of smart how he always takes girls who aren't missed immediately. Runaways, foster kids."

"What you call smart, I see as tragic." I filed through the victims' pictures from his file. "What do you think he does with the girls when he has them?"

"That's anyone's guess," Tyler said, merging onto the highway, forging the path toward the danker, grittier parts of Detroit. "I mean, with no sign of physical or sexual trauma, who knows? Maybe he gets off on the power of keeping them there."

"And motive? What could be his motive in this?" I became suddenly aware of how hard my heart was beating, vibrating through my whole body.

"Who knows. He's a sicko." Tyler's answer sounded far away, barely making it through the hammering of my pulse in my ears.

As I continued to think about Franks, as the images of the dead girls and messages written in blood flooded my mind, my breathing accelerated. I wasn't ready to drive into the lion's den. I hadn't trained enough, didn't know enough, wasn't ready.

I wasn't ready.

I tried to take a deep breath, to slow my racing heart and even out my breathing, but my lungs refused to fill all the way, sending waves of panic through my mind, which in turn made me gasp, desperate for oxygen.

I wasn't ready!

The more I tried to calm myself, the more difficult it became and then, suddenly, I was crying. My face burned hot and tears streamed down my cheeks. I fanned myself, oxygen seeming out of reach, my rapid pulse now aching with every thunderous beat inside my chest.

I'm not ready.

Was I having a heart attack?

Why couldn't I breathe?

I'm not ready.

Tyler's face contorted with worry as his gaze darted between me and the road. He veered off at the next exit and turned into the first gas station he came to, peeling into a spot. Shifting the car into park, he reached over and squeezed my shoulder.

I looked up at him, my eyes wild with panic.

"I'm...dy...ing..." I said, gasping for air between each syllable.

"No you aren't." Tyler's voice was gentle. "You're okay. Here..."

He reached over me and opened the glove compartment. Even in my agitated state, I couldn't resist the comforting aroma of his musky cologne mixed with a hint of peppermint. I did my best to focus on his smell, to ground myself with it, but I could hardly breathe, and putting my attention anywhere became an impossible task.

Tyler retrieved a brown paper bag and handed it to me. "Here," he said. "Breathe into this."

I looked at him like he was crazy. Meanwhile, my lungs threatened to shut down entirely, or at least, it felt that way. My throat constricted and now my chest not only ached—it throbbed.

"It'll help. I promise." He waved the bag at me, and I snatched it from his grip.

As if I didn't feel like enough of an idiot, I put the bag over my mouth and breathed in and out, in and out. Each breath came with slightly more ease than the last, my panic abating as my breathing regulated.

"See?" Tyler's voice was not condescending but kind. "Listen, I'm with you and we are safe. I'm not going to make you knock on his door or anything, okay? It's normal to be scared."

I let the bag go slack in my grip and rested my head against the seat. "I can't do this," I said, more to myself than to Tyler. "I'm not ready." I turned my gaze toward him and found compassion on his face.

"I don't know if you give yourself enough credit, Mason. You're working really hard."

"But I should be better than this. I should not be having panic attacks because you and I take a car ride. This is ridiculous." I didn't know which was worse—my embarrassment, or my irritation at my stupidly extreme reaction. I hammered my thigh with my fist in frustration.

"You gotta cut yourself some slack. You can't be perfect all the time, Mason. Now, are you ready to try this again?"

I closed my eyes and took a deep breath, annoyed with his brusque assessment of me, yet acknowledging that maybe he wasn't entirely wrong. Still, the way I looked at it, there was no room for error. I *needed* to do this perfectly. People's lives depended on it.

Tyler kicked the car into drive and merged back onto the highway. Three miles later, he pulled off and turned into an area that looked like the kind of place I'd imagine a serial killer would live. The neighborhood was rundown, with shabby houses crammed too close together. Some had multiple layers of paint slapped on them, making it seem as if someone had started painting with one color, then, when they'd run out, had simply continued with another. The homes were huge, once upon a time serving as luxurious dwellings for the well-to-do, but now most were converted into rundown duplexes or triplexes.

Several of the places had furniture scattered on the porches—couches, rocking chairs and the like. Despite the winter conditions, a few people stood outside, talking and smoking. Tyler drove down the street slowly, scanning the houses.

"Look for number twenty-two," he said.

"Evens are on my side. Thirty-two, thirty…" I counted down by two's, inching closer to the address we sought.

Number twenty-two was even more decrepit than the other houses in the area. Black paint splintered and chipped along the exterior. One shutter hung precariously from the second story and plastic covered a few of the windows.

"His address was 22B."

Tyler pointed to the left-hand side of the house. Black curtains shaded the window, but light filtered through and around them. Next to the front door, a porch swing crashed against the house as the wind caught it. There wasn't much else to see, but on the other side, number 22A, various children's toys lay scattered in the snow out front, abandoned for the winter.

I cringed to think about children living next door to a monster like Franks.

Tyler pulled along the road, parallel parking between two other cars across the street from 22B. The street was lined with cars on both sides, congested and busy and we nestled into the mess of them without issue.

"We're just going to sit here? Won't that seem suspicious?" I asked, casting a wary eye around the seedy neighborhood.

"Maybe. If anyone gets curious, we'll drive away. But there are so many cars, I doubt it'll be an issue."

We sat in silence, both watching the house.

My stomach let out a terrible growl. Embarrassment tinged my cheeks and I drew my hand to my midsection. "Sorry."

"I got you covered." Tyler reached behind us, his musky cologne wafting my way again and sending a strange calm over me. He grabbed a couple of grocery bags from the back and pulled out several bags of chips, some cookies, and drinks."

"At least you packed healthy for us," I said, surveying the options.

"Well, if you'd rather wait for some broccoli—?" He held the food close to himself and leaned away from me.

"Give me those!" Snatching one of the bags of chips, I tore it open and crammed a handful into my mouth.

Tyler gawked at me, his expression a mixture of delight and disgust. Finally, he burst into laughter.

"Wha—?" I attempted to ask, but my mouth was too full. I spat some chip particles in his direction, which then made me laugh and suddenly, I was caught between choking and spitting out what I had in my mouth. I put my finger up and did my best to calm my laughter so I could swallow. This light moment was a welcome reprieve.

Gulping down the chips in two attempts, I smiled in embarrassment. "Sorry. That was gross. Meet your future wife, Mr. Emmanuel!"

As soon as the words left my mouth, the jovial mood died. Tyler looked away and I slapped my hand over my lips, my cheeks burning hot.

"I'm sorry. I... don't know why I said that."

Clearing my throat, I shifted toward the passenger car door, stealing a glance at 22B. A shadow crossed in front of the curtain, one that seemed to belong to a tall man.

"Look!" I cried, pointing. "Do you think that's him?"

Tyler leaned over me, his cologne filtering through my nostrils again now that he was in close proximity. "Could be, hard to tell. That's why we're watching him."

Silence settled as we watched and waited, the shadow pacing back and forth in front of the curtained window.

"I freaked out my first time out, too," Tyler admitted, grabbing my attention.

I put my back to the door and turned toward him. "You did?"

"Oh yeah."

A few beats passed, and I was grateful to Tyler for sharing that with me. For helping me feel a bit less crazy.

"I was super pissed back then, too. I would barely talk to your dad, who was the one who took me out."

"Really? And he still thinks this whole thing's a good idea?" I waved my hand between the two of us.

"I got through it. He's a good teacher, a good man. He gave me space and I think he understood."

"What part pissed you off the most?"

He cleared his throat and turned to gaze out the windshield. "I hated the idea of my future being decided for me. I told you my parents forced me to quit the sport I loved, the thing that gave me my identity. I had to become someone else then—someone I didn't want to be."

"I know how that feels," I sympathized.

He went on as if I hadn't spoken. "And worse, I was told that I'd have to break up with my girlfriend at some point. That was something I couldn't do, so I refused."

Awareness dawned. "Ahh, so *that's* the real reason you said you didn't want things to be romantic. I'm sorry I called myself your future wife earlier. I didn't mean—"

He put his hand up to stop me. "You don't have to do that."

"Do what?"

"Apologize. They do want us to end up together. I have nothing against you, but if I'm going to spend my life with someone, it's going to be on my terms, not anyone else's."

"I'm with you there."

A hint of movement caught the corner of my eye. "Someone is coming out the front door," I said, and my heart sped up again, this time with anticipation.

A tall, lean man stepped onto the porch. He looked out of place in this rundown neighborhood, wearing fitted jeans and a button-down shirt. He checked his watch before descending the front steps and climbing into an old, beat up beige Buick. I bent and rifled through the file we'd brought so I could check out Franks' picture, though I already knew I was looking at him. It was hard to reconcile his picture with the fact that he was a merciless murderer. He was handsome, with dark hair, gray eyes, and a dimpled chin. But even in the picture, there was something missing from his eyes. It was as if he had a monster caged inside his handsome exterior and it had devoured his soul.

"It's Franks!" I exclaimed.

The Buick started up and he crawled out of his parking spot and headed down the street.

Tyler waited until the Buick stopped a couple of blocks ahead at a stop sign and then he merged onto the road and followed, keeping a block or two between the two vehicles. "Let's see where he's headed."

We didn't have to wait long to find out. Just a couple of minutes later, the Buick pulled into a gas station at the corner of Gratiot and 8 Mile. Franks emerged from his vehicle, pausing to fasten a name tag on his shirt before proceeding inside.

"He works here!" I said, feeling a new sense of boldness come over me. I took a deep breath and as I surveyed the rundown, shady looking gas station, a thought formed. "I'm going to go in there," I said.

Tyler frowned. "What do you mean you're going to go in? We're just watching, learning his routine right now."

I shook my head as the idea became clear to me. "I don't know how long I'll have before the water's demands become too much to handle. I fit the profile of the kind of girls he likes to take, and I'm an actress."

"You're a what?"

"I'll tell you more later, but I'm really good at playing different roles. Let me go in there and find out a little bit more about him." Where I'd been paralyzed with panic before, this new idea gave me a sense of purpose, of control in this thing. Given my ability to lose myself in a character, this approach was perfect for me. I may not have been able to imagine killing another human being, but I could *be* another human being for the purpose of learning about this psycho.

Tyler was obviously struggling with the idea. "I don't know, Mason."

"You can follow me in, if you want. But I will be okay. He's at work. He's not going to do anything."

Tyler expelled a resigned sigh. "Fine. But let's make it brief. I'm keeping my eye on you."

"Deal."

I waited until I saw Franks take his place behind the counter, and then I opened the car door and got out. Here went nothing.

13

Tyler

I watched her go from an utter out-of-control panic to calm, cool composure in less than an hour. The way this girl seemed to be able to pull herself together, take back control, impressed me. Still, I worried about the pressure she was putting on herself. Coming to terms with the water's urges was enough to wrestle with without the added self-applied pressure to be the perfect assassin. I wondered if she approached everything in life that way, and as soon as the question occurred to me, I already knew the answer.

I waited two minutes and then followed her inside. When I passed her in the candy aisle, I gave a curt nod of my head and made my way one aisle over.

"Sorry man, you can't buy cigarettes without I.D." Franks spoke loudly to a customer, grabbing my attention and I peered over the chip display in front of me to watch. He motioned the customer forward and said something indiscernible in a hushed tone. Money changed hands, as did the previously off-limit cigarettes, and the customer left, the new pack in hand.

When I peeked around the display, I realized I'd lost sight of Jessie. My stomach dropped but, trying to keep my composure, I hurried around the side of the aisle, locating her in line. She gave me a quick glance, and I stopped, pausing in front of an endcap, as if I was trying to decide what variety of mixed nuts I wanted.

"Hey there ma'am," I heard Franks say. "Need anything else today?"

"I'll just take these," Jessie answered. When I looked over my shoulder, I watched her slide a Caramello and a Dr. Pepper across the counter. A window separated her from Franks, and as she fumbled with her purse, he watched her. There was delight, intrigue, and a touch of lust in his gaze, and the way he looked at her stirred up nausea in my belly. I should call this off. This was our first time out, our first foray into getting to know Franks' routines. It was too early to be jumping in this way.

"I don't see too many girls like you coming in here," Franks said, smiling.

Jessie giggled. "Well, you know, I'm new around here. My foster parents don't seem to give two shits about how I spend my time, so you'll probably see me around."

Something occurred in Franks' expression. She had his attention. Well played, Mason. Speaking right to his demographic. Then it occurred to me that she had just spoken *right to his demographic. What was she doing?* I should jump in, stop this thing. I picked up a bag of chips, pretending to read the ingredient label.

"Is that so?" Franks was saying.

"Yeah, leaves me with lots of time on my hands. What do I owe you?"

"That'll be $3.75."

Jessie pulled a five-dollar bill from her wallet and slid it under the window. "With all this time on my hands, a job might be good. You guys hiring?"

Franks raised his eyebrows at her. "You want to work here?"

Jessie shrugged. "Maybe."

Franks reached behind him, never taking his eyes off her. He slid a sheet of paper under the window. "Fill this out and bring it back in. If you come back tomorrow when I'm here, I'll make sure the boss sees it."

"Okay, thanks…uh…" She pointed at his name tag. "Jimmy?"

"Yeah, Jimmy. And you are?"

"Bridget," she answered without missing a beat.

This girl could lie like it was her job, and I wasn't sure if I should be impressed or scared.

"Hope to see you again sometime, Bridget."

Jessie took her change and walked out of the gas station, seemingly aware that Franks was almost drooling as he watched her leave. I waited a few minutes, then left the gas station, taking the long way back to my car. When I opened the door, I found Jessie inside, alive with energy.

"Did you see that?" she asked, her dark eyes bright with excitement.

"Yes, I did, Ms. Liar, liar, pants on fire. What was that?"

"I told you I'm an actor. It's not hard to take on another identity. So I'm Bridget Smith, originally from Flint. I've moved from foster home to foster home and no one wants me because I keep running away. I'm just looking for a friend, you know?"

"I don't know, Mason. It's risky."

"Listen, I'm good at this. Besides, I need to feel like I'm *doing* something. More than sitting in a circle with you and Rodney or beating you up in the ring."

"Ha," I said, starting the engine and getting out of the gas station as fast as I could.

Once on the highway, I asked, "Are you going to turn in the application?"

"Of course! Isn't that the point? To get to know his comings and goings? What better way to do that than to insert myself into his life?" She opened the Dr. Pepper and guzzled it.

"We usually do that from a distance," I objected.

"Well, this is better," she concluded, and her tone told me she was closing out the discussion. "Besides, it gives me good practice for the musical I'm in."

"You're in a musical?" I asked with genuine intrigue.

"Yeah, there's lots you don't know about me," she said, sitting back in her seat.

I glanced at her. "I guess so. Can I come see it?"

"What—the musical?"

"Yeah. I want to see it."

"Do you...like musicals?"

"You could say I'm a fan of the theater."

She looked me up and down, disbelief in her gaze. "Hmm, I guess we both have a lot to learn about the other."

"I guess we do."

She watched me for a second, and I found the penetration of her gaze unnerving. "What?"

"I was just wondering about your girlfriend. Are you still with her? Is that why you are so adamant that it's strictly business here?" She motioned her hand between the two of us.

I looked at her, my gaze darting away as soon as our eyes met. I hadn't expected her to circle back to the subject of Sarah, and it was one area I wasn't ready to talk about. "No." The answer was clipped, but that did not seem to discourage Jessie.

"Whaaat....happened?"

I sniffed, and faked a glance in the rearview, but I didn't offer any information.

Jessie swatted my arm. "Listen, even as friends, we have to get to know each other. Aren't we supposed to have each other's backs? How can I trust you when you keep things so locked down?"

I rolled my eyes. She wasn't wrong, but I hadn't talked about Sarah with *anyone*. A little war stirred in my chest, and I was torn between the freedom of talking about something that was hard and the desire to keep it locked up. After a moment's deliberation, I figured it couldn't hurt to share a little.

"We broke up. Really, it only happened recently. I refused and refused, but the deeper I got into this thing, the louder the voice was inside of me, the more I realized I was putting her in danger. I loved her—I did. I might still. But I just couldn't continue to lie to her. And, truth be told, I was afraid of what I might do. Then, I found out you were coming of age and I knew that would demand even more of me."

"Sorry?" she said with an air of sarcasm, turning her body toward the passenger door. "I didn't ask for any of this either," she argued. "I had a boyfriend too, and the last thing I wanted was to break up with *him*."

"But you did?" I asked.

"Yeah, I had to, didn't I? Don't worry—it had nothing to do with you. It was for all the same reasons you mentioned. I don't like lying to people and this…this reality forces me to. How can you have a relationship when one person is hiding parts of who they are? You can't. I suppose that's why they make these arrangements." She motioned her hand between us again, her movements exaggerated, matching the bitterness in her tone.

I cringed, sorry about the way I'd come across. If I was honest with myself, maybe I did blame her for having to end things with Sarah. But that was before I'd met her. And since then, I saw things a little differently. "I didn't think that," I said, my voice lowering by several decibels.

"What?" she snapped.

"That you broke up with your boyfriend for me."

"Good, because I didn't."

I stifled a laugh, doing my best to hide it from her. I had a feeling it would not be well received at the moment.

She slumped against the back of the seat, straightening her posture and casting her gaze out the window. "You've made it very clear you're not at all interested in me," she fumed.

Despite her initial claim that she didn't feel rejected by my suggestion we keep romance out of the equation, she seemed to have reconsidered. So I thought it best to keep this thing from spiraling. After all, we needed each other, like it or not.

"I don't dislike you, you know. I don't have a problem with *you* at all. This whole thing just sucks. Even though I've had time to get into a groove and learn the ropes of how all this works, there are just some times I'm reminded of everything I've had to give up. I don't mean this in a bad way, but meeting you has brought it all back for me. So I'm sorry if you've picked that up from me. I've just had a lot on my mind the past couple of weeks, remembering everything I've lost. Immortality ain't cheap."

She stifled a laugh, and some of the tension eased from her posture. "Thanks for saying that. And for the record, I get it. To you, I was just some faceless person out there that you would one day have to deal with and now—boom!—here I am. In your face. It must be tough."

"I'll get over it," I said, the corners of my mouth twitching. And I had to admit, the process had begun sooner than I expected.

"What was her name?" she asked, tipping her head against the seat, her gaze fixed on the highway ahead.

"My girlfriend?"

She nodded.

"Sarah." My jaw clenched at the mention of her name—a name I hadn't uttered in a long time.

"My boyfriend was Jake."

Silence settled and she seemed deep in thought. After a few beats, she spoke up again. "At least my parents haven't made me give up the musical. I really feel for you. It would suck to find this out, and then have to walk away from the thing that makes you *you* in one fell swoop."

One corner of my mouth tugged upward. It had been a good decision to share some of these things with her. After all, she was in the unique position of being able to understand. And more than that, she could identify. I hated to admit it, but it created a connection between us, a sort of kinship.

"I'm thinking about letting it go, though," she added.

"What? You'd quit the musical?"

"Yeah. I lost my cool at rehearsal already, and I've missed too much time. I just don't know if it's worth trying to stay in it while I'm dealing with all of this. Then again, I feel like I *have* to, you know? It's one of the things that makes me, me."

"Don't quit," I told her, thinking of my basketball glory days. "I earned a place at state with my team and it was taken from me. You earned your part in this play. If it's within your power to stay, I think you should."

"Thanks, Tyler."

When we arrived at the training facility, she made to get out of the car, then stopped and looked at me. "Was I stupid to march in there and get up close and personal with Franks?"

I shrugged. "Did it help you accept any of this?"

"Kind of. I mean, it made me feel like I had something to contribute, some way of controlling this uncontrollable situation."

"If it helped you come to terms with what you're going to have to do, then it was the right thing. But now, you're going to have to get a job."

"Maybe, or at least interview."

"I'll take you back tomorrow and you can turn in that application. For now, we'll do it your way. We'll see just how good those acting skills of yours really are."

14

Jessie

Figuring it would probably be smart to make an appearance at school if I didn't want to fail my junior year, I grudgingly went the next day, although I was more than a little preoccupied with Tyler's promise that he and I would turn in the application after school when Franks said he would be there again. Still, I had to get through the day first, and I glanced down at my phone as I shoved my books into my locker. Four unanswered texts from Addy stared back at me, a trend that was growing. Swallowing my guilt, I reminded myself that more important matters loomed ahead of me.

Though I'd managed to dodge her in person that morning, I knew I couldn't keep avoiding her, so I texted back: *Sorry I've been distant. Things have been crazy. I'm still sad about Jake. Catch you later?*

I figured blaming my silence on the break-up was believable enough. My increased training efforts over the last week had helped me push Jake to the back of my mind. So when I saw him outside our shared third hour class with Katie Griswald hanging on his arm, I was stopped in my tracks.

That was fast.

It had been a week. A week! And already the sophomore had sunk her claws into Jake, their mutual smiles sending a wave of nausea through me. Tears filled the corner of my eyes, and something within me tried to take hold. But I closed my eyes and took a deep breath, stifling the rising emotion—quieting the whispering water's voice. I glared at the two of them, though they didn't see me, and trudged into class.

Jake proceeded the bell by seconds, taking his seat next to me. I caught him out of the corner of my eye, a big grin on his face. A grin put there by another girl, and my heart lurched in my chest.

I rallied and turned toward him. "How are you doing?"

"I'm good!" he answered with a smile. But it didn't look like the same smile I knew when we were together. This one lacked sincerity. It was if he wanted me to *know* just how good he was *without me.*

"Good," I responded, doing my best to hold back a sarcastic remark. I couldn't believe this. How could he say he loved me a week ago and be happily entangled with someone new so soon? A part of me recognized that I had no right to be upset. After all, I had dumped *him.* Still, that didn't make this any easier. I fought back the tears stinging behind my eyelids, as Jake sat beside me, unaware, uncaring about the pain he caused.

I reached across our shared chem table and grasped his arm. "I'm really sorry, Jake. I never wanted to hurt you."

His eyes traveled from my face to my hand on his arm and back up again. He withdrew his arm from underneath my palm. "It's fine, Jessie. I'm good."

His rejection to my touch, along with his denial that this was hard for him too crushed me. I cleared my throat and turned my attention to the front of the room as the teacher took his place. As I sat there, zoning out the teacher's instruction, I brooded over the fact that Jake was so quickly...over me.

But then, I had to consider how freeing it felt that I no longer had to hide anything from him. Still, that didn't excuse him from happily moving on without me. I had legitimate reasons for breaking up with him. It was for *his* protection, for the sake of *his* happiness and safety.

How dare he move on so fast! I clutched my chest, the pain manifesting physically near my heart and swallowed hard.

I glared toward the front of the room, the hurt and rejection swirling in my belly. Did I really mean that little to him? Why had I tortured myself over breaking up with him, when I was so easily and urgently replaced? Stewing over the situation, my pain planted a seed of anger, and that anger put down roots. Demanding roots. And then, they spoke to me.

Take. The word resounded louder in my head than ever before.

"Take what?" I responded in my mind.

Life. Life for life, came the answer.

"NO!" My protest rang loud in my mind and on the heels of that thought, a scourge of punishing pain struck the back of my skull and burned down my spine. I grabbed my head and hissed.

"Are you okay?" Jake asked and when I met his gaze, I found worry there. But now, his concern only proved to irritate me.

"Fine, I'm fine," I spat at him. It took a great deal of effort to utter those words, to fight through the pain to say them. This was nothing like the headache before, when I'd resisted and my mom had cradled me through it. All my energy went into keeping myself upright instead of falling to the floor in agony. The chem teacher droned on in the background, as I fought against my growing murderous impulses and the burning torture my refusal inflicted.

But the voice wasn't finished with me yet. Variations of "Take", "Life for life", "Obey", and "Kill" swirled in my thoughts. Only they weren't *my* thoughts. Something else was calling to me, and that same thing tortured me every time I resisted, building in volume and intensity at my refusal to comply.

How was I supposed to *work* with this? When I could take no more, I sprung to my feet and ran from class, my stunned teacher's calls for me going unanswered. I sprinted down the hall, no destination in mind, when I passed Addy, sitting on the floor outside of her class, filling out a sheet.

"Jess?"

Her voice sounded farther away than it was, but I had enough of my wits about me to stop, and for the moment, I did my best to refocus my attention on her.

She jumped to her feet and gripped me by shoulders, as I covered my ears in a feeble attempt to drown out the voice coming from inside of me. "Are you okay?"

My ears rung and her question sounded muffled, despite her proximity to me.

Think, Jess. Think. I focused on Addy's face, on the new colorful combination of colors in her hair. Purple, pink, blue. Blinking hard, I heard myself say, "Jake has a new girlfriend. It's so fast."

Admitting this out loud quieted the ire within me, morphing it back into the sadness it had grown from, and the tears I'd worked so hard to hold back spilled down my cheeks.

"Oh sweetie, it's okay." Addy embraced me, squeezing me tight. "I have just the thing for you." She snuck a glance at her class door and added, "Keep watch. I'm supposed to be working on a quiz I missed." She tiptoed to her locker down the hall and returned with a bag of freshly baked cookies. "I made these for you."

I regarded the bag, appreciating how Addy always took care of me. "What are those for?"

"I haven't heard much from you over the last week and I've missed you. So I made them for you. Gotta keep my girl fed."

"That's really sweet."

Addy sobered then. "What's been going on, Jess? I mean, I know you're sad over Jake, but I've hardly seen you in the last week. I'm your best friend."

"I know, I—"

"We have never kept secrets, Jess, but it's starting to feel like I don't know you at all."

I nodded, a fresh reserve of tears welling in my eyes, discomfort kicking up in my stomach at her unexpected confrontation. She had no idea how true her statement was.

"I have no excuse," I sputtered, the tears now falling down my cheeks. "I'm sorry, Addy. I love you."

She pulled me in for a hug. "Aww, I love you too, boo," she said as she rubbed my back. "So what's the deal?"

We both slid to the hall floor, and I felt a desperate desire to tell her everything. For a solid thirty seconds, I seriously considered spilling every secret I'd been holding onto since I turned seventeen. She was my best friend in the world, and she was right—we had never kept things from each other. But as I looked into her expectant gaze, I knew I couldn't tell her this. *This* was different. So instead, I wracked my brain for something I *could* tell her.

"So, there's this guy. His name is Tyler and he's been giving me self-defense classes. You know, to get my mind off of things."

She smacked my arm. "You've been holding out on me!"

"No, no, no. It's not like that. He is SO not into me. Trust me on this one."

"Is he hot?"

"I mean, he's...okay."

"Uh-huh... How is 'self-defense' going?" she asked, finger-quoting the words in mockery.

"Seriously! He's teaching me self-defense! I'm getting pretty good at it too!" I argued unconvincingly.

"Mmm hmm... And just how many 'holds' has he had to demonstrate on you?" She paused for effect and all I gave her was a shrug. "Yeah, he's into you," she concluded.

"Whatever, Addy. We're more like...business partners."

"And just what business are you two a part of?"

Her question held a jesting tone but my defenses immediately flared. I tensed, shifting my body away from her by a minuscule amount, aware I'd said too much.

Addy sensed the shift in my demeanor and the smile fell from her face. "What'd I say?"

"Nothing."

What could I tell her? I wracked my brain, trying to think of a way to recover, but I came up blank.

"I thought we'd just established that we were done with secrets."

Addy's tone was harsh and when I met her gaze, she frowned back at me.

I shook my head. "There are certain things I just can't tell you, okay?" I felt the flare of irritation deep inside of me, another whisper of the water's call, but I told the ugly beast within me to calm down. I had this.

"That is just so wrong, Jess." Addy got to her feet and planted her hands on her hips. "I tell you everything, but here you are—holding out on me again. I even baked you cookies!"

"I can't tell you, okay?! It's not that I don't want to. I just can't!!" I got to my feet too, matching her posture.

"Why, Jess? Why *can't* you tell me!"

My anger flared, feeling like a flame licked me from the inside, an inferno beginning in the pit of my stomach and crawling up my spine, springing alive in my chest. I suddenly lunged toward Addy, invading her space. I glared down into her face, my own stature a couple of inches taller than hers, our noses almost touching.

"I. Said. I. Can. Not." The words came out through gritted teeth.

The commands flew through my brain, one on top of the other, until it sounded like a cacophony of voices, words muddled together but the *feeling* they provoked was very clear. The water inside of me was here to collect, and it wanted my best friend's life.

"No," I whispered to myself.

"No what?"

Addy hadn't backed down, despite my threatening advance toward her.

"No," I said again. "I won't do this."

I was talking to the water but Addy took it to mean our current fight.

"Of course, you won't do it. You always back down from confrontation. Just fight with me, Jess! Let's have it out. Get it all out on the table."

She stretched her arms out as she talked, as if challenging me. Everything about her right now—her words, her body language—provoked me. It was almost as if she was deliberately baiting me, hoping to bring out my killer instincts.

At least that's what the water whispered to me. *Do it!* it screamed inside my head.

"NO!!"

This time I screamed back, and an instant punishing wave of pain circulated around the base of my skull and tore down my spine, doubling me over.

"What, Jess? What now?"

Irritation colored Addy's tone, and I looked up at her with contempt in my gaze. If only she knew how I fought for her life in this instant.

I had to get out of there, now. The agony was reaching unbearable proportions. I backed down, darted one more callous glance at Addy and took off running. The bell rang just then, and students filed into the hall. I fought my way through the growing crowd of people, desperate to disappear.

Then I ran right into my sister, Talia.

"Ouch!" she yelped. "What are you doing?"

Our collision snapped me out of the battle inside my mind. And just in time—it was getting harder and harder to discern my own thoughts from that of the voice within me. Still, the pain persisted, blazing a fire through my skull. With pleading eyes, I said, "I have to get out of here!"

Talia nodded, taking my hand and leading me through the crowds and into the girls' bathroom. Thankfully, it was abandoned. She watched me sink to the floor and bury my face in my palms. I had won the war for now, but it had left behind battle wounds. My head had never ached so severely.

"Are you—are you okay, Jess?"

When I lifted my gaze to meet hers, tears stung my eyes again. "No," I said. "I am so not okay." I burst into a full-on ugly cry and my sister—bless her—wrapped me in a much-needed, though uncharacteristic, hug. We'd never connected like this before, but I decided not to overthink it.

"What do you need?" she asked quietly in my ear.

"I don't know," I sobbed in response.

"I'd offer to take you home, but you know…can't drive yet and all."

I laughed through my tears. "Can you…can you just stay with me until the next bell rings?"

"I can do that." Talia lowered her arms and sat next to me, our shoulders touching. Neither of us said a word, and I found her presence to be a surprising comfort. With my head on her shoulder, we remained that way for almost half an hour.

When the bell ran, I got up slowly, my head still aching with a dull discomfort, and gave my sister a feeble smile. "See you after school?"

"Yup," was all she said as she got to her feet and walked toward the door. I smiled after her, seeing her in a whole new light.

Once she'd gone, I splashed cool water on my blotchy face. Coming to school had been a huge mistake. I had to get out of there. With a shaky sigh, I left the restroom and made my way to my locker to grab my bag and go home. But when I opened my locker, something fell out.

I bent, retrieving the folded piece of paper from the floor. My hands shook, and I knew before I opened it that this was another threat. Confirming my suspicions, I unfolded the sheet of paper, and read:

You're losing control. The time is near.

Shaking violently, I snatched my backpack from the locker and ran from the school. First, they'd come to my home...and now, my school. I wasn't safe anywhere. But they were wrong about one thing: I *was* in control. I would not let this thing get the better of me. But to make sure of that, I had to get out of there. Had to find Tyler.

Had to get Franks.

15

Jessie

"So you found it in your locker?" Tyler narrowed his eyes as we drove down 1-94 toward Detroit.

"Yes. They're obviously watching me."

"Or you know them already."

That statement sent a shiver down my spine. Even though Tyler and my parents had both warned me to be leery of everyone, I'd imagined that this person threatening me was a stranger, someone who was stalking me the way I was stalking Franks. I couldn't even consider the idea that I knew the person who wanted to hurt me. The people I knew just weren't capable of it. Then again, I'm sure no one would have imagined what I was turning into, either.

I shook out my hands, my knee shaking with nervous energy. "I can't just sit around, Tyler. I can't go to school and sit through my classes when this is happening. I need to get this thing done with Franks so I don't have to worry about it so much. And I need..." I broke off just in time, before I made my embarrassing confession, averting my gaze out the passenger window.

"Need what?" he asked, combing his hand through his hair and casting me a quizzical look.

Oh, what the hell. "You, Tyler. I need you. I need your help, your eyes, your protection. Whoever wrote that note is wrong. I won't lose control. But I need you there to help me make sure of it."

Something crossed his expression, and he averted his eyes. "I'll do my best to keep you safe, Mason. But remember, you and the water are one entity as much as you are separate. You have to work as a cohesive unit. You've been given the tools—now it's a matter of putting them to work. And that's something only you can do."

I rolled my eyes at his insistence (and everyone else's, for that matter) that I submit to the demands within. It was a ridiculous notion. This was my body, my mind, and I would decide what I did with those things, not some invisible age-old magical parasite living inside of me.

Luckily, it wasn't long before we reached Gratiot and 8 Mile, and a spark of anticipation lit in my belly. When we pulled into the parking lot, Tyler killed the engine and turned toward me. "Are you sure about this? We can just follow him a little longer, learn his patterns better."

"Nope, I'm sure," I said, a defiant tone in my voice.

He lifted his hands in surrender. "Okay. I'm right out here, though, if you need anything."

"Thanks. I won't be long."

A flutter of nerves kicked up in my stomach as I climbed out of Tyler's car. I exhaled a long breath and tugged on the hem of my shirt. Double checking that the application was in my purse, I made my way inside. When I walked through the door, the bell dinged, announcing my presence. Franks didn't see me at first—he was helping another customer. I got in line and waited.

When the guy in front of me finished his dealings, a practiced smile appeared on my lips and I looked up into the deceivingly handsome face of Franks through the glass partition. "Hiya, remember me?" I said, with a bat of my eyelashes.

He smiled at me, revealing perfectly straight, white teeth. "Couldn't forget." He checked his wrist. "But shouldn't you be in school?"

"I never told you how old I was," I answered, sliding my application under the window. "Anyway, I'm here to drop off my application."

Frank picked it up and took a minute to read it over—probably a little too thoroughly. "So, you are seventeen. You should be in school."

"Listen, are you going to go all truancy officer on me or hand that to your manager like you promised you would?"

He eyeballed me for a sec, his eyes drinking me in, traveling from my face down my front in an obvious and utterly creepy fashion. "Yeah, he's out back. Give me a sec." Franks disappeared, and I glanced around the empty store. Peeking out the front doors, there was only one car filling up.

When Franks returned to the window, he gave me a big smile. Another man came out of the protected back counter fortress and approached.

"Hi Bridget. I'm Trevor, the manager. You want to work here?" He narrowed his eyes at me, like he didn't believe it.

"Yeah, this guy said it's a good place to work. I have a lot of time on my hands and not much to do with it. Might as well make some money." I glanced at Franks when I said this and found him watching me with great interest.

"Alright, do you have time for an interview?"

I glanced at my wrist. "Now? Yeah, let's do it."

Trevor led the way to a little closet-sized office in the back and asked me a few typical interview questions, like strengths and weaknesses, availability and five-year plan kind of things. Honestly, it was about the easiest thing I'd ever done, slipping with little effort into this role I'd invented for myself.

"Okay then, this all looks good. Let me just get a copy of your license and we can discuss your schedule when I return."

I froze. My license. My license with my *real* name and address on it. I smiled, doing my best to conceal the alarm rising in me. "Okay, sure." I rifled through my purse. "Oh shoot, I guess I forgot it. Is it something you really need?"

He considered for a moment, and then waved his hand in the air. "Just get it to me when you have a chance. Now, what days are you available?"

Just then, Franks poked his head in. "Hey, there's a customer out here who wants to see the manager."

Trevor sighed and threw me an apologetic smile. "Be right back."

While he was gone, I glanced around the office. A corkboard hung on the wall behind his desk with the employee schedule pinned to it. I tipped my head out the door to ensure the coast was clear and snapped a picture of the schedule with my phone. This would come in handy in figuring out Franks' routine.

When Trevor returned a moment later, he sat down across from me at his desk. "So, when can you start?"

* * *

"You got the job, just like that?" Tyler looked at me in disbelief.

"I did. I start tomorrow. I told him I could only do one evening a week and Saturday mornings to leave time to practice my training with you and participate in the rest of my life. I saw the schedule; Franks is on every Saturday." I flipped to the picture of the schedule on my phone.

Tyler pushed his dark blond hair back and let out a low whistle. "You're a natural, Mason." I swear I saw admiration in his eyes.

Having taken the bull by the horns, I felt better about everything, even the note. And when Tyler dropped me at my house, I was relieved to have something useful to pour my focus into. I pulled up the employee schedule and memorized when Franks' would be there. As I paced my room committing this to memory, my phone dinged.

A glance revealed a text from an unknown number. Curious, I clicked on it.

hope you don't mind. I took your number from your app. this is jimmy

Stunned, my mouth fell open at the bold gesture. Still, this was an invitation to jump right in, to get to know him. I debated for a minute on what to do, if I should engage. But wasn't this what I wanted? To insert myself in his life and get this thing done? Warning bells rang in my mind as pictures of his past victims—young girls who looked a lot like me—floated through my head. But I was safe here, behind the shelter of my phone screen.

Me: Hey there. Thanks for help getting the job!

Franks: no prob. congrats on getting it. not surprised. i'd have hired u if it was up to me

Me: Thanks.

I paused, uncertain how to respond from there. But I didn't have to wait long.

Franks: How many foster homes u been in

Me: I've lost track. They all suck.

Franks: Tell me about it

Was he confiding in me? Building a bridge? Is this how he connected with his victims? I rummaged through my backpack and found his file, remembering something about his own foster care experience. Maybe he targeted runaways and foster kids for reasons other than their anonymity.

Me: How would you know?

Franks: u and I have more in common than where we work

Me: Oh really? You were in foster care, too?

Franks: yes and I know the hell it is

Then, before I could decide how to respond to that, another text came through.

Franks: don't worry. I'll keep you safe

My heart sped up when I read that, deciding to go all in. I'd never get another chance like this.

Me: That's awfully kind of you. Life's been hard. My parents died when I was two and I've bounced around ever since. No one wants a troublemaker around—at least, that's what they call me. Luckily, I've been able to take off when I see them starting to turn on me. Because they always do.

As I waited for his response, I thumbed through the file. After many brushes with CPS in his early years, his parents' rights were terminated, and he was put into foster care at the age of six. By then, he was an angry boy who acted out a lot and no one had much patience for him. He moved from home to home until he was implicated in a house fire when he was a teenager. At that point, he was convicted of arson and spent his years from sixteen to nineteen locked up. From what the police could tell, he started killing shortly after he was released.

Franks: I bounced around too. doesn't feel good when no one wants you. but we foster kids need to stick together

If this was typical for him—if he went for girls in foster care because he felt a sense of affinity with them, a desire to protect them—that confirmed my suspicions that there was more to this. For him, it didn't seem to be totally about choosing victims who were easy to lose in the shuffle, girls with no real family to care if they turned up or not. But then, why did he kill them?

Me: I like how that sounds. You can't trust too many people these days.

Franks: you can trust me

Me: I'd like to, Jimmy, but I hardly know you.

Franks: I know you. you're like me. lost, alone, rejected. I won't let you feel like a nobody Bridget.

If I had been someone who felt lost, alone and rejected, I imagined Franks' words would feel good. Now I understood how he wormed his way into the lives of the girls he eventually killed.

Me: What do you like to do for fun?
Franks: talk to pretty girls
Me: Oh, am I interrupting??
Franks: you are the pretty girl
Me: Aww! That's really sweet. Thanks Franks. Tomorrow's my first shift. See you there?
Franks: see u then

At this I sent a blushing emoji and left it at that. I'd see him soon enough. And in the meantime, I would work on polishing my story.

Just then, another string of text messages came through, this time from Addy.

We need to talk. That fight was dumb. You're my best friend and I love you.

I put my phone down, leaving her appeal unanswered. For now, I needed to stay away from Addy. She wasn't safe with me until I could get control of myself. So instead, I'd focus all my energy on mastering my emotions and getting to know Franks. The water wanted someone served up. And if I wanted to have at least some of my life back, it would have to be him.

* * *

I had briefed my parents on the new job with Franks and, though it made them nervous that I'd be so close to him and in such a bad part of town, they were comforted by Tyler's assurances that he would drop me off each time and wait for me through my shifts.

Skipping school was becoming my new norm, and it was my goal to get back there in time for rehearsal afterward—I'd missed too many of those, and if I wasn't careful, I'd get kicked out. I didn't have to be at the gas station until 10 a.m., so technically I could have gone to the first few hours of school. But I figured that time was better spent priming my mind. I sat on the floor in my room, the house quiet following the departure of my dad and sisters, my mom downstairs working happily away in her craft room making her bug jewelry.

I started with my focusing exercises, bringing my mind to the present, noticing my breath first. As I sat there in the silence, I heard a stirring, like the water waking up within me. As I counted my inhales and exhales, a whisper traveled from the base of my spine up to my head and into my ear.

Audibly, as if someone sat next to me and spoke, the word *Take* formed in my mind.

Inhale, 1-2-3-4

Exhale, 1-2-3...

Time now to take

My attention snagged mid-exhale on the fact that the word had turned into a phrase.

I refocused, placing my hand on my stomach so I could feel my body filling and emptying with air.

Inhale, 1-2-3-4-

Life for life. You owe a debt.

My eyes snapped open, and I realized my slow steady breathing had turned into frantic, ragged panting. A cold sweat broke out on my upper lip.

"A debt?" I asked. I felt my sanity slipping and wondered, as I had a few times before, if there was no water. Maybe I was merely losing my mind.

You owe a debt. Life for life. Take...Take!...TAKE!!

The last command rang loudly in my head and was accompanied by a blast of excruciating fire. "NO!" I shouted, jumping to my feet. If I hadn't been crazy before, the madness was really closing in on me now.

"I will pay my debt!" I shouted into thin air. "But you obey me, not the other way around!"

In answer, a shaft of pain ran up my spine and split my head in two, throwing me to my knees as I grasped my throbbing skull. *TAAAKKKKKEEEEE*

Something gripped my head, the force so extreme that I heard my own bones start to give, cracking under the pressure of whatever invisible force held on. I screamed, and just when I thought I couldn't take it anymore, just as my vision started to blur, the hold on my head yielded its grip with an instantaneous release. I fell on the floor, weeping. The force within me had gotten the point across—I was at *its* mercy.

I crawled on all fours, tears on my cheeks and sweat dotting my forehead, then pulled myself to my feet. Glancing in the mirror, I glared at my own reflection. Ringing sounded in my ears and the room went dark around me, focusing my vision on my reflection. The time was drawing near and as I stared at my image, I made myself a promise: the water within would not win. When the ringing subsided and I felt a little more normal, I dressed, performed the rare application of makeup and brushed my long, dark hair. It was time to see Franks.

16

Jessie

"**A**re you sure you're ready for this?" Tyler's expression held concern as he watched me psych myself up to get out of his car and walk into the gas station, my new place of employment.

"I have to be, Tyler. I feel my control slipping, which means I need to focus *more*, not less. Now is the time for me to get hold of this thing."

"And if you lose control while you're there?"

I smiled at him. "I won't. I beat it this morning, didn't I? It went away after I refused."

"That's not exactly how it works, Mason. It doesn't just 'go away.'"

"I'll be fine and if, for some reason, I'm not, you'll be here." I patted his arm and got out of the car before he could object. Expelling a deep breath, I straightened my black t-shirt, channeling my inner Bridget, and walked up to the store. Inside, I found Franks and Trevor stocking an endcap.

"Good morning Bridget!" Trevor said. "I'm going to have you train with Jimmy today for your first shift, if that's okay with you."

I smiled at Franks, and his gray eyes narrowed, assessing me with obvious hunger. "That sounds great."

After showing me where I could stow my belongings and giving me a few instructions, Trevor set me loose under the care of Jimmy Franks. Franks turned out to be a pretty capable teacher and a knowledgeable employee. He was patient as I learned the cash register and bailed me out when I couldn't answer a customer's question. If I hadn't known better, I'd have said he was a nice guy—charming even. It was hard to reconcile the guy I saw with the murder victims my dad was so sure were his. But then, wasn't this how he got those poor girls to trust him?

"You're doing great so far," he encouraged, as I restocked the chip aisle.

"Thanks. I have lots of practice with packing and unpacking."

He chuckled, joining me in my task since there weren't any customers in the store.

I decided to take the opportunity to learn about him. "Did you grow up right in Detroit?"

He placed some Doritos on the shelf. "I grew up here and there in Wayne county."

"How old were you when you went into the system?" I did my best to keep my tone casual, aloof. Just making conversation here.

"I never knew my dad. My mom decided she loved drugs more than me and signed me over to the courts when I was five."

A tremble of emotion tickled the back of my throat. How tragic. "I'm—I'm sorry to hear that."

He shrugged. "Not much you can do, right? You know that better than anyone."

"Yeah, I do... I'm just surprised no one adopted you. You were pretty young when you went into the system."

"No one wants a hellion. And I was a hellion. An angry one." He sliced open a fresh box of chips.

"I can relate. Foster parents don't seem to appreciate it when you act out. But what do they expect? How's a kid supposed to tell you how they feel when their whole world has been torn away from them?"

He paused, turning his attention on me. "You get it. But they're so quick to dispose of us, aren't they? No patience for our complicated emotions, no love for children not their own." The last phrase came out through gritted teeth, but he got a hold of himself quickly, giving me a smile. "I think we're going to get along just fine, Bridget."

"Yes, I think we are," I answered, allowing my gaze to linger on his, trying to see the sad, abandoned boy inside him. "You asked me how many homes I'd been in. How about you?"

"Thirty-two."

My jaw dropped.

"What? I was a hellion, like I said."

I wondered what he could have done in those homes to be cast aside so frequently. "There wasn't a single home you liked?"

He was thoughtful and didn't answer for a moment. Then he said, "Well, there was one."

"How old were you?"

"Fifteen. I was actually there about a year."

"And what happened?"

Franks smiled at me. "You're curious, you know that?"

Heat filled my cheeks, and I waved my hand. "Just making conversation."

"Hm..."

He watched me for a minute, unspeaking, sending a wave of unease through me. Just then the door dinged. "Customer!" I exclaimed, relieved for the interruption.

We passed the remainder of my shift in near silence—no more small talk, no more bonding. I wondered if I'd screwed up, touched on some nerve, right off the bat. Two o'clock, when the end of my shift finally came, I ran to the shelter of Tyler's car, thankful for the safety he represented for me. After a debriefing on the way home, he dropped me in my driveway, and I drove straight to music rehearsal, rolling in just five minutes late.

I busted through the auditorium doors and immediately noticed everyone's eyes turn toward me. Colin was on stage with my understudy, Misti Moore. I took in the scene, my heart accelerating as it slowly dawned on me what I was seeing.

Mrs. Ferris made a beeline for me. "Hi Jessie. Mind if we have a word over there? Keep running the scene, folks!" She pointed to the corner of the auditorium and started walking toward it. I followed her and we sat, side by side. She drew in and released a big breath while struggling to hold my gaze.

"Jessie, I've been concerned about you. Before anything else I want to ask—are you okay?"

I nodded without hesitation, to convince both of us. "I'm sorry, Mrs. Ferris. Life has gotten…complicated lately. I haven't meant to miss so much practice, but I promise I have all my scenes and songs memorized. I could perform them tomorrow if I had to."

She gave me a sad smile. "I have no doubt you could, Jessie. You're a star." Her eyes welled with tears. "But I'm sorry. This is a big commitment and unfortunately, you've shown that you just aren't up to it."

My mouth fell open. I hadn't expected this. I thought I was keeping it together, thought I was managing everything.

"But…this is my passion, my dream, Mrs. Ferris. I'll do better—I'll be at every rehearsal from here on out." Even as I promised, I wasn't certain I'd be able to keep my word.

She shook her head. "The decision has been made. Misti will perform as the baker's wife. If you'd like, you're still welcome to be in the chorus. We could use your soprano voice."

My cheeks filled with heat as my heart raced, the tears already forming in my eyes.

She had given me an out. She saw what a lunatic I was becoming. I should just accept my fate, take her up on her offer, thankful to be relieved of this commitment so I could focus all my energy on Franks, on containing the murderous impulses in me. But then I thought of Tyler. How he'd been forced to quit basketball. How he'd lost himself for a while because of it. How he'd called me courageous for sticking with the musical, the thing that brought me joy.

And I thought about Jake and Addy and everything I'd already lost because of what I was becoming. Unable to speak for fear or crying, I only nodded, gathered my belongings, then fled from the auditorium. In the hall I passed Jake, who was at his locker, making out with Katie Griswald. The sight was a punch in the gut and a further reminder of what my existence as an immortal killing machine had robbed me of. Unable to contain my tears any longer, I ran, not able to get out of that place fast enough.

But when I reached my car, I found Addy perched on the hood.

I couldn't do this now. I just didn't have it in me.

I put my hand up before she could speak. "Addy, not now," I said, desperate to get out of there. I didn't even slow my pace, just brushed past her, trying to get to the driver's side door.

Addy grabbed my arm, stopping me. "What's wrong, hon?"

I sniffed. "It's been a bad day, and I just want to go home."

"Jessie, please. Can we go talk somewhere? I brought a peace offering. She thrust a twenty- ounce bottle of Dr. Pepper and a Caramello at me, my two favorites.

Addy's gift softened some of my anger. She always showed her love with food and, truth be told, I needed some love just then. "Fine," I said and opened my palm. She dropped her peace offering into my hands and smiled.

"That's my girl. Let's go somewhere and make up. Meet at Lakeside park?"

"See you in five," I conceded. Against my better judgment, I hopped in my car and headed in the direction of the park. I really wanted to go home, to take a few minutes to myself and nurse my wounds but the girl had brought my favorites. She clearly wanted a chance to clear the air, and I figured I should give her the opportunity. After all, she was my best friend and, truth be told, I was in dire need of her friendship.

When I pulled into the parking lot and got out of my car, Addy was already swinging idly on one of the swings. The Dr. Pepper bottle hissed as I opened it and took the swing next to her.

"So you got pretty mad at me earlier," she noted.

"I guess we're launching right in," I said, throwing back a swig of pop and swishing the sip in my mouth, enjoying the fizz of the carbonation before I swallowed.

"You owe me an apology, Jessie."

My defenses flared and I held the bottle up in midair. "This peace offering is a lie. You don't want to make up. You want to fight more," I accused.

My ever-present internal companion woke within me, eager to pick up where we'd left off earlier—igniting me from the inside and egging me on. I let it in just a little; the energy it imbued was a nice exchange for my emotional exhaustion.

"Whoa, easy Jess." Addy put her palm in the air. "I don't want to fight with you. I just want to understand."

"You have a funny way of approaching understanding," I said with a sneer.

The companion within me pushed me to my feet.

"Why did you get up? Are you leaving? I thought we could talk about this."

"You don't respect my limits, Addy. I tell you I don't want to talk about something—or, in this case, I *can't*—and you push anyway. It's always been that way. But friends don't do that. They don't impose their own desires on someone who isn't comfortable with them!"

Addy sprung to her feet. "You think I'm imposing?!" Her voice took on a hysterical note. "I've left you alone while you blatantly avoided me all last week. After I was there for you when you broke up with Jake! After I've *always* been there for you! I've given you all kinds of space, but the moment I try to have a conversation with you about it, you blow up and storm off."

"SHUT UP!!" I screamed.

The outburst was directed at her and I meant the words. But even more than that, I was hollering at the water, to the commands ringing loud and clear in my mind, deafening me.

I could control this again. Just like I had all the times before now. I would control this.

Addy's eyes welled and she took a step back. "I don't even know who you are right now."

"No one does!" I screamed, and then, "I said, 'SHUT UP!'"

Though the second statement was aimed solely at the water's deadly directives, Addy narrowed her eyes.

"So, this is how it is now, huh, Jess? I open my mouth and you shut me down? You think you're better than me! You always have! With your straight A's and your lead roles and your stupid perfect hair!" she spat. "You think you're perfect. And that's your problem, Jessie. There's no such thing as perfection. You can't control everything and everyone in your life!"

Desperately fighting the water's compulsion, I plunged my bare hand into the snow. Anything to detract from what was being asked—demanded—of me.

"What are you doing?" Addy screamed as she jumped back.

Kill

Take
Feed me
Your debt to pay
She doesn't know you
She hates you
KILL!

The directives flew through my mind, one on top of the other, repeatedly, pulling me down into insanity. I tried to think about the cold snow on my hand.

I tried to focus on my breaths.

I tried to key in on Addy's voice asking me what I was doing.

I tried.

But I couldn't stop it.

Something fought for control of my body. I resisted, the scourge of pain a reminder that I wasn't in control. But I would get control.

This was my body.

My mind.

My sanity.

Mine.

Only that was a lie. Everything was a lie. My life. My friendship with Addy.

I was at the mercy of the water's demands.

Through my resistance, the pain awakened a new desire in me—to obey, to find relief, for this to be over. Now there were promises attached to the demands for the very things I craved.

For the voice to quiet.

For the agonizing fire creeping over my skull and reaching down my spine to stop.

I grasped my head and fell on my side as excruciating waves of torment pulsated through my brain.

A hand reached for me, landed on my shoulder.

"Are you okay?"

The question echoed in my head, and I could barely focus on it. The harrowing punishment for my refusal was drowning out Addy's voice.

I glared up at her, but her expression showed only compassion. "Do you need help? Should I call 9-1-1?"

I wanted to send her away, to warn her, but something clamped my mouth shut. I tried to maneuver my tongue, tried to convince it to form the words, but nothing came out. I fought for control of my body, but some invisible force lifted my arm, curled my hand into a fist, and brought it up toward Addy's face, to strike. But I pushed my right fist down with my left hand, clawing at my own skin to feel something besides the water, to stop myself from doing what I was being asked to do.

The water was displeased with me, and it threw me to the ground, knocking the wind out of me. I resisted, tensing my muscles, but my arms, my legs, moved without my permission. I was on all fours, trying to pin myself to the ground. Despite the cool temperature, sweat soaked my forehead and dripped down my temple. But even as I fought, I found myself crawling across the ground toward Addy, making my way to give the monster inside me what it wanted.

NO!

I was in control. I stopped myself, every muscle in my body tensed in resistance.

But the force inside of me was stronger and I began to move again.

Addy was my best friend.

She doesn't know you.

I won't hurt her.

She hates you. Take. Life for life. Her life.

With stiff movements I crawled across the ground, fighting my own body the whole way.

Addy backed away, her fearful eyes pooling with tears. "What's...happening...Jess?" Her voice shook, disbelief written on her face.

"You have to go," I managed to say, but the words came out quiet, weak.

She took a step toward me, extended her hand.

I smacked her arm away. "Go, Addy! You have to get out of here! We're done, okay? We're done. Just go..." I sobbed as the words left my lips. I didn't know how much longer I could hold on. The water's demands were getting stronger by the second, and my ability to keep myself from lunging at her—from throwing her head into the pavement and being done with this—was almost gone.

Suddenly, against my will, I got to my feet and started to pursue her. I braced my own leg, even dug my nails into my skin, to slow my advance on Addy.

"GO!!" I screamed at her. "GET OUT OF HERE! WE'RE NO LONGER FRIENDS, ADDY, DO YOU UNDERSTAND? GOOOO!!"

An injured expression froze on her face, and tears trailed down her cheeks. She opened her mouth like she was going to say something but stopped short.

Meanwhile, I fought, tearing at my own flesh, holding myself off. But the water was stronger.

Addy shook her head, then turned and ran away, scrambling into her vehicle and driving off.

Relief filled me, but it was short-lived, followed by even more unbearable punishment. I fell to the ground and a rage that didn't belong to me reverberated through my body. I couldn't move. I could only suffer. And the water was making sure I did.

I fingered my cell in my pocket and dialed Tyler's number.

"Hello?" His voice sounded like salvation.

"I need you!" I screamed into the phone.

Then I passed out.

17

Tyler

I peeled into the driveway where my 'find my friend' app told me Jessie was, and panic ripped through me when I saw her crumpled form on the ground. I jumped from my car and shook her.

"Mason, Mason! Wake up!" Her head sloughed to the side, and I scooped her freezing frame into my arms and carried her to my car. Once I had her inside, I rounded to the trunk and found the fleece blanket I kept there for emergencies. I wrapped her up, blasting the heat in her face to warm her.

"You're going to be okay," I assured her as I made my way toward her house, dialing her dad on the way.

It went straight to voicemail.

"Yeah, Mr. Mason, this is Tyler. Jessie is in trouble. Call me back." My gaze flitted toward her still unconscious body as concern welled.

A couple of eternal minutes later, she stirred, fingering the fleece blanket I'd wrapped her in. She looked at me, her eyes heavy. "How'd I get here?" she asked in a groggy voice.

"Don't push yourself. We're almost there."

She rested her head against the seat. "Where are you taking me?"

"Home," I said, my eyes focused on the road, my mind on getting her to safety.

"No," she objected.

I frowned. "Why not? You'll be safe with your parents."

"I don't want to go home. Not yet. I don't have the energy to deal with my family yet. That's why I called you. I need a minute. Isn't there someplace else you can take me? Some place safe?"

Conflict raged in my mind as I pulled to a stop at a light. The left turn signal blinked the direction of her house. I thought about her request for a few moments, then wanting to do whatever was in my power to make Jessie Mason feel safe, I turned right when the light changed, redirecting the car toward my apartment.

Once there, I pulled into my parking spot and opened the door. "Stay there," I told her, then got out, ran to the other side and opened the passenger door. Reaching in, I helped her from her seat, wrapping my arms around her waist and supporting her steps. She wobbled under her own weight, her jelly legs insufficiently doing their job of holding her up. I led her across the parking lot and up some stairs to the second floor. Balancing her weight on one side of my body, I rifled through my pocket for keys, then unlocking the door, I led her through.

Inside, I guided her to the leather sofa in the middle of my living room and clicked on the lamp next to it. Lowering her down, I unwrapped the blanket from around her and spread it over the length of her body. Then, I disappeared into the kitchen to retrieve a glass of water and a washcloth.

Minutes later, I pushed the glass into her hand. "Drink this. You need to stay hydrated."

She eagerly took the water from me and downed it. I took it back to the kitchen and refilled the glass, then gave it back to her.

"Tip your head back," I said, examining her face. There were no visible signs that injury had occurred and then healed.

She did as I'd asked without question, leaning her head on the soft leather of the sofa. Washcloth in hand, I wiped her sweaty, dirty face with gentle strokes. She shut her eyes at my touch, at the warmth of the cloth on her face. She was beautiful this way—long lashes framing her closed eyes—looking completely vulnerable there on my sofa.

When I finished, I simply watched her for a few moments, averting my gaze when she opened her eyes and caught me. When I looked back, her expression was filled with sadness. Without her saying anything, I knew what had happened. "It came collecting, didn't it?" I asked.

She nodded, drinking from the refilled glass of water. "I almost killed Addy." Her voice cracked under the weight of the words, under the acknowledgment of what had come close to happening. "She's my best friend, and I almost killed her. She got away."

Tears streamed down her face, and she made no effort to stop them.

I patted her shoulder, feeling her pain. I remembered how this felt, that moment when you realized you weren't the one in control. That's why I'd tried so hard to tell her to let go, to learn to work *with* instead of *against* the voice of the water. But I also understood that people had to learn for themselves. Still, I wished that I was able to take the pain of the lesson away from her. Which meant...I cared about this girl, about what happened to her.

"Do you understand now?" I asked her.

She nodded, too fragile to speak. I fought the impulse to wrap her in my arms, to protect her, assure her she would get through this. I pushed my hair back and crossed my arms. "On the bright side, you said you *almost* killed her. So, she's not dead." I raised my eyebrows, trying to lighten the mood a bit.

She gave me a feeble smile before she sobered again. "It was close."

"It's been building for you. If you were able to resist at all, that's something. Once the water reaches its full power within you, it's almost impossible *not* to give it what it wants."

"I believe it."

"This is what we've all been talking about. Me, your dad, Rodney. This doesn't come down to control. It's about surrender."

She lifted her shaky gaze to meet mine. "I don't know how to do that." She blinked her eyes hard to halt another rush of tears.

Something moved inside me, and it took me a moment to recognize what it was. I watched her cry, broken, almost defeated by this immortal burden we bore together, and I felt...helpless. Seeing Jessie this way stirred something in me that had long been dormant, something I'd forced myself to tuck away because feeling it—for anyone—made me dangerous to that person.

But maybe not to her.

In her, I saw myself—the scared, uncertain grieving immortal, full of power not yet understood with no view of the bigger picture, no knowledge that it would be okay in time. I wanted to make her feel better, to bring a smile to her face, to help her recognize her own strength.

But realizing this, at this moment, broke me, too. Because I couldn't fix this for her. All I could do was be here.

I leaned over her, my eyes fixed on her sad, beautiful face, and retrieved a tissue from the end table. But for a moment, before I grabbed the tissue, I froze, and our eyes locked in some intense exchange of kinship. She knew I understood what this was like. I saw it in her gaze.

When I leaned away, I dabbed the tears with the tissue. She gave me an appreciative smile and something else woke up in her eyes—a brightness. She bit her lip, her gaze trailing just for a moment to my mouth, then back up again. This, of course, dragged my attention to her lips.

I gave myself a mental shake. "It gets easier," I assured her.

A weak but appreciative smile lifted the corners of her mouth. "What was it like for you?"

I folded my arms behind my head, remembering my own journey. "I didn't want to accept any of it either. It's hard to acknowledge what...we are."

"I mean, who wants to be a ruthless murderer?"

I chuckled, turning my gaze back to her face where it lingered a little too long. "Exactly." Then I remembered, and a tangible darkness followed the memory. "I was terrified—when my parents first told me and when I started to hear the voice myself. You know, there's no way to prepare for the actual experience of hearing the water speak to you, even when you know it's coming. Can you imagine not knowing? Just having those impulses and ugly thoughts?" I shuddered.

"Anyway, once my parents made me quit basketball, I sank into a depression. I totally withdrew—mainly because I'd lost something I really loved, but also because I was just plain scared. I didn't know how this would manifest or who I could hurt. You know, I have to tell you that I'm impressed with how you haven't let this end things for you. You've gone on with your life. That takes guts."

Her face dropped.

"Oh no, what'd I say?"

"It's over for me, too. I got kicked out of the musical today."

I let out a low whistle, regretting my words, the pain they'd put on her face. "Mason—I...I'm really sorry."

She put her hand up to stop me. "I think it's for the best. I was determined to hang on to everything, you know? To not let my parents' birthday revelation change anything about my life. My boyfriend, my best friend, my straight A's, my lead role...all those things I held on to for dear life."

She trailed and a dry sob shuddered through her. "But what today taught me is that I never had any control to begin with. Addy said something to me at the park when we were fighting. She told me that I think I'm perfect. She couldn't be more wrong. I try *so hard* to be

178

perfect, but I always fall short. Truth is, I'm terrified of failure. And now, I've let everyone I love down, including myself. And I don't know how to recover."

She was quiet for a moment, and I watched her process the events of the day.

"It totally took over my body today. I couldn't speak at one point, could hardly move. I was stupid to think I could control it."

"It has to, to get its way. If you fight it for control, it will win—every time. Jessie, no one is perfect, okay? And to hold yourself to that standard is an ongoing setup for failure. You're much better off admitting where you fall short. Start with the water. Admit to yourself that you don't have control. And then admit to yourself that that's okay. There's freedom in surrender."

She slid up in her seat and raised her eyebrows at me. "You're kind of wise, you know that, Tyler Emmanuel?"

Her gaze lingered on me, and I slid closer to her on the couch as heat radiated between us.

"Thanks," I said, before clearing my throat and dropping my gaze to my hands.

"Is that another reason you started teaching self-defense to seniors?"

Confused by her abrupt change of subject, my eyes snapped up to meet hers. "Is what another reason?"

"Just…because you had to give back. To deal with being a killer."

I nodded, considering the question. "Actually, it was. Because of my first victim, who I told you about and because I saw a need. It seemed right to give back, to redeem some of what I am, in a way."

She smiled, tipping her head against the sofa. "I think that's very noble."

I shrugged. "I never really thought of it that way." When my eyes drifted back to her, I found her watching me. "What?"

"I don't know. In a lot of ways, you're not what I expected."

I tilted my head. "Oh?" How's that?"

She shrugged and fiddled with a loose string on the blanket cocooning her. "I don't know. You seemed cold at first. Who knew there was a kind, thoughtful, charitable person in there?"

I fought the smile her compliments produced. "Well, I happen to think you're alright too…" I trailed, our gazes locking with intensity. I licked my lips, fighting the urge to taste her.

"I want to thank you, Tyler. You've made me feel…safe."

"You got it, Mason."

Our gazes locked again, the intensity almost unbearable. Thankfully, Jessie broke the connection, studying her fingers in her lap. "Can I ask you something?"

If she asked if I wanted to kiss her, I was screwed. "Of course."

"Do you promise this gets easier?"

"It does, Mason. As you continue to learn to listen for the water's voice and teach yourself to surrender, that process becomes natural for you. You will be able to channel it in the right direction. What happened tonight—" I reached over and squeezed her knee before I could stop myself. "—won't be a regular occurrence."

She dragged her gaze to where my hand and her leg met. "That brings me some relief." I sat back, knowing that if I didn't move, I was going to kiss this girl. And we needed to be focused.

She shivered on the couch and her eyes welled up with tears again. "What is it?" I leaned in closer.

"It's just been a rough day. I got dropped from the musical today, witnessed my recent ex-boyfriend making out with someone new and, to top it all off, I think I've lost my best friend."

"Oh…" I looked out across the room. "Some friendships can survive these things and some…can't. But if you guys have been friends for a long time, she might forgive you."

"I said some really awful things to her." She closed her eyes, like she was seeing the scene in her head. "And I saw the terror on her face as she watched me go insane."

Jessie's mention of the things she'd lost triggered my own grief over what my immortality had taken from me. A sadness shadowed us, and I guess she could see it because she reached over and squeezed my hand.

As if she knew my thoughts, she said, "If your parents are anything like mine, they don't talk a lot about the losses. But I'm sorry you had to give up the sport you loved and I'm sorry you had to break up with your girlfriend."

I gave her hand a squeeze and looked into her dark, compassionate eyes. "Wounds heal."

We sat there, hand in hand for a solid minute. It wasn't a romantic gesture, but one of solidarity, of mutual support, of understanding. I hoped I helped her feel less alone, as she had done for me.

"You've had a long, hard day. We should probably get you home and bring your parents up to speed." I reached into my pocket and checked my phone, discovering two missed calls from Mr. Mason. "Yeah, they're probably worried."

"Good call—I think I'm ready now. I'm exhausted and my head still hurts a little."

"Oh yeah, that'll last a bit. But once the water figures out that you're going to give it what it wants, it's 'encouragement' lessens."

"I look forward to that."

Ten minutes later, I drove her back to where she'd left her car. She froze when she saw the place I'd found her, an abandoned Dr. Pepper lying on the ground, its contents spilled around the bottle.

Urging her to get into her vehicle, I followed her to her house, to be there for her as she conveyed the night's events to her parents. This was becoming more than a job, a business partnership. I *wanted* to support Jessie Mason, wanted to be there for her. But first, we had to get her through her first kill.

18

Jessie

February 19, 2012

Dear Diary,

Tonight it almost happened. I almost killed my best friend.

Writing those words makes me hate myself. If I could turn my killer impulses toward myself, I would. I'd rather die than hurt Addy. Or anyone, for that matter. What is happening to me?!

I scratched my own skin raw. Thank God it closed up instantly. The scary thing was that I didn't even feel it. I tore my own flesh with my fingernails, and I felt nothing. I was too busy fighting back the urge to kill her, trying to drown out the voice commanding my every move.

Thank God I didn't strike her. Thank God most of our fight consisted of nasty words. Still…the things I said to her… I'm a terrible friend.

All of this feels like it's for nothing. Who cares if I stop this Franks guy if it means I might hurt those I love? It doesn't seem like a worthwhile exchange. I can't control myself or this thing inside of me. And I'm terrified.

I don't know myself anymore. I've lost myself to the water I never chose to drink. This wasn't my choice!!!!!!!

Ugh, it makes me so mad, so sad, so…

I hate myself. I hate what this is making me. I don't recognize my own face anymore. But I feel trapped. Trapped by another being inside of me, threatening to take me over. It almost did. Tonight.

Poor Addy. She'll never forgive me. I'd never forgive me either.

If I learned one thing tonight, it's that I am not in control—of anything! This thing has broken me.

Everyone's been telling me I need to surrender, to let go. That sounds almost as impossible as killing someone, but I understand now that I have to figure out how to make it happen.

You win, cursed Fountain of Youth. I'm at your mercy.

Teach me now how to let you lead.

* * *

Exhausted from the day's events and from the debriefing with my parents, I trudged up the stairs to bed. As much as I felt defeated by everything that had happened that day, I also felt grateful that Tyler had been there for me, that he had made me feel less alone. And I could have sworn he was thinking about kissing me. As much as I'd tried to fight it, I couldn't deny my growing attraction to him. And tonight, when he took care of me and made me feel better, I realized something.

I liked Tyler.

My affection for him was inconvenient, to say the least. I had to be focused, pouring my time and energy into Franks, into figuring out how I was supposed to work *with* the water so as not to be overcome by it. I didn't have time to worry about how I was coming off to him. Yet somehow, that wasn't really a concern—after all, he'd seen me at my worst. At least, my worst so far. I had a feeling tonight was just the tip of the iceberg.

My parents had been worried, of course, about my ability to direct my impulses to the appropriate outlets in time. I already felt as though the proverbial clock was ticking down to my ultimate descent into madness without their added pressure, as well as their daily check-ins about any out-of-the-ordinary happenings.

I stopped halfway up the stairs at this thought. In all the madness of the day, I'd forgotten about that last threatening note. I knew that the person sending me these missives was dangerous to me. But right now, I was more frightened of the threat inside of myself. That took priority.

At the top of the stairs, I saw light streaking out from beneath Talia's door. Remembering how she'd been there for me the day before, I decided on a detour and knocked on her door.

"Come in," she answered.

I pushed the door open and she looked up at me from her laptop with a surprised expression.

"What are you doing?" I asked her.

"Can't sleep. Where you been? Tonight, or every night, for that matter? Or is that classified?"

I huffed and walked into her room, plopping down on her full-sized bed. The walls in her room were a deep purple, a sharp contrast to the pastels in mine. Where I had musical posters hanging everywhere, Talia's room reflected her love of the Marvel universe. I smiled, appreciating the huge superhero nerd that was my sister, the innocence of it all.

She regarded me with curiosity and perhaps a hint of suspicion. I couldn't remember the last time I'd sat in her room to talk.

"Soo…is there something you need at this late hour?" she asked, her attention focused on whatever she had displayed on her laptop screen.

"My sister," I said in all seriousness.

Talia crinkled her eyes and set her laptop to the side. "Really?" She looked at me with disbelief in her expression.

"Yes, really." I don't know if it was the crushing exhaustion or the reminder that I had lost everyone I cared about lately, but tears started to fall before I could stop them.

"Oh," said Talia, closing her laptop and drawing closer to me. "You really are not okay, are you?"

I shook my head 'no' as the tears fell. "I'm really sorry to come blubbering into your room." My voice cracked under the pressure of all the emotion and I laughed in embarrassment.

"You don't have to apologize," said Talia. "I've wanted this for a long time."

I frowned at her through my tears. "To see my cry?"

"No," she laughed. "No." The second denial came out softer and I saw an openness in my sister that had been missing for some time.

"Talia, I wanted to thank you for yesterday, for being there for me. I've thought you hated me."

"Seriously? How could you think that?"

"Well, you do have a knack for picking fights with me."

She bit her nails and looked away. "I know. But you gotta understand what it's like living in your shadow. You literally get everything you want—everyone loves you and Mom and Dad bend over backward for you. I guess I've been a little jealous."

That confession catapulted me into a fit of laughter and Talia drew back, looking offended.

"No, no," I explained, patting her arm. "It's just funny because I've been such a royal screw-up lately. If you only knew *what* you were jealous of!" Where extreme emotional exhaustion may have played a role in my tears a few moments ago, now it seemed to bring me into delirious hilarity.

Talia grimaced and then smiled. "Um...what have you screwed up, Jess? From where I'm sitting, everything looks pretty good."

That statement killed my exhaustion induced buzz. I cleared my throat. "You've been right to be suspicious. I've learned some things recently—things you'll learn, too, in time. But for now, I'm bound to secrecy. And these aren't good things, Talia. They've...caused me to change and I haven't handled that process very well."

I looked up at the ceiling, recounting all the humiliating things I'd done of late.

"I broke Jake's heart, even though I didn't want to end things with him."

"Then why did you?"

"I had to. It was easier that way. Safer."

Her eyes narrowed. "Safer? What's that mean?"

Ignoring her question, I reached for her hand. "Just promise me you won't get a boyfriend before you turn seventeen."

"You want me to stay single for the next two years?"

"Yeah. Trust me. It'll be better for you if you do."

"Oooo...kay. Care to share a few more details?"

"I wish I could. Trust me, Talia, I would. You're my only friend right now."

She tilted her head to the side. "Friend? You think of me as more than your sister?"

"I mean, I would like to. If you could stop picking fights with me."

She laughed. "I'll work on that. But...what about Addy?"

The mention of my bff's name sent a jolt through me, and I shook my head as my throat constricted.

"What happened?"

"We had a big fight."

"Well, she'll get over it."

"No." My voice had dropped to a whisper. "This isn't the kind of thing you get over. I don't see her ever forgiving me for what I've done."

"That doesn't sound like Addy. You guys have been inseparable forever."

I could only shrug.

Talia reached forward and took my hand, squeezing it with hers. "I'm really sorry, Jess. I'd like to be there for you, if you'll let me."

I gave her an appreciative smile. "I would like that. Oh, and the list of failures goes on. I'm pretty sure I am failing the majority of my classes because I've missed so much school and today Mrs. Ferris kicked me out of the musical. So, you see? Not much to be jealous of here." I opened my arms wide.

Talia's jaw unhinged and her eyes bulged.

"Yup," I confirmed.

We sat in silence, shoulder to shoulder.

"Talia?"

"Hmm?"

"I'm really sorry if I've made you feel as if you're in my shadow. It's never been intentional. I am *not* perfect, by any stretch. I've tried to be, accepting nothing but the best from myself. But the problem is that it's only when I've been able to deliver—the straight A's, the lead parts in musicals, etc.—that I feel like I am worth anything. So, understand, dear sister, that what you see as perfection is really a very fragile self-esteem, hinged together by deafening demands to do everything right. I have a yardstick, you know? A way to measure myself.

"But lately, it feels like life has taken the yardstick and snapped it in half. I don't really know who I am, anymore. But I want you to know that I'll try harder to see you, and make sure you're seen. You deserve your own spotlight."

Talia gasped. "Wow, Jess. I had no idea about the pressure you felt. I'm sorry I've been such a jealous pain."

I shrugged. "We all cope in our own ways."

"I guess." She drew her hand back and propped pillows behind her, adjusting her posture so that she leaned against the headboard.

"Can I tell you something? Something I've been dying to talk about?" I laid on my stomach, kicking my feet in the air behind me.

"Of course." Talia leaned in, obviously curious.

Without Addy to talk to, this juicy tidbit had been left to fester inside of me, growing almost unnoticed. And now that I realized the truth, I was dying to set it free. "I like Tyler."

"I KNEW IT!" Talia screamed, far too loudly for the hour.

"Shh, shh! You'll wake up Cora!" I hushed her.

She covered her mouth and we both giggled, this rare moment of bonding deeply needed by us both. I felt some of the heaviness lift from my heart.

We each finally managed to catch our breath as the laughter died down.

"Has he kissed you yet?"

"No, I don't think he even likes me."

"Yeah, right. Of course, he does. What do the two of you do in all that time you spend together?"

I froze. "Um, self-defense. He's like a teacher, a mentor. And he's made it perfectly clear that that's all he wants to be. But still, those eyes...that hair..."

"Your kids would have the most gorgeous hair...."

"HA!" I looked at the clock as a big yawn hit me. "We have school tomorrow," I said. *Well, she had school.*

"I know." Talia yawned then too. "I'm glad you stopped by tonight."

"Me too, sister." But I didn't leave, and we both drifted off to sleep right there on her bed, until her 6 a.m. alarm went off, waking us to another new day.

Talia scrambled to get ready for school, and I dressed like I was going too. I drove us both, as I always did, but after she got out of the Vibe in the parking lot, I pulled out of my spot and headed home. There was nothing for me at school now. I didn't want Jake's new relationship rubbed in my face and I couldn't see Addy. Not yet, anyway. The musical was off the table, and as sad as that made me, I had to also admit that I felt a bit relieved. The pressure had definitely been getting to me.

Learning to focus was my singular mission now. I needed to figure out how to submit to the water's demands so I could get this thing done with. Before pulling out of the school parking lot, I performed a quick scan of the cars. Addy's usual spot sat empty, and I wondered how long she'd skip school to avoid me. I wished I could tell her she didn't need to—that I wasn't there anyway. And then I thought I might.

Shifting into park, I plucked my phone from my pocket and shot her a text:

I'm really sorry about our fight. I love you.

I left it at that and headed home to my quiet house. Mom had gone to the vet with Arnie the snake for a check-up, and Dad and my sisters were at work and school. Sitting in the middle of the floor of my bedroom, I closed my eyes.

"Okay, you bastard. I'm listening. I will work with you. I will...submit to you. Speak to me."

I waited, but my appeal was only met by silence.

"Water within me, speak!" I felt kind of stupid talking to some invisible magical force, but I figured if I could hear it, it could hear me.

But still, nothing.

Painful though it was, I took my mind to the night before, when I fought against the water's urges for Addy's life. I remembered what it felt like, how loud the water's demands had become, how resisting had become more difficult as a new desire, one to acquiesce, sprung forward.

I opened my eyes, remembering that detail. That scary detail. Not only did I fight the water's demands, I fought my own bending will. And I understood right then what Tyler had meant about either submitting or being submitted to the water's hunger for blood.

I opened my eyes as I realized my breathing had accelerated. The memory had punctuated my need to figure out how to communicate with this thing, how to be one with it. Here I thought I'd been practicing all those mindfulness exercises to control my mind, to manipulate it. But really, all along, I'd been learning how to connect to what was inside of me. Now, I understood that my only choice was to embrace the killer within if I wanted any influence over who my victims would be.

I closed my eyes a second time, and pictured the scene from the night before, trying to connect to the hunger that was inside of me. A whisper stirred, a response to my attempts to call it forward. I had the water's attention.

Next, I brought Franks' face to mind and then I pictured all of his victims and what he'd done to them, just to pour some fuel on the fire.

"Him," I said and pictured his face again, showing the thing that stirred inside of me what I wanted.

I felt a vibration of understanding as the hunger made itself known to me as its presence came alive.

Take?

The word I'd come to associate with pain now formed in my mind as a question, an attempt of understanding.

"Yes, take," I answered.

Rather than the bloodthirsty wild animal uncaging inside my brain, or the punishing pain that accompanied my refusals, a sigh of contentment echoed through me, filling me with peace, with clarity, energizing me with a sense of purpose and direction.

"Yes, take," I repeated. "Soon. I promise to give you what you need, soon. Okay?"

Another sigh of appreciative understanding filtered through my mind, down the length of my body, leaving me feeling almost euphoric.

I smiled. Tyler, Rodney, my parents—they'd all been right. Letting this thing in, rather than keeping it out, was the key. I only had to set up the right circumstances to unlock the door.

* * *

It was only my second shift with Franks, but I hadn't heard from him since he shut my questions down the last time we worked together. He hadn't even bothered to text me. I hoped I hadn't lost his interest already, hadn't made my job harder.

I'd checked my phone a million times before going into the gas station, only to find that my message to Addy had gone unanswered. I typed out a second one: *I hope you're okay*, and left it at that.

When I walked through the door and Franks' gaze fell on me, I was reassured. He peered at me with the same hungry look in his eyes I'd seen that first day, and his lips formed a welcoming smile at the sight of me. I couldn't decide if his expression signaled attraction...or bloodlust. Either way...

"Afternoon, Jimmy. How are you?" I said, coming around back and stowing my belongings.

He gave me an easy smile. "Good to see you again."

"Hey listen, I hope you don't feel like I overstepped the other day, asking about your experience. It's just—we have a connection, you know? About our shared foster kid status? And...well, the truth is that I haven't had anyone to talk to about it. It's been kind of lonely. So if I seemed like a nut job just launching in like that, I apologize."

The satisfaction my appeal gave him was apparent on his face. Since he'd spoken early on about me being able to trust him, I decided approaching him from that angle might give me a better way in.

And I was right.

Franks stood up tall, his thin, lanky frame towering over me, a subtle smile on his lips. He searched me with his gray eyes. "I get that," he said at last. "Some things are just hard to talk about."

"Yeah, I know," I answered truthfully, although we definitely weren't talking about the same thing. "And you have to be careful who you trust with those parts of yourself." I took a step closer to him, keeping my eyes locked on his gaze. "You told me I could trust you so I was just hoping...I was just hoping you'd trust me, too."

His eyes were beautiful, the prettiest I'd seen. It was difficult to reconcile their beauty to the monster in whose head they were. Franks reached forward, running his fingertips down a tendril of hair that had escaped from my ponytail and tucked it behind my ear.

"You're lovely, Bridget."

I feigned embarrassment, looking down at the floor before meeting his eyes again.

"You remind me of someone...someone very special to me."

Was this why I was his type? Young and in foster care, dark features?

"Who?" I asked, hoping he'd tell me more, something I could use.

Franks opened his mouth to answer, but the dinging of the doorbell interrupted him. Our mutual attention snapped to the door, to the customer walking through.

Franks released an irritated sigh, then his expression softened when he looked back at me. "I have to take this. Hey, listen..."

The intensity had returned to his gaze, and he came close, close enough to share my air.

"Would you like to meet up outside of here sometime this weekend? Could you get away from your foster home?"

This was it—I was in. I gave him a smile. "Oh, I'll figure out a way."

"I'll text you the time and place. Can't wait." And with one last hungry glance, he turned his attention to the customer.

19

Jessie

Three days later, and many sessions of interacting with the water's voice within, I prepared myself to go visit Franks at the address he sent. He had given me a public place, probably to build some trust first, and I would just have to see where the night took me. I pulled on some ripped skinny jeans and a fitted black sweater.

Before I tucked my phone in my pocket, I checked again to see if I had any response from Addy but found my five attempts to reach her unanswered. I pushed through my disappointment, unsure it was even a good idea to try and reconcile, despite how much I wanted to.

A knock sounded on my door and my parents pushed the door open, walking into my room. "Hey there, just wanted to check on you."

I gave them a smile as I smeared lip gloss over my lips. "I'm good."

My parents exchanged a look and my mom sat down on my bed, Liza perched on her shoulder and Arnie coiled around her wrist. I was always amazed how they left each other alone when on her person like this, bonded by their mutual love for her.

My dad spoke first. "This makes me nervous, Jessie. You have yet to answer your first call to kill and I'm not sure spending time alone with a serial killer is wise. We prefer to hunt from the shadows, only opening ourselves up to the water's demands when absolutely necessary, keeping ourselves as anonymous as possible."

I turned, irritation crawling up my throat. "Dad, Mom, I get it. I fought this thing, thought I could control it, but it taught me that I'm at *its* mercy. I feel like I know how to work with it now. You have to let me do some of this my way. I almost feel like acting has set me up for this, you know? It's been easy, almost effortless, putting myself into this role of sad foster child. I just need to get him alone and get this over with."

They exchanged looks.

"Okay," my dad said.

"Okay?" I echoed.

"Yes, okay. We trust you, Jessie. Each person has to figure out how the water works with them. We just want you to be safe... I trust Tyler will be there?"

"He'll be there, watching. There's nothing to worry about."

"There is one thing." My mom's face held a pained expression. "Have you gotten any more notes, Jessie?"

"I would have told you if I had, Mom. But they're not my primary focus."

"I know, and that's what concerns me. It should be *a* focus. Just promise me you'll be careful, okay? Don't eat or drink anything anyone gives you."

"Because they could be trying to slip me some of the antidote?"

"Precisely. This is a serious threat, Jessie. It's literally the only thing that can hurt you. I just wish we knew where these notes were coming from..." She stroked Arnie and cast a desperate glance at my father.

"I told you. I couldn't find any fingerprints on any of them," My dad said to her.

"Mom," I said, grabbing her attention again. "I promise I won't take any candy from strangers—"

"—or even anyone you think you know," she interjected.

"I won't eat or drink anything. Tyler will be there, and we will both keep an eye out."

Mom shivered. "The whole thing makes me uneasy. I wish I could just do it for you, send you back to your normal teenage life."

"I wish you could, too. But it's too late for that, Mother."

* * *

An hour later, Tyler and I were making our way toward the address Franks had texted me. Thanks to Google Maps, we knew it was a bar close to downtown, and I wondered just how I'd manage to get in, since I was obviously underage. Tyler parked two blocks away from the address, giving me the opportunity to approach on foot.

He turned to me and squeezed my arm, the heat of his fingers on my skin distracting me. "Are you sure you're okay?"

His question cooled me down quickly. I nodded. "I am."

"Okay. I'll give it about five minutes or so and then I'll follow you in. And don't worry, I'll keep my distance."

I nodded again and left his car, my heart racing with anticipation as I made my way toward The Garage, a warehouse-looking bar. My shallow, rapid breathing fogged the air as I got closer, and I heard a tiny rumble of satisfaction inside me, as if the water knew I was headed to see our intended victim.

Walking through the door of the place, I was met with a warm blast of heat and a smiling hostess. Franks was inside, and I immediately noticed the way his hungry gray eyes roved over me. He'd dressed up for me, wearing jeans and cream-colored sweater. He stepped in front of the hostess before she could greet me, and a waft of spicy cologne met my nostrils.

197

"Is this a bar?" I asked, looking around. The space was wide open—a long bar counter ran the entire length of one side, there were pool tables in the middle and tables took up the space along the wall across from the bar. The atmosphere was dark, the music loud and the place teemed with activity. If Franks had lured me here to kill me, he'd definitely made a mistake. Nothing would go unnoticed in this place.

"You can come in, but they will want to see your ID, so they know not to serve you. You'll have to wear a special bracelet to signify that you're underage. Do you have a license with you?"

My heart gave a start—my license displayed my real name. I'd managed to avoid ever giving Trevor his promised copy, and he hadn't seemed to care, as long as I'd shown up for my shifts.

"Um…" I pretended to search through my purse. "I guess I forgot it. I don't drive much." I gave him a nervous smile, but he watched me with an almost suspicious look in his eye.

"Why don't you look again? We can't go in without them carding you." His smile was patient and he gave a wave of his hand with his suggestion.

"O—okay." This was not going well so far, and my heart kicked up as a sweat broke out on my forehead. I pulled out the contents of my purse one at a time. Opening my wallet, I found my license right where it always was. "Oh, here it is after all," I said with a chuckle.

"Your wallet. That's the last place I would have looked, too." One corner of Franks' mouth turned upward, but I wasn't convinced that he found any amusement in this at all.

I turned toward the hostess and handed her my license, my pulse now pounding loudly in my ears, drowning out the music and chatter of patrons. Franks stood on his tiptoes, as if he was trying to sneak a peek.

Do something, Jessie!

"Hey, so…" I grabbed his arm, snagging his attention. "I like this sweater. It looks really good on you."

He tilted his head, a soft smile reaching his lips. "Thank you." And then his gaze swept the length of my body. "You look good, too." Franks licked his lips; that hungry look in his eyes had returned.

"I'll just need your wrist, sweetie," the hostess said.

I gave Franks a smile, extending my wrist toward her and allowing her to fasten the plastic bracelet. I was relieved to see she'd placed my license on the stand upside down. As soon as my bracelet was secured, I reached out and snatched it back. "Thanks," I told the hostess and plunged my license—the proof I wasn't who I said I was—back into my purse.

Franks' appraising eyes lingered on me for a full five seconds before he said, "Shall we take a seat up at the bar?"

"Sure," I said, allowing him to lead me inside, my nerves kicked into overdrive by the close call. I told myself to get my head in the game and mentally threw myself into the role of Bridget, the sad, lonely and lost foster kid, desperate for this guy's attention.

We sat down, side by side, on bar stools, then Franks ordered a beer for himself and a Coke for me, without asking what I liked. I found this interesting. Was this part of his attempt to take care of me?

"How old are you?" I blurted when the bartender set his beer down in front of him.

"Old enough for this." He raised the glass to his lips and watched me as he took a draw.

"So...twenty-one, then? You know I'm only seventeen, right?"

Franks put his beer down and smiled. "Jailbait, are you?"

In more ways than one, I supposed.

"I'm not bothered by your age, Bridget. Are you uncomfortable with mine?"

"No, not at all," I lied, though I glanced quickly toward the door. A moment of relief surged through me when I saw that Tyler had just walked in and was getting his own fancy plastic bracelet.

"Did you have any trouble sneaking out of your foster home?" Franks watched me closely, and the question felt like a test.

"Not really. By this time, Mr. Johnson is usually three beers in and Mrs. Johnson is sneaking out to meet with her "bridge team," I said, finger quoting the words.

"And there are no other kids in the home?"

"Just me for now."

He raised one of his eyebrows, his gray eyes searching. I gave him a shrug and smiled, as he drew another sip of beer.

When he set the glass back on the bar, he said, "You asked me about the home I was in for a year."

"Oh, yeah. I assumed you didn't want to talk about it."

He narrowed his gaze and smiled. "I don't mind. You told me some of your story, so I'll share mine. This is just a more…suiting environment in which to tell it than work is." He paused. "Don't you like Coke?"

I eyed the glass in front of me, my mother's warnings loud in my head. "I'm not thirsty right now. But please, I want to hear your story," I asked, waving my hand for him to continue.

His gaze moved between my face and the glass of Coke on the bar before he started talking. "So, yeah, I was in this one house a while. It wasn't great—none of them are. The only thing that made it tolerable was…this girl. My foster sister. Her name was Bo."

"Oh, that's nice you had someone," I said. "You two were close?"

He nodded. "I had every intention of getting out of that home as quickly as I had the others. But then I met Bo."

"Are you still in touch with her?"

A darkness fell over his face. "No," he answered simply.

"Oh, that's too bad." I didn't know what else to say.

"She passed away a few years back."

"Wow, that sucks. I'm sorry, Jimmy."

He waved his hand. "Everyone dies at some point. It was her time." The words were cold, devoid of emotion, and he locked eyes with mine when he said them, as if there was a bigger message underneath his choice of words.

I cleared my throat. "So…after she died, did you go to a different home?"

"She died after we left the home."

Man, getting details from this guy was like pulling teeth. I glanced briefly toward Tyler. He'd taken a seat at a table across the warehouse space and was pretending to look at a menu. I was comforted by his presence and I exhaled a shaky breath, turning my attention back to Franks.

"Jimmy, is she the girl you said I remind you of?"

His gaze faltered at my question, but he recovered almost immediately. "In fact, she is. You bear such a resemblance to her." There was a mixture of admiration and muted rage in his tone, and I wondered what she'd done to him.

"So what happened? Why did you both leave the foster home?"

Another shadow crossed his face. "There was an accident. A fire. The couple lost their home, and their license to foster was stripped from them for negligence."

"That's awful. Everyone got out okay?"

He nodded. "Tell me. How old did you say you were when you got into the system?" He tilted his head, his question sounding like a challenge. Another test.

"Two," I answered without skipping a beat, though I had a sinking feeling that he was on to me. Or maybe he was just making sure, double-checking to see if I was worthy of being his next victim.

"So young, you poor thing. You need someone to protect you, don't you Bridget? Someone strong, who understands what you've been through."

I gulped and nodded.

"Someone who will keep you safe, the way I pulled Bo from the fire and saved her."

My eyes grew wide.

"But you'd be more grateful than she was, wouldn't you? You'd understand that I just wanted to protect you—from getting hurt or from feeling pain."

I nodded, words failing me, trying to read between the lines to uncover the rest of the story. "I—I need someone to look out for me," I stammered. "I'm sure you did everything you could to protect your foster sister. She was lucky to have you."

Franks smiled at me, angling his body toward me on his stool and leaning in. "Wanna get out of here? Let me show you just how safe you'll be with me?" He licked his lips, his gaze traveling to my mouth and back up again, lust—blood and otherwise—obvious in his expression.

Did I want to leave with him? Was I ready? Could I count on my internal companion to show up if I needed it tonight? I glanced at Tyler—at least I knew he'd be near. My nerves rattled inside my body, the thought of being alone with Franks making my skin crawl.

Just then my phone buzzed. "Excuse me," I said to Franks, my finger in the air. "Better make sure it's not the foster parents."

Glancing at my phone, I saw the long-awaited response from Addy. *Jess, I need you. I know we've had a fight, but I want to talk. I miss you.*

I could refuse to answer or not show up—that would seal the fate of my friendship with Addy. And maybe that was a good thing. But I didn't want that, and she said she needed me.

In the last few weeks, I'd lost all control, my former life fading away with each passing day…but I wanted to preserve this. I also needed my best friend, even if I couldn't let her in on what I was. But first, I had to deal with Franks. I would go with him; I would do what was needed and then I'd make things right with Addy.

"Everything okay?"

I looked up to find Franks watching me closely.

"Yeah…um…I do want to go with you. I just need to use the bathroom first, okay?"

His jaw tensed and his hungry eyes sparked with dangerous excitement. "Of course," he answered softly. "Take your time."

"I've had a really great time, Jimmy. I'm excited for what's next."

From his expression, I could tell he took pleasure in my statement.

I slid off the bar stool and made my way to the bathroom, happy to find it empty. In the stall, I tapped out two texts.

To Addy: *I'll be there soon, Hang tight. Miss you too.*

Then to Tyler: *Going somewhere undisclosed with Franks. Follow at a distance.*

His response came back immediately: *You get fifteen minutes. Then, I'm coming in.*

I rolled my eyes. On the one hand, I understood his need to keep me safe, as his partner in literal crime. On the other, I didn't feel like I needed a babysitter. I flushed the toilet and left the stall, my phone clattering to the floor when I looked up at the mirror. An expo marker lay on the counter and across the mirror it read:

It's over, Jessie. Tonight it ends.

I glanced around in every direction, searching the bathroom. I pushed every stall door open, finding each of them empty. No one to my knowledge had come in or gone out of the bathroom since I'd entered, but then, I had been preoccupied with my phone. Still…was this the final threat from the OMD?

I gulped, stunned. My ghostly white reflection stared back at me. On wobbly legs, I squatted down to retrieve my dropped phone. No

one knew where I was, except for Tyler and my family.
And, of course, Franks.

20

Jessie

I couldn't feel my legs as I awkwardly walked out of the bathroom, finding Franks waiting for me by the hostess stand.

His expression drooped when he saw me. "Are you okay? You look like you've seen a ghost."

I forced out a laugh. "Oh yeah, I'm fine." With a leery sweep of The Garage, I saw nothing out of the ordinary. Tyler remained seated at his booth.

Either Franks had put that note on the mirror, or it had been left by the OMD member who'd been following me. Could they be one in the same?

I scolded myself for overreacting. What were the chances that my first designated victim was a serial killer of innocent girls *and* a member of a secret order of immortal slayers? Not likely. But then, that only left my parents and Tyler who knew where I was. Obviously, my parents weren't trying to kill me. But what about Tyler?

As I gave myself a moment to consider this, my gaze landed on him. His dark blond hair fell in his eyes as he looked over the menu. No. I refused to entertain that as a possibility.

The wintry air outside refreshed my burning skin as Franks and I left The Garage, and I tightened my jacket around my body.

"You sure you're okay?" He watched me again with appraising eyes.

I shook my head to clear my mind. The situation at hand required focus. As unnerving as it was, I would have to worry about that last note later. If Franks was leading me to what he thought would be my death, I would just have to make sure I killed him first.

There was a certain empowerment that came from understanding my own invincibility. If he tried to hurt me, I would heal. I could not die. At least, not by his hands.

So I gave him my most fabricated smile. "I'm fine." To seal the deal, I linked my arm through his and snuggled close.

He wore a wool jacket and squeezed my interlocked arm in his. We strolled down the sidewalk, the chilly wind whipping my hair around my face.

Franks was a good seven or eight inches taller than me, and he gazed down at me while we walked. "Your hair is so lovely," he said, daring to finger the strands blowing wildly.

"Thank you." We rounded a corner, and the bright city lights grew dimmer as we turned toward a shadier part of the city. I always marveled at how quickly the landscape changed around here. Wealth on one block, poverty on the next. A few minutes later, we turned down a dead-end street that contained a row of abandoned houses. Some of them had even been condemned. And Franks was walking me toward them. "Where are we going?"

"I want to show you my home."

I looked up at him, confused.

"Well, it was my home for the longest period of time. It's the one I lived in for a year—the one that burned down. It's just down this road."

"Oh!" I exclaimed, awareness dawning. And as we drew nearer, I noticed the small row of houses weren't just in disrepair—they'd all been torched, as if a massive fire had blown through the whole block.

Franks must have seen that realization on my face. "You're wondering why it looks like *all* the houses burned."

I nodded.

"The fire in our home was uncontainable. It spread so fast, none of these other places stood a chance."

"That's awful," I exclaimed as we approached the first one. The roof was half caved in, and a child's singed bike sat eerily on the half of the porch that remained.

"It was so bad they had to shut the entire block down."

"And your...your foster sister, Bo. She almost died?"

"She should have died in there, but I couldn't let that happen."

I found his wording curious and I shivered—maybe from the cold, maybe from the way he talked about her death. I wondered how she ended up dead after escaping the fire that had destroyed this block.

We stopped at the last house at the end of the short street. I glanced from it, and looked down the rest of the row. The path of the fire was still evident in the wreckage.

"The fire spread right down the line, engulfing the entire block," Franks said, confirming my thoughts. "The fire department fought it, but it was a nasty one."

"That must have been so sad for you," I said. "Losing your best home."

"'Best' is relative when you're in foster care, though, isn't it?"

He stood on the bottom step of the porch, making the wood bow.

"Are you sure this is safe?"

He turned to me, darkness in his expression, but a smile on his face. The smile was meant to soothe me, but I saw the monster lurking beneath. I had one inside of me too, making it easier to see Franks' demons. "I told you...I'll protect you."

He extended his hand, and, pushing aside the uneasiness in my stomach, I took it. He led me up the stairs, each one creaking under our weight, and we made our way onto the porch. One side of the house was open to the air outside, showing the singed walls inside and some of the framing, while the rest of it had fallen in, surrendering to the ravaging flames.

The other side of the house stood intact, though charred to a crisp. Franks led me through what would have been the front door. The path was clear, as if someone had moved the debris out of the way.

"Why are we here, Jimmy?"

He turned toward me and smiled. "I wanted to show you this place, Bridget. Or shall I say...Jessie Mason?"

He fixed his gaze on me now and I saw the hungry darkness in his eyes.

I gulped, my heart racing. "Did you leave that note?"

His face twisted with confusion. "What note?"

I heaved out a breath and studied him. "The one that was on the mirror when I came out of the bathroom. Did you follow me in?"

"I don't know what you're talking about. But tell me the truth. Why did you lie to me? You're not Bridget; you're not even in the system." The last statement came out with a sneer.

"What makes you think you know anything about me?"

"I followed you," he said, like it should have been obvious.

"You—why?"

"Let's just say, I have a bit of a trust problem." He picked at his nail and looked around the place. "So, what do you think, Jessie? Do you like my home? The neighborhood's a bit rougher than the one you live in."

"You know where I live?"

"I know many things." He took a couple of steps toward me. "What I don't know is why. You were so perfect."

"Haven't you heard? Perfection is an illusion."

He smiled. "I also know your dad's a cop. Is this some kind of sting operation?"

"This has nothing to do with my dad's job."

"Then what are you up to?" He took another step, closing the space between us. "You can't fool me, Jessie Mason. I've survived this long by always being one step ahead."

"Were you one step ahead of Bo too, Jimmy? Making her think you'd saved her...only to turn around and kill her in the end?"

His jaw tensed and his hands fisted at his sides. "How dare you—?"

"Am I wrong?"

He puffed out a breath of air and said through gritted teeth, "She needed to die for what she did. For how she—" He gulped, emotion momentarily choking him before he recovered. "For how she betrayed me."

"She started the fire, didn't she, Jimmy? She started it but you took the fall for it." A detail from his case file sprung to mind—that he had served time as a juvenile for arson.

His face contorted with rage. "The fire was her idea. A way out. We were going to run away together. But it got out of hand and then she got trapped, so I helped her. Once the smoke had cleared, and the authorities had determined that the cause was arson, she went to our foster parents and told them I'd concocted this plan to burn the place down. How she'd tried to stop me, tried to tell them but I wouldn't let her, that I'd beat her to keep her quiet. But now, the guilt was tearing her apart, so she had to tell," he spat. "I should have let her burn."

"Why'd she want to set the fire then?"

"She wanted out, wanted to be on her own. She was just using me. In the end, she figured that I could be of use to her by taking the blame."

"How'd she die, Jimmy?"

He cast a mournful look at me. "I didn't want to kill her, but I had to. I had to save her from herself. I was *her* safety net; she'd told me that. But when she sent me away, I couldn't look after her anymore. So I knew what she needed me to do."

"Was she the first girl you killed?"

An evil smile curled his lips. "When I got out of juvie for an arson charge that got negotiated way down, I looked her up. Then I brought her here, reminded her of what we had planned, what she'd done. She apologized of course, but she didn't mean it. I knew she'd never be safe from her own urges, so I rescued her."

"And have you rescued other girls, Jimmy? Girls like her?"

"Why yes, yes I have Jessica."

"It's just Jessie," I corrected.

He smiled. "Does it matter? Bridget? Jessie? Jessica? Does it matter what you're called?"

"Tell me about the other girls, Jimmy."

After spending time focusing my internal directives at Franks, the water lit with excitement in my belly, asking to come out and play.

Soon, I thought. *Patience. It's coming.*

The whisper echoed through me, but instead of words spoken, it left me with a feeling, an awareness of its intention to wait for my signal and a promise of what might happen if I didn't deliver.

"There are always girls who need rescuing. This system is broken. It chews kids up and spits them out. And so, for a select few, I offer salvation."

"Do you intend to save me, Jimmy?"

"You look like the others, but you aren't one of them. You come from privilege, from a family that wants you. But you're a liar and you're trying to trick me. I don't know why, and I don't much care. Like Bo, you can't be trusted. And you need me. You need me, Jessie Mason, to save you, too."

Inside, a power ignited, adrenaline firing up my hands, my feet, energy bursting out of every pore of my body. My moment had come, and I was ready...

"Jessie!!" My name, screamed through the air outside, snagged both my attention and Franks'. We exchanged confused looks.

"Did you have someone follow you here?"

"Not that someone," I answered. What was she doing here? I turned and made my way on the porch but didn't see anyone. "Is there another door?"

"Just on the side of the house." Franks led the way through the rubble, and on the side of the house that still had a roof, there were stairs that led down to a door. He threw it open, and my best friend peered back at us.

"Addy? What are you doing here?"

She gave me a feeble smile. "You didn't show, and I got worried."

21

Jessie

"How'd you find me?" My gaze volleyed between Addy and Franks, desperate for her to get out of there, to get to safety. The water within lurched, propelling me forward. It was *asking* if it was time, reminding me of my promise.

No, I thought to it. *Not yet.*

Addy lifted her phone into the air. "I used the 'Find my friend' app," she said.

"Yeah, but here?" I pinched the bridge of my nose. "Never mind. Addy, this isn't a good time. Please go. I'll call you later."

"Is this your friend?" Franks said, taking a step forward, his eyes roving over Addy.

I turned to him. "Yes. And *this* is between you and me." My gaze pierced his and he held it, a subtle snarl on his lips.

"She's welcome to stay. This is my home," he said. "C'mon, *Jessie*. It could be fun."

"*This?!*" Addy blurted with a look around the charred house. "Doesn't look like anyone has lived here for years."

I bulged my eyes at her, silently telling her to shut up. "You have to go," I said.

Franks descended the stairs toward the back door before my sentence was complete. He approached Addy, taking the longer strands of her asymmetrical hair, now teal and purple, between his fingers.

"Short," he said.

Addy's gaze lifted to Franks' face as he towered over her. "Dude, personal space," she told him. With a hand to his chest, she forced him back a step. Franks turned to look at me, the hunger in his gaze now turned to fury.

"Jimmy," I negotiated. "Just...let's go back inside. We'll finish our conversation. Addy, GO HOME. I will come to you when we're done here."

Franks' mouth lifted in an evil smile and then he turned back to Addy and grabbing her by her short hair, he dragged her up the steps into the house.

"Ahhh!" Addy screamed, trying to loosen his fingers from her hair. "Stop, that hurts, you maniac!"

"Jimmy, let her go," I pleaded, following behind them. "This is between you and me. You and me, Jimmy. Jimmy! Look at me!"

"You traded Jake in for this abusive SOB?" Addy screamed when he released her, throwing her to the black singed floor of the house.

"I'll take care of both of you—you both need saving. After all, you're so lost," he said, a look of disgust on his face. "So lost," he whispered again. Franks paced the small space and I ran to Addy's side.

"What are you doing here? You should not have followed me. This place is dangerous."

"I know, but I needed to see you," she whispered back, a tremble in her voice.

"SHUT UP!!!" Franks screamed. Then he walked over to us and grabbed Addy, yanking her to her feet and putting a knife to her throat.

She screamed, her eyes filling with tears, the terror evident on her face.

With my best friend in his grip, a knife to her throat, Franks directed his words to me. "The night I met Bo here, when she apologized and I knew she didn't mean it, I knew I had to free her. You're the same, Jessie Mason. You're a liar and worse. But don't worry. You won't have that problem for long."

His gray eyes bulged wildly, and spittle misted into the air as he spoke. Despite the cool temps, sweat dotted his brow and upper lip.

The water within me lurched, patiently waiting for permission, moving my footing just slightly.

Almost. Almost time.

"Yes, Jimmy, yes. You're right. I'm the one who needs saving, just like Bo. But she—" I gestured toward Addy. "She's not like me, okay? She's honest and loyal and an overall amazing person. I haven't been a great friend to her lately, but she's always been there for me. Always stuck by my side. She's not like me, Jimmy, or like Bo or any of the other ones you had to save. Just let her go, okay? Let my friend go and you and I will finish this thing."

As if in agreement, the voice of the water issued a hissing *Yessss* inside my head and pulsated energy throughout my body. It was ready to be called upon, ready to feed. And I would deliver. A similar desire to comply that I experienced the night I almost hurt Addy sprung alive in me, and a cohesive agreement circulated through my veins, my own blood and the water mutually working to keep me alive, to make me something else—something more than I was by myself.

Something complete.

It wouldn't be ideal to kill Franks in front of Addy—hell, it would take a lot of explaining—but what choice did I have? I wouldn't let her die for me, and I couldn't leave here with Franks alive.

Addy whimpered in Franks' arms, and his expression wavered. I took the opportunity to lunge, driving my body into both of theirs with a sloppy crash, knocking all three of us to the ground. Franks' knife clattered on the floor, and I sprung to my feet between Addy and Franks with arms spread, shielding my best friend.

Energized by the water flowing through my veins, empowered with a supernatural strength that pushed me forward, by the water's need to feed on the life of another, my body catapulted into Franks' stomach, and knocked him flat on his back. He scrambled for the knife, but I got there first, kicking it away.

I squared my posture, calm as ever. Everything around me became clear, all my senses heightened at once. My vision cut through the darkness with clarity, and the faintest, most distant sounds registered in my ears. The scent of Frank's fresh blood on his lip coalesced with the smell of Addy's fear and the nighttime Detroit air, all of them filling my nostrils simultaneously.

The companion within threw my body at Franks, who was so surprised by my sudden attack that he had yet to get back up. I landed on top of him, straddling his body, and pressed my hands to his throat.

Strength not my own pinned him to the ground and he sputtered for air and clawed at the floor beneath us. He reached up and grabbed a handful of hair, giving it a forceful yank that threw me off balance.

But that was all he needed.

He hopped to his feet, recovered the knife that had clattered out of his hand and rounded on me, a cruel snarl curling the edges of his lips.

"Bo fought too. She lost."

The water inside of me was displeased with the fact that he'd escaped my grip and it lunged inside of me, sending bursts of energy coursing through my body and making me throw myself at Franks again. Remembering my lessons with Tyler, I ground the palm of my hand into the base of Franks' nose. His head shot backward, his nose spurted blood. Stunned, he stumbled away, and I chopped his wrist with my arm like a hammer, knocking the knife from his grip a second time. Then I ran at him, pushing his body with my own until it was up against one of the singed walls.

Pinned and unable to wriggle free, Franks sputtered, "How…are…you …doing this?" Though he was bigger than me in every way, immobilizing him against the wall required little effort on my part, while he flailed and squirmed and fought to get free. He clawed at my face, my flesh tearing under his fingernails and closing back up again, one gash after another.

I watched as Franks witnessed my supernatural healing, his face contorting with confusion, and he momentarily stopped his assault on me as shock widened his eyes. The water took advantage of this, urging me on, taking control of my hand and tightening my hold on his windpipe a second time. Franks reached for his throat, clawing desperately to get free.

"Go to sleep" I said. "Go to sleep and never wake up so you can't ever hurt anyone again," I crooned, bearing down on his throat.

The color drained from Franks' face, and he looked to passing out. In one last effort, he reached for a loose stud hanging from the caved-in ceiling, grabbing on and swinging it toward me. I blocked his attempt, but he threw me off him again. Now free, he circled me, a burned wooden stud in his hand, snarling. His gray eyes filled with a deranged madness and his once neatly slicked-back hair now fell into his sweaty face.

"You're worse off than I thought," he taunted. "You need to be saved more than I knew." With the wooden stud in his hand, he circled me, as a jungle cat would trap its prey. Only, for all his confidence, the water's voice assured me we would emerge from this place victorious. The sadness I'd experienced since turning seventeen, the losses I'd endured—the water showed me that those things had been a worthwhile sacrifice for what it made me now, for what it gave me in return: courage, strength, clarity. It truly was a gift.

"Jessie, watch out!" Addy screamed. She had shuffled toward the wall, her knees pulled in protectively against her chest, watching in helpless horror.

The water sensed Franks' attempted blow before my conscious mind registered it and I found my hand reaching up to catch the stud before he could bring it down on my head. But Franks was fast, and he wrestled the wood out of my grip before aiming at me again. This time, it made contact with the side of my head, knocking me to the ground. Warm fluid leeched from my skull and trickled down my temple and the entire side of my head seared. My ears rang, and I shook my head. But the moment I registered all these painful sensations, the wound Franks had inflicted closed up, and I was good as new. I got to my feet as he came at me again, caught the stud in one hand, and threw it to the floor.

At that, Franks finally seemed to realize what he was up against. Fear joined with surprise in Franks' expression, as he scrambled on the floor, desperately trying to get his hands on the stud again.

This gave me the opportunity to reach for the knife I'd knocked away earlier. I stood between the weapon and Franks and took two backward steps, then squatted and snatched the knife.

The water inside me lurched with nearly uncontainable excitement—the moment it had been waiting for was so very close. Holding the knife aloft, I grasped the handle of the blade with both hands. Franks saw what I held, and he got to his feet, the stud back in his hand. But he was too slow.

With the strength endowed by the water, I ran, throwing myself into him, knocking him to the ground, onto his back. Franks looked up just in time to watch the blade come down, landing square in his chest, right into his beating heart. The penetration of the blade in his flesh sent a sigh of satisfaction inside of me—the water was pleased with my work, but it wasn't done.

Yet.

My arms lifted of their own accord. I looked into Franks' eyes. All arrogance and malice were gone, leaving only fear. Not only could I see the terror in his eyes, I could smell it on him, feel it almost palpably. Inside me, the demanding water was delighted to have its prey cornered, its life stores so close to replenishment.

Where some men would plead for their lives, Franks' narrowed his eyes at me, daring me to finish him.

The power of the eternal Fountain of Youth, bloodthirsty and unsatisfied until the job was finished, pulsated through me, egging me on. The world went black around me, my surroundings seeming to fade into nothingness. Franks and I were suddenly alone in the abandoned, fire-ravaged home. The only sound my ears registered was the faltering beats of his dying heart. I could hear it in his chest, in his neck, his carotid calling to me, asking for a quick end to the suffering.

The energy within buzzed, thrumming through me, giving me a sense of invulnerability, telling me that this was the moment we'd been waiting for. Me and the water.

Take.

This time the word was spoken in a whisper, in a quiet agreement between the water and me. The time had come.

With a final strike of the knife, I ran the tip of the blade across Franks' throat, landing it against that carotid, the one that called my name, that asked for the relief from its duty of pumping blood through Franks' worthless form. And in thanks, the artery broke free, spewing blood like a released dam.

Franks' clawed at his throat, arrogance now replaced by panic as life left his body, but there was nothing he could do.

I stood back, watching him struggle, gasp, writhe on the floor until finally, he stopped flailing and lay motionless.

Dead.

A party sprung alive inside of me, the water sending bursts of energetic power and licks of happy energy all through me in thanks for delivering what it so desperately needed. For finally understanding how to work with it, instead of against it.

"What the hell, Jess?"

Addy's voice pulled me from my reverie, flooding light back into my vision, returning me to the dank and cold house where she'd watched me murder Franks.

I looked down, my hands, covered in blood, still grasping the knife. I came to my senses, cast the weapon onto the floor and crawled across the charred floor to Addy.

She shied away from me.

"Relax, I just want to see if you're okay."

Just then, Tyler ran through the door. "Time's up, Jess. How did—?"

He froze, taking in the scene. The upper half of my body, stained in blood, huddled next to Addy and Franks' lifeless form, saturated in red, lay motionless on the floor. His gaze volleyed between Franks, me and Addy.

"Looks like you're okay," he said, putting his hands up. "Who is this?"

"Tyler, Addy. Addy, Tyler," I said, waving my hand between the two of them. I stood and approached Tyler, saying in a hushed tone, "She's my best friend, the one I told you about."

"*What* is she doing here, Jess?"

"You didn't see her come in?"

"No, I've been watching the whole time. This isn't good. We can't have witnesses."

I closed my eyes and sighed, uncertain what to do. The adrenaline-charged joy of my victory was now clouding over with a new problem.

"DON'T. MOVE."

I turned to find my best friend standing there, the discarded, bloody knife now in her grip.

"Addy? What are you doing?"

"I can't let you leave," she said. "We aren't done here."

I exchanged glances with Tyler, then put my hands up in surrender.

"On your knees," she commanded.

And I obeyed.

22

Jessie

"Addy, put the knife down," I commanded. "You're not in danger anymore."

Her eyes narrowed and her grip tightened around the knife. "I watched you," she said. "I didn't want to believe it was true, but it is. You wanted to kill me a few days ago. And you *did kill* him." Tears welled in her eyes and she sniffed them away, shifting on her feet with nervous movements.

"I'm sorry about what happened at the park. I am. I never wanted to hurt you. You have to believe me. But him...?" I pointed my finger at Franks' corpse. "He was a monster. And he was going to hurt us. He did hurt you."

"*You're* the monster. You killed him!" she screamed, her voice echoing off the empty walls of the house. She kept the knife pointed at me, her hands trembling.

"I'm sorry you had to see that, but I was defending us."

"Were you?" Her voice cracked under the weight of her question. "Because I think you've been planning this."

And then a thought occurred to me. "Why did you come looking for me, Addy?" I cocked my head. "I told you I'd be over."

Addy flinched, her gaze flickering away before meeting mine. "I told you already. I was worried, so I tracked your phone," she admitted.

"Why? Why would you follow me here? You had to know what kind of area you were venturing into."

"Because, Jess. Because I knew you were getting close."

"Close?'"

She gulped, shifting her stance, her arms shaking violently in an obvious struggle to hold the knife still. "Yes. I knew you were fighting the impulse to kill me at the park. And I knew then that it was only a matter of time."

"What? How?"

And then it dawned on me. "It was you. *You* left the notes."

Her eyes narrowed into a glare, even as tears continued to fall. "Yes."

"Why?" And then I gasped and covered my mouth as the truth became clear. *"You're* part of the Order? The Order of the Mortal Defenders?" Saying those words out loud cut me to the quick.

Tyler shifted in my periphery; the revelation putting him on the defensive.

She didn't answer me, and her silence confirmed my suspicions. The betrayal seared so deep, I felt as if she'd run the knife she held through my heart.

"I don't understand. We've been friends since kindergarten."

"Yes, on purpose."

"But you're adopted."

"Only since the 3rd grade. Things were already in motion by then. My birth parents had already started grooming me, and they left me to Ralph and Janet on purpose, to give me a strong cover. But when I turned fifteen, per their will, I was given access to a storage unit they'd left for me. The Order reached out and they've been training me for this. And they expect results."

"Two years? You've known about this for *two years*? Before I even

learned about it, you knew what I'd become?" A myriad of emotions struck me all at once—confusion, betrayal, relief...and then anger sprang up with sudden force. "You lied to me! All that time, you lied. And you knew why I couldn't tell you what was going on, yet you made me feel bad about it!"

"I wanted you to tell me yourself."

"How would I even open a conversation about this, Addy? I love that new shade of lipstick. Oh, and by the way, I just found out that I'm going to kill people. Yay!" I threw my hands in the air to emphasize my sarcasm.

Hands shaking, Addy kept her gaze fixed on me as she rifled through her pockets. "I followed you here because I knew what you were up to and I thought maybe I could stop you. And if I couldn't, I would make you eat this!" She thrust her hand forward, a Caramello in her grasp.

"My favorite candy bar? Is this really the time?"

"Oh, this isn't just any Caramello, Jess."

"Mason, don't touch that!" Tyler shouted at me.

"My parents left the antidote to...*what you are*...growing in their storage unit. All those years. It's a robust little plant, but the Order keeps it alive, keeps it growing. Their unit is just one of many. They gave me clear instructions on how to cultivate it and what it's used for. And the Order has been like a second family to me, taking me under their wing in place of my parents, making sure I was trained." Addy took a couple of steps toward me.

"So, all this time, when you've always shown me your love with gifts of Dr. Pepper and chocolate and cookies..." The truth dawned on me in painful bursts.

"You had to trust me. You had to be willing to take anything from me, so that when the time came, you wouldn't think twice. It would have been so easy. And it still can be. All you have to do is eat the chocolate, Jess. It's your favorite." She shook the bar adamantly with a waver in her plea.

"If I take that from you…if I eat it…it will turn me to dust, Addy. I will be gone."

She shrugged. "I know, but what's the alternative? You'll kill, just like you did my ancestors long ago."

"Okay, first, I didn't kill anyone in your family. And second, we have a system here. Did you see what kind of guy Franks was? He kidnapped and tortured girls—girls like us—and the authorities couldn't get him of the streets. But I could. I did that." I gestured to his corpse.

"Oh, I know what you did." Addy's arm had not moved from its outstretched position, though her hand still shook. "I'm glad I got to see it myself, so that I had confirmation of what you were." She gulped, a fresh reserve of tears spilling down her cheeks.

I rose slowly to my feet. "And I'd do it again, Addy. I'd kill him again if it meant saving you. If it meant saving other girls like *you*. Tonight, you and I were on the menu and I served him up instead. I can't help what I'm becoming. I didn't ask for this. But I am doing my best to work with it, to find a use for it so that I can live with myself. Will you punish me for something I have no control over? Something that's a part of me? Addy, come on. This is hard enough. I don't want to lose you, too. And I certainly don't want to die. You told me control is an illusion, remember? You were right! I never had any control over what I am, and I still don't. I surrendered to this…*thing* inside of me. And it made me strong. It made me able to do what I did tonight."

I took a step toward her, standing directly in front of her. Tyler shuffled off to the side, and from the corner of my eye, I saw him approach, his movements careful. He was ready to intervene should things go south.

"More than sparing me, Addy, spare yourself. Trust me, it's hard enough to live with the fact that I hurt you. You don't want to live with the knowledge that you killed me, your best friend."

Uncertainty flickered in her expression. She licked her lips and darted her gaze between me and Tyler, her resolve wavering. Her sobs shuddered through her body. "But my parents…my lineage, their legacy… It's all I have left of who I am."

I wanted to throw my arms around my best friend, to comfort her and tell her she was more than some ancient mission her parents had left her with. "I didn't get a choice in what I'd become but you get to decide what your life will be like, Addy. What do you want it to be?"

Her gaze met mine, conflict and sadness mingling in her eyes. "I don't want to be a killer," she murmured. "You're right—he was going to kill us. You saved me. I don't want to do this."

Addy froze, her shaking hands still clutching the chocolate and the knife. "But if I don't go back to them…if I refuse to do this…"

The knife clattered onto the floor and she dropped her head to her hands, sobbing.

I crossed the remaining distance between us and embraced Addy. She wrapped her arms around me, weeping into my shoulder. When she pulled out of my embrace, she tucked the candy back into the safety of her pocket. "I love you, Jess, and I don't want to hurt you. But they've done a number on me and I don't know what I'll tell them if I come back and you're not dead."

"Tell them I got away. Or tell them I haven't shown any killer compulsions. We can think of something. We can talk to my dad."

"NO!" She took a step back. "You *can't* tell him. He'll come after the Order and it'll be my fault."

I sighed and glanced at Tyler, who gave his head a subtle shake.

"If there is a sect in this area that is alive and well, our Community isn't safe. *I'm not safe.* Do you understand, Addy?"

"I do. But exposing them is not safe for *us*. These people are my family as much as you are, Jess."

I cast a pleading glance at Tyler, but he shook his head. "I don't know this person, Jess," he said.

"But I do," I answered, my gaze moving from Tyler to Addy. "And I trust her."

Tyler took a step toward me, looking me in the eyes. "I trust *you*. But we're not leaving here without an agreement."

"What kind of agreement?" Addy asked.

Tyler directed his response to Addy. "We have to tell Mr. Mason. He can protect you, coach you through whatever you need to tell the OMD. I realize this puts you somewhat at risk, but it keeps your people safe and it keeps ours safe, too."

I took Addy's hand. "And I will keep *you* safe. My parents love you as much as I do. You know my dad will protect you."

Addy looked from Tyler to me. Heaving a sigh of submission, she said, "Okay. I don't like it, but okay. If this will protect us all, I'm in."

With a glance toward Franks' corpse, Tyler added, "We need to call your dad to get this cleaned up." He whipped out his cell and hit a couple of buttons, then walked away from us to make his call.

I nodded. "Addy, you go first, okay? Get far away from here before my dad shows up. I want to tell him everything without you here."

She nodded sadly.

"I'm really sorry you got caught up in this. Really," I said. "I'm so sorry this…thing got the better of me at the park. I never wanted that. I did everything I could to protect you from it."

Addy nodded. "I know you did. And I'm sorry I've been lying to you for the last couple of years. You are my best friend in the world, Jess, and that's made this secret almost impossible to bear. I'm glad it's finally over."

I squeezed Addy's hand, grateful that the lies between us could now come to an end.

"Oh!" she exclaimed. "And I'm sorry I jumped the gun on outing your impending break-up to Jake. I figured this was the reason your dad told you to end things and I kind of figured Jake needed to be out of the way. And that maybe, he wasn't safe. But it wasn't my place to say anything, and I should have trusted you to take care of it in your way."

I laughed. "That feels like a lifetime ago now, water under the bridge. I don't know where we go from here, but I love you, Addy, and I'm going to make sure you're protected, okay? We can trust each other…" The bathroom incident came to mind.

"Can you I ask you a question?"

"Sure."

"Why the notes? Why warn me? I mean, you could have just given me candy. I would have eaten it and died."

Addy shrugged. "I guess maybe that's not what I wanted?"

"Did you leave the note in the bathroom?'

Her cheeks burned pink. "Guilty."

"You are sneaky and that was devious," I accused, mutually creeped out and impressed.

"I followed you. I knew you were there, and it was a last-ditch effort to scare you, so you would leave. Jess, I was terrified. I felt like I had to carry this out, but when it came right down to it, I couldn't."

Tyler reappeared. "I talked to your dad."

Addy jumped at the sound of his voice.

Tyler palmed the air. "I kept my word and didn't tell him you were here. But he's on his way, so you gotta leave. Jess, you and I will stay behind and give them our report."

Nodding, my gaze shifted from Tyler to Addy. "Are you okay to go alone?"

She shrugged and huffed a laugh. "I came alone," she said.

I walked her to the porch and watched her make her way down the block before rounding the corner to wherever she had parked her car.

When I returned inside, I found Tyler bent over Franks' corpse.

Getting to his feet at the sight of me, he turned a soft smile my way. I stopped directly in front of him, my stomach churning in anticipation.

"How are you feeling?" he asked, as he reached up and smoothed a runaway piece of hair behind my ear. The intimacy of the gesture sent chills down my spine and my stomach flip-flopped000.

"Never better," I admitted. "Does that make me a terrible person? I just committed murder."

"Not at all. It's natural. You worked with the demands and you took out an exceptionally bad guy."

I nodded, and in place of the guilt I'd expected to find, I felt a sense of pride about what I'd just done. Justice had been served. I refused to allow myself to feel badly about killing a man who preyed on innocent young girls who'd already had enough grief in their lives. Maybe I should take up Talia's habit of wearing superhero t-shirts. Because, today, I definitely kicked ass.

Tyler's eyes locked with mine, and he licked his lips. "Remember when I said we should keep romance out of things?"

I nodded.

"At the time, I didn't like how you reminded me of my past, of the pain that becoming what we are brings. And honestly, I found you way more attractive than I thought I would. I was worried that if we went for it, it would distract us from what we needed to do."

I licked my lips, too, as anticipation grew in my stomach. "And now?"

"Now I think that's dumb."

I took a step closer, wanting his kiss more than I'd ever wanted anything. He reached forward and braced my chin between his forefinger and thumb. His fingers were hot on my face, and they sent tendrils of fire through me. Where I had been unstoppable just moments ago, Tyler's touch weakened me, making me vulnerable. He wrapped his arm around my waist, pulling me close, the weight of my body supported by his grasp.

My heart kicked into overdrive, and I feared he'd hear it thrashing around in my chest. His grip was soft on my chin, the texture of his fingertips smooth against my skin. Then, *finally*, he gently guided my face toward him and lowered his mouth to meet mine.

I parted my lips, inviting more, and he flicked the edge of my mouth with his warm tongue. Then he shifted, moving his hands to either side of my face, deepening the kiss.

It was better than I'd ever dreamed of and I wanted it to last forever. When we finally had to come up for air, he tipped his forehead against mine, and we stayed there, panting, enraptured in this moment, our first kiss.

Tyler looked into my eyes. "I hope that was okay," he said with a smile.

"I think so. But maybe we should try it again, just to make sure."

He laughed and took me back in his arms, showing me that our chemistry wasn't a fluke. Personally, I would have been happy to stay there, smooching the night away in Franks' dirty, charred old foster home, next to his corpse—my first murder victim. But our make-out session was interrupted by the sound of car doors slamming outside.

We pulled out of our kiss and stared into each other's eyes. Tyler took a step away from me but held onto my hand. "We'll pick up with this later. They're here. Are you ready to be briefed?"

I nodded, unsure of what I was agreeing to. But I knew one thing—if Tyler was asking me, the answer was yes.

23

Jessie

pplause filled the room and everyone sprang to their feet as the school musical, *Into the Woods*, concluded. I stood, flooded by genuine pride for the cast who'd executed a flawless show. I had tried to hold on to everything, to keep it all the same while I was changing, only I couldn't see how wonderful it felt to let go and step into my birthright, until this thing inside me had brought me to my knees and showed me the truth of who I was.

And now, standing here, watching Misti Moore take the bows that would have been mine, I knew I'd made the right choice. I couldn't hold on to who I was—not if I wanted to become everything I could be.

Now that I had the murderous impulses behind me, I could be myself again. I had my best friend on my left, Tyler holding my hand on my right and my family seated beside him—what else could a girl ask for? Sure, no one grows up aspiring to be an immortal serial killer but we don't always get a choice, do we?

As we stood in line to greet the cast following the show, Addy squeezed my hand and played with her now bright pink hair. "You okay?" she asked. She knew this evening could have been difficult for me, and I loved her for checking in.

"I am. I'm better than okay." I smiled and she gave me a hug.

"My turn," Tyler cut in, nudging Addy out of the way. He pulled me into a kiss, something we'd been practicing every night since my first kill. If practice made perfect, then I was pretty sure no one could kiss as well as we did.

"Ahem." My dad cleared his throat and elbowed Tyler. "That's quite enough, young man." He gave him *the look* and Tyler lifted his hands in surrender, backing away.

My dad gave me a stiff hug and a kiss on the head. He'd been such a Rockstar the night I'd taken Franks out, showing up with a whole crew in tow, and giving me a new respect for him and what he does.

I saw his uneasy glance at Addy. He'd agreed to protect her in exchange for intel on the OMD—just enough to keep our people safe. Addy had been willing to comply, but I knew that finding out her true identify had broken my dad's trust. From now on, he'd be watching. I was okay with that, as long as Addy was safe. She had seemed relieved to have everything out in the open. I knew exactly how she felt.

Mom came up next to Dad as we waited in line, her latest bug hanging from her neck. "Jessie, I'm sorry it didn't work out for you. You would have been magnificent!"

"Mooo-oom!" I said. "People can hear you. Misti did a great job."

Mom covered her mouth in embarrassment. "I know she did, I was just saying."

Just then, I reached Misti and Colin and gave each a warm hug. "You guys were amazing."

Colin's smile was tentative, as if he still wasn't quite sure of me. "Thanks. We missed having you there." It was nice of him to say that, though I wasn't buying it. After all, he'd had a front-row seat when I'd had one of my now infamous meltdowns.

"I'm not saying I'm glad you dropped out, but I was thrilled to have the chance to play this role. So in that way…thanks?" Misti's statement came out sounding like a question.

"Anytime," I said. I greeted the rest of the cast and when I reached the end of the line, I spotted Jake and Katie Griswald hanging all over each other. Even now, my heart lurched at the sight of him draped around Katie, and I wondered why he was here with her. He spotted me too, whispered something in her ear, and released his hold on her.

As he approached, my insides constricted. "Hey," he said.

I nodded. "Hey."

"I expected to see you up there."

"Yeah, well, things don't always work out."

My comment hung in the air between us, the double meaning evident. "Speaking of that," said Jake, "I just wanted to say I'm sorry about what happened between us, but I hope you're happy. I know I am." He cast a look in Katie's direction.

I took Jake's hand and gave it a squeeze. "I'm really glad for you, Jake. You were a great boyfriend, and I'm glad I had the chance to know that. Katie's a lucky girl." I pursed my lips in a tight smile.

"Thanks Jess." He gave me a hug and made his way back toward Katie. I smiled, satisfaction rippling through me as I watched Jake happily take his new girlfriend's hand, as Tyler nudged Addy and the two of them broke out laughing, as my family joked around with other parents who'd come to see the show. Yeah, I was happy. I knew I didn't have it all figured out yet, but it was going to be okay. I could handle whatever came my way, especially with the support of my family, Tyler, and the larger Community. I may not have chosen immortality and, was still coming to grips with what that meant for me… But I could accept this part of myself. I could continue to work with the beast inside of me, channeling it toward good.

At least that's what I told myself.

For now, I resolved to enjoy this moment. My murderous impulses had been tamed, the opening show a success even if I hadn't been a part of it, my friendship with Addy was solid, I had a new understanding with my sister Talia, and a new boyfriend to boot.

Life wasn't so bad.

For an immortal, bloodthirsty serial killer, that is.

About the Author

CS Kendall first sparked an interest in writing in the third grade and has been toying with various story ideas since.

Finally, a few years ago she decided to put pen to paper and really give it a go. The Killing Cure Series is her debut work.

In her day job she feels honored to serve as a therapist in a private practice setting where she is daily inspired by the stories of struggle, courage. and overcoming her clients entrust to her. Walking through the difficulties of depression, anxiety and major life transitions is a privilege she feels humbled to be a part of. She incorporates themes she sees in her work, of humanity warring with aspiration to be better, of suffering and triumphing. She believes it truly is the story of humanity, those common experiences and struggles—sometimes endured in silent desperation—that connect us all. And she loves to find creative ways to convey that to her readership.

CS lives happily with her family in southwest Michigan.

You can connect with me on:

🌐 http://www.cskendall.com

⬛ http://www.facebook.com/cskendallbooks

Subscribe to my newsletter:

✉ https://mailchi.mp/8b049e9c7c20/booknews

Also by C.S. Kendall

The Killing Cure Series—our first brush with the murderous Fountain of Youth—follows Julia and Charlie, whose love may be the only thing stronger than the water's murderous impulses.

The Killing Cure: Drink
The story that started it all!

Childhood friendship turns to love in this dark reimagining of the fountain of youth. In 1919, Charlie returns from WWI and gives his heart to Julia. As their love story begins, tragedy strikes when Julia contracts a deadly illness. On her deathbed, dreams of a future together shatter, but Charlie refuses to give up, convincing Julia to drink from a vial of "healing waters" his war buddy swore would bring spontaneous healing. Julia's miraculous recovery brings hope, but the water's murderous side effects snuff out the couple's short-lived joy. Can Charlie help Julia fight the water's call to kill? All their efforts may be in vain when Julia has to choose between running from the curse or embracing it in order to save Charlie. Journey with Julia and Charlie through a love story that spans a hundred years and an age-old curse that spans more and worse, puts Charlie's life and Julia's soul at risk.

The Killing Cure: Heal

After completing the one hundred year-long mission Julia was forced to carry out, she returns to the island where it all began. But rather than finding her beloved Charlie where she left him, the island which houses the cursed fountain of youth is abandoned. In her frantic search for Charlie, Julia will enlist the help of an unlikely ally—someone from her past whom she believed to be dead. This new partnership is rocky, but together they will work to solve the mystery of where Charlie has gone. But even more perplexing than his disappearance is what Charlie has become. With extraordinary abilities of his own, Charlie's talents are valuable, and they've been found out by a dangerous foe. Journey again with Julia as she finds Charlie, unearths a wealth of secrets contained within the fountain of youth's waters, and discovers that a mission she thought completed...has only just begun.

The Killing Cure: Redeem

Finally, after a century apart, Julia and Charlie begin building a life together. But once again, their plans for a future are thwarted when Charlie displays puzzling side effects of his supernatural existence as the Phoenix. As his symptoms progress and Julia runs out of options, they are forced to seek out the only other immortal they know—Charlie's former captor, Amara.

Darius and Amara go back millennia. Having drunk from the murderous Fountain of Youth, their history is marred by deadly choices. Amara is desperate to have Darius back but he cannot forgive her for the part she played in unleashing the Fountain of Youth on the world or for what the water made her do.

When Julia gets wind of Amara's insidious plan to redeem herself, she finds that an enemy of an enemy is a friend. After saving her life, Darius reveals the truth about Charlie's existence as the Phoenix, including the fact that this time, Julia can't save the only man she's ever loved. Armed with nothing but a shadowy foretelling about the Phoenix, Julia discovers that with Charlie and his newfound abilities they may be able to stop Amara from unleashing her treachery on the world. The only problem is they have no idea how. Even if they could figure it out, will the cost of bringing Amara down be too high?

The Killing Cure Origins (prequel novella)

What if Ponce de Leon was right, and there truly exists a fountain of youth somewhere? Would you take a drink? Indeed, everything you've heard is true, but only half-true. Such a fountain exists, and the water gives life. But it demands it too. Once a sip is taken, the waters within come calling, awakening a need within those who have had a drink to kill so the water can replenish the stores of life giving power flowing from the fountain. But there is a safeguard—a family who has passed down guardianship of the water from generation to generation. Guardian tells the story of Norman, who struggles to come into his new role and ultimately makes a decision that will alter the course for those across the generations who have taken a drink from the deadly spring.